At Plains University, they are graduate students.

But when they enter Wascana Park after midnight, they become something much more.

SHELBY is MORGAN,
a sagittarius, expert with bow and arrow.

INGRID is FEL,
a miles—a sword-wielding gladiator.

CARL is BABIECA,
a trovador, skilled at music—and theft.

ANDREW is ALEO,
an oculus who sees spirits.

At the university, their lives are dull and predictable. In the city of Anfractus, they use their wits, their skills, and their imaginations to live other exciting and sometimes dangerous lives.

And now that danger has followed them home. . . .

PRAISE FOR

PATH OF SMOKE

"Cunningham's expert storytelling, inventive plot, and fascinating characters will hook readers right away, engaging them until the very last page."   —*RT Book Reviews*

PILE OF BONES

"An absorbing tale of role-playing, magic, and the danger that can ensue when boundaries between the real and the make-believe disappear . . . Intelligent storytelling and compelling characters add to this fascinating read."   —*RT Book Reviews*

Ace Books by Bailey Cunningham

PILE OF BONES
PATH OF SMOKE
PRIZE OF NIGHT

PRIZE OF NIGHT

BAILEY CUNNINGHAM

ACE BOOKS, NEW YORK

ACE

An imprint of Penguin Random House LLC
375 Hudson Street, New York, New York 10014

PRIZE OF NIGHT

An Ace Book / published by arrangement with the author

ISBN: 978-0-425-26108-8

PUBLISHING HISTORY
Ace mass-market edition / July 2015

PRINTED IN THE UNITED STATES OF AMERICA

10 9 8 7 6 5 4 3 2 1

Cover art by Gene Mollica.
Cover design by Lesley Worrell.
Interior text design by Kelly Lipovich.

Penguin
Random
House

To the city of Regina,
and the park in its center, on borrowed land

Acknowledgments

It's difficult to end a series—difficult to know what is owed to the story, and how to let go of these people, who have occupied my life for the past three years. I wouldn't have been able to do it without the help and presence of several individuals. Rebecca Brewer offered insightful advice along the way, and her assistance in streamlining the manuscript was invaluable. Lauren Abramo remained patient and responsive to all of my queries. Alexis McQuigge allowed me to steal her chair (and her living room), and together we discovered just how many episodes of *House Hunters International* we could view in a single sitting. Medrie Purdham and Mark Lajoie calmed my nerves with grog and conversation. Rowan Lajoie provided several informative lectures on dragons, space, and poetry. Bea listened to a five-minute song that I left on her answering machine, and still consents to take my calls. My dad suggested that I include a glossary, which was probably the most practical piece of advice that I've ever received on a manuscript in progress. My mom sent me precious books and chocolate—the hat that she knit me while I was working on *Pile of Bones* is still keeping me warm. Jeet Heer gave me the initial idea to write about Wascana Park, and Garry Sherbert convinced me to read *The Satyricon* by Petronius, which has influenced this series more than any other text. My creative writing students inspired me with their work and reminded me why I love what I do.

There is a glossary of terms at the back of the book.

PRONUNCIATION

Most of the terminology in the book comes from ancient Latin. We have scant knowledge about how people in first-century Rome may have actually sounded, but classical linguists have done their best to reconstruct this. I base my own pronunciation on the recordings of Wakefield Foster and Stephen G. Daitz, which can be streamed here: www.rhapsodes.fll.vt.edu/Latin.htm.

The vowels *a* and *o* are generally long, while the short vowel *i* sounds like *EE*. The consonants *c* and *g* are always hard, as in *cat* or *gold*. The modern-day term *Sagittarius* would sound more like *sag-ee-TARR-ee-us*. The consonant *r* is rolled slightly when singular, and more strongly when doubled, like the Spanish or French *r*. The word *Anfractus* has a slight growl to it: *an-FRRAC-tus*. The *um* ending is nasal, resembling the French *u*. French would elide the final syllable, but in Latin, it's voiced. The consonant *j* more closely resembles *y*, so *Julia* becomes *Yulia*. The consonant *v* is never pronounced as a hard *v*, but rather as *w* or *iu*, which means that *impluvium* would sound like *im-PLOO-wee-um*.

The only exception is *trovador*, which comes from Occitan rather than Latin.

I've tried to obey rules of grammatical gender and plurality, except in the case of *nemones*, an invented plural form of *nemo*.

PART ONE

SAGITTARIUS

1

THE PLAINS UNIVERSITY CAMPUS WAS LOCKED in snow. This wasn't unusual, save for the fact that the snow was on the inside. Shelby made her way carefully along the ice-locked linoleum, trying to avoid the drifts that covered everything in silence. This wasn't right. Winter couldn't get through the doors. Weren't there protocols and storm glass? In a province where the cold lasted for seven months, the one thing you could count on was the weight of doors, the barriers that people formed against the wind. How was this possible?

Shelby saw Ingrid walking calmly across a snowbank. She wore slippers.

Shelby blinked, and crystals flared against the white. Sparks that might have been eyes, bleached bones, or flashing LEDs.

She was willing to admit that this might be a dream.

Ingrid grabbed her hand. They'd been together for a few months, but touch was still a miraculous circuit. Plus, she always smelled like pomegranates.

"You're late for registration," Ingrid said.

"What? When did that start?" Shelby blinked once more. "And why is it snowing in the Innovation Centre?"

Ingrid sighed. "That's been happening for centuries. Come on."

"Where are we going?"

"To get you the proper forms."

Now they were in skates, dancing across the ice floes. Ingrid casually executed a triple Lutz jump. Now Shelby was certain that she was dreaming. They reached the main office, and the ice turned into hard-packed snow. Her skates were gone, and so was Ingrid.

"*Tansi*, dear."

Shelby turned. Her grandmother was sitting behind the desk. Her hair was plaited in two silver braids, and she wore turquoise earrings. The phone began to ring.

"*Nokohm?*" Shelby looked at her uncertainly. "Are you going to answer that?"

"Answers are overrated." Her grandmother looked at the phone. "This is my first day on the job, though. I could be going about it the wrong way."

Shelby picked up the phone. She heard a voice. It was the cold of bleached roots and silt beds, a growl rising from Precambrian basalt. She hung up.

"You'd better register," her grandmother said. "If you wait too long, there won't be any uncolonized space left."

"I know. Ingrid was—" She looked behind her, but Ingrid was gone. The only light came from her grandmother's Tiffany lamp.

"She left, of course. She has far more important things than you."

"That's not true. I'm part of the collection. I've got my own shelf."

Her grandmother approached the faculty mailboxes, holding a wet cloth. "You should go. I've got my work cut out for me."

"Is that blood?"

The cloth had become a dagger.

"There's blood on everything. Now *go*, or you'll miss it."

Shelby left the office. She punched the down button on the elevator. The cables groaned, reminding her of the dark voice. She'd recognized a word. She knew that she could remember, if it would only stop snowing. But the flakes continued to gather in her hair as the drifts swallowed her feet. She should have bought those boots at Cabela's, the ones with the rivets. Her toes were starting to go numb.

The elevator doors opened. Her supervisor, Dr. Trish Marsden, emerged.

"I need your help—"

Trish grabbed her arm. Shelby felt winter in her blood. Claws brushed the surface of her skin, waiting to dig deeper. "You're not going to pass. We can't find anyone willing to examine your thesis. None of the usual sacrifices have worked."

"But I'm nearly finished."

"No." Her eyes were yellow. "You haven't even started."

Shelby sat up, breathing hard. It took a moment for the room around her to resolve itself. She wasn't in a blizzard. The sheets were familiar. Down the hallway, she could smell waffles.

A boy in dragon pajamas looked up at her, expectantly.

"Neil." She rubbed her eyes. "Morning. What did you say?"

Ingrid's five-year-old son held out a picture. "I have brought you whispering death."

"What?" For a moment, she went pale. Then she saw the drawing. It was of a dragon, smaller than average, with several rows of teeth.

"Whispering death," she said.

He climbed onto the bed. "Can I tell you something? They are like little saw blades, when they are born. Then they start to burrow."

"That's nice and unsettling."

"Don't worry. They are quite rare."

"And you'll protect me, right?"

He looked nervous. "Don't you carry a shield?"

"I've already got a lot of textbooks. It won't really fit."

"Your bow fits."

She stared at him. "What did you say?"

Shelby thought about Anfractus—the city beyond the city. She'd discovered it two years ago, while walking through Wascana Park in downtown Regina. She'd taken a wrong turn, and suddenly, she was standing naked in an ancient metropolis. No bow then, just burning feet. She'd earned the bow later, as a sagittarius patrolling the battlements. In Anfractus, Ingrid carried a sword. They were shadows of themselves, distinct, yet never wholly different. They rolled with living dice that unleashed dangerous possibilities, guided by the fickle turn of Fortuna's wheel. Shelby could almost feel the bow in her hand, the name that came with it. Morgan.

Was it a character that she played, or was Morgan the real one?

More importantly: what did a five-year-old know about any of this?

But it was too late to ask. He was already heading toward the kitchen. She let him pull her down the hallway, bouncing. His small feet pounded against the hardwood floors.

"*Mum!* Shelby is awake and ready for burrowing class!"

"Waffles first," she said. "Then . . . maybe some light burrowing."

The kitchen was full of light and smells that brought her back to her own childhood. She expected to see Ingrid's brother, Paul, in the thick of it, fingers slick with yolk, but it was Ingrid who stood at the sink. The blast radius around her was considerable and included a spray of eggshells, glass bowls, and an upturned bottle of vanilla extract. She smiled as she caught sight of them.

"I see the dragonrider woke you up."

"I did it gently, Mum," Neil said. "Like you asked."

"That's good, my sweet. Your waffles are at the small table."

"Where's your brother?" Shelby asked.

Paul didn't know about Anfractus. When Ingrid returned home in the middle of the night, he assumed that she was studying for her comprehensive exams. They were all academics, tripping over themselves from lack of sleep, and the image worked to conceal their dangerous extracurriculars. They'd fought a homicidal satyr, rescued an empress, and chased a dragon made of smoke, all while Paul was asleep. Ingrid refused to tell him. Neil was also in the dark, though Shelby often suspected that he knew something. His comment about the bow only served to confirm this. She watched him spear a waffle. Maybe he knew more than all of them.

Ingrid dried her hands on a tea towel. "He's out with Sam. This is one of the four meals that I can cook without supervision. Impressed?"

Sam also knew about Anfractus. In that other city, she crafted devices that were beautiful and dangerous. Here she was an engineering student. Ingrid, who moonlighted as a warrior named Fel, hadn't quite come to a decision about their relationship. Whenever she mentioned her brother and his new girlfriend in the same sentence, Sam's name had a certain intonation—as if her existence hadn't yet been confirmed. *Paul's out with "Sam." They're dating. Allegedly.*

Shelby wanted to touch her, but she was wary of Neil's presence. Ingrid had never laid down any rules about public affection. Shelby sensed that she didn't want to answer certain questions, and Neil was a question factory. He accepted their occasional sleepovers, because Shelby would always read him extra stories before bed, and she had a passable talent for doing animal voices. But how to explain what this was becoming? And was it becoming anything at all? It felt both comfortable and fragile. Loads of laundry, stolen kisses, breakfasts on the run, limbs tangled in pomegranate sheets.

Neil sometimes slept between them, when neither felt like carrying him down the hall. What surprised her was how natural it felt. Was she becoming some kind of stepmother? A fairy godmother with a quarrel full of arrows? She'd always had ideas about settling down. Plans and scenarios with illustrations. But they all dissolved when she crossed the street, hand in hand, with Neil and Ingrid. *Parking lot rules,* she'd find herself shouting as he burst forward. It was a perfectly reasonable thing to yell in public. And nobody gave them a second glance, because they might have been sisters, or friends. The more complicated questions remained forever on the horizon.

Her phone buzzed. She checked it and saw that it was Carl, but the text was just a string of characters. In Anfractus, Carl was a musician named Babieca with a knack for screwing himself into corners. He was drifting on the other side. Not just graduate student malaise, but something more fundamental. She didn't know how to talk about it.

"Who's that?" Ingrid asked.

"Butt-text from Carl."

"Ah. So nothing out of the ordinary."

She texted him back: To Carl's left butt-cheek. Are you hosting the game tonight?

He answered a few seconds later: My place is too small and smells like cheese.

Shelby sighed. "How would you feel about gaming here tonight?"

"After the dragonrider's in bed."

"So, around eleven?"

Ingrid made a face. "Let's be optimistic and say ten thirty."

"That doesn't leave us much time, but we can make it a quick session."

"I'm under the thrall of a five-year-old. We'll have to take what we can get."

She sent Carl a message: 10:30 at Ingrid's. Bring chips.

"I remember when I first discovered the park," Shelby said. "I wanted to be there all the time. To be part of that impossible magic. It seemed to have all of the answers. Now I just want a break."

"*I* would like a break."

She suddenly realized that Neil was standing next to her, holding out his plate. She handed it to Ingrid. "A break from what, sprout?"

"From the many demands of whispering death. And I am *no* sprout."

"My mistake. Your dragon sounds pretty high-maintenance."

"And I thought that he was *low*-maney-ance." Neil sighed. "On the plus side, he has new rotating teeth. Can you believe it?"

Ingrid handed her a plate of waffles. "Eat fast."

They finished breakfast in record time. Neil didn't want to get dressed but ultimately agreed to wearing sweatpants and an oversized fleece shirt. Shelby glanced at her own outfit—jeans with a staple in the knee, an unwashed blue top that smelled like stale bread—and realized that she wasn't doing much better. She was supposed to meet with her thesis supervisor, but the dream had shaken her. It felt best to avoid the campus.

Outside, the snow was melting. She knew that it wouldn't last, but it felt delicious all the same. A slushy reprieve from their winter captivity. Ingrid buckled Neil into the booster seat. He was coloring a picture of a monster with two heads.

"Are you editing today?"

"Yeah," Shelby lied. "I'll be done before sundown, though."

"Best of luck. Text me later."

"Absolutely."

She almost leaned in for a kiss, but just then, a neighbor walked by. Ingrid waved to him. Shelby ended up brushing the hem of her jacket, in a gesture that must have been a mystery to everyone involved. Then she got into her icebox of a truck and rubbed her hands together. The heater was acting up, but she had no money to throw at the problem. It reminded her of every online payment that she needed to make, and all the phone calls that she'd be receiving when she didn't click send. All the stone-cold voices, demanding the bare minimum, which she couldn't even give them.

Shelby could still see her breath, but there was no use in waiting any longer. She pulled out of the driveway, her teeth rattling as she hit every rut in the snow. It was like being on a disappointing roller coaster that ended in vicious potholes. She merged onto Albert Street and joined the flow of traffic heading downtown. Ingrid would be arriving at Neil's school, listening to his warm chatter. She would watch as he ran toward his very own locker, remembering the time—not so long ago—when he had to be peeled, crying, from her arms by the teachers. *He has . . . things now,* she'd said to Shelby, her expression bordering on wonder. *Lunch in a paper bag, a space all his own, friends. When did it happen?*

She remembered getting lost on the first day of seventh grade. Wandering through the rows of lockers, which resembled Dante's sinister grove. She was too old to be distraught but felt it anyway, silently. When the secretary finally called to her, smiling from behind her glass partition, the sensation was indescribable. Found. She'd flushed with relief, unable to explain her shivering as the woman in the broomstick skirt led her to class.

The lie that she'd told Ingrid wasn't gnawing at her, as she'd expected. Wasn't that a bad sign? One day, you awoke to find a blemish on the skin of the relationship. For the first time, you found yourself doing harm, and the lies—however slender, necessary—didn't keep you up at night. Of course, they were all in the business of telling lies. Ingrid still lied to Paul about where she went, after dark. Shelby's grandmother may have suspected what she was up to, but her mother had no idea. There was no easy way to say it. *At night, I go to a magical park and nearly die. I walk through a city of infinite alleys. It's sort of like a role-playing game, only you forget who you used to be. And the forgetting is the sweetest, the most dangerous part.*

It had been Carl's idea to play the game-within-the-game. He thought using paper and dice would allow them to try out scenarios before entering the park. Anfractus, the city beyond the park, was governed by the knife edge of chance. Your role was your prayer. In the safety of Ingrid's living room, they would roll the translucent red die they'd bought from Comic Readers and imagine that the goddess of chance was there with them, peering through a diaphanous curtain. Behind her, the wheel turned on its primordial axle, pulling stars and lives and betrayals along with it.

Strange to begin a role-playing game that you knew was real. They rehearsed the moves on paper, knowing that they would become reality, after dark. It gave them some semblance of control as they wrote down possibilities and saving throws. It may have been a lie, but at least it was a lie with nachos. A lie that their chosen family told each other. Perhaps Carl needed it most of all. He'd watched his companion die and carried what was left of him across the worlds. Like all of them, he feared what Andrew had become. What he might do. They'd lied to him for months, told him that his dreams were neurotic, that there was no such thing as a hidden city where powers moved beneath your desire.

Maybe they'd even wanted it to be true. It ended, strangely enough, in a room full of old pianos. Andrew's eyes were open, his hand stretched out to the woman who'd tried to destroy them. Now they were together, and she needed to know what that meant. If he could still be saved. If he even cared.

Shelby found a spot on Rae Street, next to Andrew's place. Everyone looked gleeful as they walked through the slush. The temperature was above zero, which signaled a citywide celebration. As Shelby watched from inside the truck, a young man unzipped his coat, slightly nervous, as if he might be breaking the law. Then he grinned at the blue sky, just standing at the corner. Paralyzed by sunlight. It was still cold, but people were dressed for a spring day. When winter lasted for seven months out of the year, as it did in Regina, you had to seize upon mild days. They were slushy little miracles.

She should have brought a coffee. It wasn't the first time that she'd done this. Maybe it always felt like the first time, because she was so close to turning back. All she had to do was drive away. It wasn't as if she'd discovered anything. But curiosity drew her back. Would it be just the same? Or would he look up this time?

Andrew exited the apartment. Like the young man on the corner, he looked at the sky. It swallowed his shadow. A couple walked by, pushing a baby in a giant stroller, with extra-large cup holders. Both fathers were trying to maneuver the pram around melting islands of snow. Andrew watched them as they passed. His expression was difficult to read. He rubbed his arm lightly, which ached in the cold—he'd told her that much. Then he zipped up his jacket and walked toward Thirteenth.

Carl texted her: What kind of chips?

Shelby stared at the message.

Then she laughed. She sat in the truck, laughing until her sides hurt, until she could barely breathe. Then she stepped out, landing in a boggy puddle that devoured her boots. She followed Andrew. It was easy—he never turned around. *Stalking is simple,* she thought, and instantly regretted it. This was what programs liked *Criminal Minds* referred to as "escalation."

Andrew stepped into a nearby café. For a while, he just read at a table by himself. Then a man sat down next to him. It took Shelby a few moments to realize who it was. When she did, her stomach turned to ice.

In Anfractus, he was called Narses. A fallen general—

the former right hand of the woman who wanted them dead. Shelby's hands were shaking. Any minute now, she would burst into the café. Any minute now. But she didn't move. She watched them through the fogged glass, speaking like old friends. When they were done, Andrew grabbed his bag and left without another word. The man stayed behind to pay for their coffees.

It would have to be now.

Shelby stepped into the café. She sat down at the table, just as he was leaving a tip.

"What are you doing here?"

He looked at her mildly. "I believe it's called lunch, Shelby."

"Sit down."

He assented. "You've been following us."

"Following him. This is the first time that you've turned up."

In Anfractus, he was a spado. A eunuch who'd served his mistress faithfully, on the other side. In the city of Regina, he owned a club. It was a place where they'd often gone, to dance beneath the lights, to vanish into fellowship and the pulse of music that begged them to be higher, better, stronger, younger. They hadn't known that he owned the club until recently. It was a collision of worlds that nobody was pleased with.

"How's business?" she asked.

"Not great. I'm this close to bringing back the snowmen."

She frowned. "Isn't that more of an outdoor activity?"

"They're dancers."

"Oh. Clever." Shelby folded her arms. "Why are you here?"

"The last time we spoke, you weren't interested in hearing what I had to say."

He was right. The spado had tried to give her advice, but she'd walked away. She remembered that warm night. Her first kiss with Ingrid. They'd still assumed that Andrew remembered nothing, that they had so much time to figure things out.

"I suppose you're working together now. Taking advantage of those trusty eunuch skills. Can you administrate someone to death? Fluff their pillows in some fatal way? I think there's a capon in some play who gives poison ice cream to Cleopatra."

He didn't move, but something shifted between them. His voice was granite. "Have a care, child. I've commanded armies. I saved your life."

"That was Narses. If we were all the sum of our characters in the game, then I'd be a crack shot with a longbow."

He shook his head. "You still haven't accepted it. There are no characters. There is no game. The park doesn't take you to another world. It shows you what's beneath the surface of this one. All the dark seams." Now he leaned forward. "Everything is wilderness. The city most of all. That's where the really fantastic betrayal happens. But not every park leads to a place like Anfractus. Some lead to forgotten corners. Oubliettes of shadow and half-truths. One park leads back to the beginning, though nobody can find it."

Shelby frowned. "Like the little park on Osler Street?"

She remembered that park. Barely a green footprint laid over the site of a warehouse fire. Cozy and overgrown. That was where she'd kissed Ingrid, while sitting on an art installation that may have just been pulverized stone. That was where she'd seen Andrew slipping sideways into a patch of darkness.

"If it's not a game, then what is it? Did some part of Andrew really die? Does anything we do there matter?"

He stood up. "Meet me in Victoria Park at midnight. I'll take you to someone who can answer at least one of those questions."

He walked out.

Later that night, they met at Ingrid's. It was only a practice run, but the whole company was there. Sam, who became an artifex when she stepped into the park at midnight, trailing sparks and machinae behind her. Carl, who made a passable trovador, when he wasn't snapping strings. Ingrid, who wore a single bronze greave and carried the chipped blade that had protected them countless times. And Shelby herself, the sagittarius, who aimed her bow at horrors. They had lost their auditor, the one who fed bread crumbs to hungry spirits. Andrew had slipped away, just like that. Now he belonged to a different company. He was in league with Latona, the ruler of Anfractus. A month ago, she'd tried to raise hell with an ancient horn. Now she was watching their every move.

It wasn't a game. Shelby knew that, even if she couldn't admit it. The parks led to different places, all of them real and dangerous. The magic didn't choose everyone. She had no idea how it worked. But every night, people were carried off to treacherous cities, where salamanders breathed flame and worshipped Fortuna in her exquisite disarray. Nothing escaped the shadow of her wheel. And she loved games. So they rolled with their lives. They rolled for power, and salvation, and sometimes—predictably—for desire. Who wouldn't? In the city of Regina, they were graduate students, overcaffeinated and burning with imposter syndrome as they marked endless papers. After midnight, in the park's grip, they could be anything. Heroes. Monsters. Even whole.

They played the pen-and-paper game on Ingrid's floor. Neil watched in silence, eating his crustless grilled cheese with ketchup. His eyes danced as Carl described wine-soaked alleys, where assassins hid like rubies among the debris. The game was both false and impossibly real. It was a dream that they tried to catch hold of. She saw it in Carl's eyes. The need for control. *Let it work, just this once.* The dancing die, the baited breath. This was the ritual that connected their ordinary lives with the extraordinary darkness beyond.

When it was time for Neil to go to bed, they took a break, so that Shelby and Ingrid could read to him about Scaredy

Squirrel and his fear of unexpected parties. After he was asleep, they returned to the campaign. Paul made appetizers. He took their game in stride, having no idea that it was connected to anything real.

After the quest was completed and the dishes were done, they said their good-byes. When Shelby said that she wasn't sleeping over, Ingrid's expression was hard to read. Not disappointment, exactly. Something else.

"Text me when you're home safe," she said. Keeping her dice covered.

Carl pulled on his toque. "I think we're ready for tomorrow night."

"Right now," Ingrid replied, "I'm ready for the five hours of sleep that the universe has decided is my reward."

Shelby kissed her on the cheek. "Night. See you soon."

Carl politely looked the other way, as single people sometimes do. Shelby didn't quite understand it. He used to go out every night. He was charming, when he didn't try. There was no reason for him to be alone. She wanted to ask, but she couldn't do it without raising dust and shadows. Instead, she said: "Careful. The stairs are slippery."

Albert Street was still at this time of night. She listened to A Tribe Called Red, nodding along to their drumbeats. In the dark, everything was honest. Music, fogged breath, maple, slush whisper, tire beat. Cars passed her, blind to her fear.

She parked on the edge of Victoria Park. It felt perfectly empty, but she knew better. In the distance, she could see the giant light sabers, winking just beyond the trees. They were part of an installation, but from here, they could have been foxfire. Every blink turned the park a different color, rendering the trees as stained glass. Shelby let the dancing lights lead her to the war monument, where he was waiting.

"There may be some turbulence. We aren't going to Anfractus."

"Then where?"

"Farther," he said.

Shelby tried to pierce the line of trees. All she could see were flashes and the white silence of the monument. This was more than a lie of omission. Like so many of life's unexpected turns, it was a roll that she couldn't take back.

She began to undress.

2

THE ALLEY WAS THE SAME. YELLOW MOSS CREPT across the sun-warmed brick, trembling slightly, as if startled by her presence. The cobblestones were sharp against her bare feet. In the distance, she could hear the city's thunder. The oaths and footfalls and thrum of flies were all familiar, but there was something strange about them. A new accent. It took her a moment to interpret everything that she was hearing. Sunlight made patterns at her feet, and as she watched them, some of the details returned. She remembered the spado's invitation, the unfamiliar gateway, the metallic taste of her own lie. On the very edge of knowing, she felt the velveteen flutter of the other, the woman who was a part of her. Not her opposite, nor her complement, but rather a silent sister. They stood on different shores, gesturing to each other across fen-locked darkness. If she looked closely at the needlework of sunlight, she could almost see the woman's face. If she listened past the din of imprecation and hammer-song, there was a word, perhaps a name. But it stayed out of reach.

This was not her city. Anfractus was a world away. Even if she'd wanted to escape, she wouldn't last long beyond the walls. Not with the silenoi hunting her after nightfall. The rest of her company had no idea where she was.

I'm naked and alone, in a foreign city. My ally owes me nothing. He could sell me to the highest bidder and make a tidy profit. I've come full circle, to the vicious beginning.

Only, this time, she knew her name. Morgan. She knew what she was capable of. Unfortunately, she also knew the array of fatalities that waited for her, just beyond the alley. Ignorance might have been sweeter. When you transitioned for the first time, it was like waking up in a different body. This was different. More like waking up in an unfamiliar house, with the unsettling knowledge that everyone in the next room had been up for hours.

The first time had been a mixture of panic and wonder. She'd nearly died on several occasions, and escaped through some rogue turn of the wheel. This time, she was prepared. She knew most of the things that might kill her. That was something, at least.

Morgan scanned the brick wall in front of her. It offered no secrets. But there was still a chance. She ran her fingers along its surface until she came to a loose brick. She managed to work it free, scratching her hands in the process. Another brick came away more easily. She set them both on the ground and peered into the hole. It looked empty, save for an outraged beetle that came skittering out. But nothing was as it seemed in this place. Offering a silent prayer to Fortuna, she reached in with her hand. Nothing but cool air. She reached in farther, until she was nearly up to her elbow. Something tickled her fingers, but she chose to ignore it. The darkness was heavy, like a shawl wrapped around her hand. Closing her eyes, she reached farther, until most of her forearm disappeared. That was when she felt it.

Praise the wheel. I was right. Sometimes cities do keep their promises.

She withdrew a familiar bundle. It was her bow and painted quiver. A small clay jar held wax for the bowstring, and there was also an assortment of poisons in glass vials. She laid these carefully on the ground and reached into the wall once again. This time, she nearly dislocated her shoulder. But in the end, she came out with the rest: sandals, cloak, boiled-leather hauberk, and smallclothes. They had transmigrated somehow, from her original alley to this one. Maybe this was her alley now. She had only the fuzziest idea of how it worked, but it didn't surprise her that both cities were in correspondence with each other.

As soon as she was dressed, she began to sweat. Morgan chuckled. She supposed that had she been a real lady, all those pretty jars would be filled with cosmetics rather than poison. In the end, she preferred to stink and stay alive. The weight of the bow was reassuring, even if it was more suited to the battlements. As long as she could find a breath of distance, she'd have no problem turning her attacker into a pincushion.

She wondered if Narses was waiting for her at the mouth of the alley. She had no reason to trust him. But his fortunes had fallen. Now he was little more than an exile. Perhaps neither of them had much to lose at this point.

Morgan took a breath and walked into the sunlight.

The market was a wave of color and sound. Awnings fluttered beneath a stale breeze, providing little scraps of shade. The stalls dealt in every item imaginable. There were stacks of golden belt buckles, rich summer wines, blades, embroidered cloaks, and fine gloves. One stall was piled with birdcages, while another dealt in brooches made of amber and rock crystal. A domina was bartering with one of the vendors. Behind her, three servants waited, carrying baskets already laden with expensive cloth. She was smiling as she spoke with the vendor, but her hands moved swiftly, describing a number of complex shapes. The domina was fluent in the hand signs of the market, and whatever she was actually saying, the vendor didn't like it one bit. He scowled as his own hands flickered a counteroffer. Finally, he stared at the ground and mumbled something. He'd lost the battle.

Morgan looked up, expecting to see a familiar network of stone skyways, but they weren't there. The city must have an alternate mode of transportation. Here, the sky was the pale yellow color of the domina's stola. It shimmered like a newly minted coin beneath the heat. The cries of the vendors filled her head. She was thirsty but had no money. Fel had kept the coin purse. It had seemed like a wise idea, but of course, she hadn't anticipated being stranded, penniless, in an unfamiliar city.

Meet me at the hagia.

Those were the spado's words, before the world dissolved. She didn't even know what a hagia was, let alone where it might be located. Her mouth was dry. Not for the first time, she had to question her shadow sister's choices. A little preparation would have made this a lot easier. But she'd never been one for planning. If there was some twilight world in which they could meet, face to face, Morgan resolved to give the woman a piece of her mind.

She saw an aquarius, hurrying by with a giant amphora of water. He was quite thin. Upon arriving in Anfractus, Morgan had tried out a variety of jobs, including water-bearer. It was dusty, exhausting work, and it had barely kept her fed. However, running up and down flights of stairs, in order to deliver water to rich clients, had made her quick and strong. That certainly helped when she approached the Gens of Sagittarii for the first time.

Some people never joined a gens. They labored beneath the powerful, waiting. She used to wonder why they bothered. Why leave a comfortable life to work as a water-bearer? The answer seemed to revolve around power. If you wanted something badly enough, you'd start over, scrape the tablet clean.

Morgan stopped the aquarius, making certain that her

bow remained visible. She could still look as if she had money, however false that might be.

"I have a question," she said.

The boy looked uncomfortable. He didn't have time to dawdle, but he also couldn't afford to be rude. After a moment, he inclined his head.

"Yes, my lady?"

"I've just arrived here, and I'm a little disoriented. Could you perhaps give me directions to the hagia?"

She wasn't even sure if she was pronouncing it correctly. The aquarius tried to hide his look of disbelief, but it was still obvious.

"Where is your ladyship from?"

Morgan froze for a moment. She couldn't risk saying Anfractus, since Basilissa Latona had spies everywhere. But she didn't know any other cities.

"I move around too much to settle anywhere," she replied. "I'm meeting a member of my gens at the hagia. What's the quickest way there?"

"All roads lead to the great hagia, my lady." He made a vague gesture, as if directing her past the market. "Follow Via Scintilla until it widens. The song of the bells will lead you to the hagia. Have a care, though. Ambers are wild today."

He left before she could decipher what that could mean.

"Ambers are wild," she murmured. "Well, at least I'm armed."

She continued down Via Scintilla until the market was behind her. Wagons and litters clogged the street. Morgan kept to the edge of the paving stones, careful not to twist her ankle on the deep wheel ruts. People gathered by large white stones, waiting for traffic to disperse so that they could cross. Morgan passed by a taverna whose sign depicted a scarlet cock. She could smell pungent fish sauce and roasting chickpeas. Her stomach growled, and she tried to ignore it. Her next adventure would need to be better funded, that much was obvious. She didn't even have a spare coin to buy a cold lemon sharbah. If the water boy hadn't paid obeisance to her uniform, she might have wandered around the market forever, searching for a building that she couldn't even describe.

The song of the bells will guide me. That sounds rather nice. I can't imagine being killed in a place with bells.

She passed by a lararium, a shrine to the elemental spirits. The altar was pale green marble, and oil lamps burned upon it, their wicks freshly trimmed. Engraved bowls held scraps of bread and meat for hungry salamanders. Even spirits needed to eat. Representations of the lares had been carved into the surface of the altar. The undinae resembled little waves with sharp eyes, while the gnomoi clustered beneath a mountain slope, digging through the dark matrix of rock with their claws. The shrine was well tended, more so than any that Morgan had seen in the city of Anfractus. People stopped to throw in a coin or a bit of oil. They paused to look upon the faces of the lares, whose expressions were impossible to read. Shrines in Anfractus were generally worn-down, and a few had even been graffitied, but this one was burnished and well loved. Perhaps these people valued their ghosts more.

A few tinted clouds moved overhead, and sunlight kissed the back of her neck. Morgan passed beneath the shade of the lime trees and followed Via Scintilla until it began to widen. Crowds of people were moving in the same direction. An artifex walked while studying a tablet, her coterie of mechanical spiders chittering behind her. She was oblivious to the heat and the sounds of life around her. The world had narrowed to lines drawn with a stylus, gorgeous formulae that might change everything, if she could only give herself fully to them. Morgan understood the impulse. Beside her, a medicus puffed as he carried his bag of instruments. Maybe he was late to a surgery. Two furs were stalking him, while maintaining a respectable distance. She gave them a long look and made as if to reach into her quiver. They took one look at her bow and scattered. The medicus was oblivious. He was probably thinking about how to lift a shattered bone, or what prayer to engrave on his polished brass instruments. If Fortuna bent an ear, the pain of a wrecked body might be softened. His patients needed luck more than anyone.

Morgan spied a miles, keeping to the other side of the street. For a moment, it might have been Fel. But then the woman stepped into the light, and Morgan saw a long, puffy scar, like a rend in fabric, that traced its way down her neck. The miles saw her looking, and Morgan tensed, ready for some kind of altercation. But the woman merely nodded. Her eyes were strangely kind. Morgan nodded back. It was unusual for a miles to acknowledge her. Although their gens weren't precisely enemies, there was no love lost between them. A sagittarius was expected to protect the battlements, while the miles patrolled the grounds below. One gens could quite literally look down upon the other. This had bred a healthy resentment for longer than anyone could remember, and Morgan was used to a much colder reception. At the very least, she expected the woman's expression to harden as she placed one hand lightly on the pommel of her gladius. The flash of amity was unexpected.

This really is a different city.

In the distance, she heard cheering. There must have been a chariot race at the Hippodrome. They weren't always bloody, but a race without at least a minor accident was considered a boring affair. That was where she'd first met Fel. The miles had fought after a successful chariot race. Blood on the sands always made people spend more freely. Morgan remembered watching her gladius dance, the sun flashing against her greave. The curious way that she refused to accept any praise for winning the match. And later, that same sword, parting bone as easily as an ivory comb might part hair. The look on her face, a cloudless sky, as she whirled in the heart of chaos. The nightmares would come later. A miles wasn't supposed to regret. Polish the chips from the blade, oil the armor, test the cunning brass straps. In and out. That was the purpose of the gladius. The short sword had been invented to make combat quick and easy. In and out, like adding a line to a ledger, a stone to a mosaic. Simple. But grief remained. Morgan could see it in the lines around her eyes.

She had killed, as well. She could never forget that night on the battlements. Watching the silenus come at her, eyes guttering like lamps in the dark. The *click* of hooves on wet stone, and the smell of him. It was deep earth, and water carried from the profound shadows of a forgotten well, and rust settling on the surface of a dead world. She'd won her die that night. The symbol of her gens. And regret was there too. She felt it against her chest. Morgan reached beneath the leather hauberk and touched the die. It was hers. This magic that she scarcely understood. She might choose to roll, so long as she was willing to pay.

Morgan heard the bells. Soft at first, then louder. They moved through her in trilling vibrations that seemed to leave a mark on her body, a fleeting touch. Three streets intersected, and now people were merging into a large crowd, following the sound. The mechanical spiders nipped at her feet, but she paid them no attention. Even the medicus had stopped looking worried and was now staring straight ahead. The hagia rose before them, its bronze cupola gleaming like a second sun. The entrance was supported by massive pillars, carved with reliefs that depicted scenes from the city's history. The façade was a mosaic, where Fortuna appeared in all of her guises. Her eyes were impenetrable black stones, while colored tesserae burst to life around her. A few vendors had set up stalls by the entrance, selling worship wheels and tablets of common prayer. The doors were blushing marble, and two miles flanked them. Rather than scanning the crowd, they were playing a game of mora, which involved rapid hand movements and guesswork. The miles on the left was clearly losing, but he didn't curse. He just smiled sheepishly as people walked past him.

She couldn't shake the confusion that had been gnawing at her. Everyone in this place was serene, as if they'd just taken a draught of nightshade. They smiled politely and made room for each other. She could detect no smoldering grudges, no sense of real danger. Even the furs kept their distance. The shrines were well attended, and as people entered the hagia, she could almost feel their piety. In Anfractus, people cursed Fortuna and pissed on her relics. Here, she was the object of their devotion. As Morgan watched, two spadones entered the hagia, carrying painted icons of the goddess and her wheel. They didn't whisper or nudge each other. Neither carried a flask. Something other than politics had brought them here.

Morgan followed them in. She expected dim light and incense, but the dome of the hagia was full of oval windows that admitted the sun. At the apex of the dome, a sheet of painted glass had been installed, and light poured through it. Added to that was the coffered ceiling, which reflected the glow of a hundred hanging lamps. The brilliance fired vast mosaics, until every stone gleamed like an ember. She saw forests of winking emeralds and packs of hunting silenoi, their eyes made of sinister carbuncles. There were lares of smoke, made from pale stones that made them resemble gathering storm clouds, and Fortuna in full armor, raising her gladius to one of the shining windows. Every legend, every scrap of song or dream worn smooth by time and the wash of memory, was displayed on the walls. Penitents gathered within the narthex, lighting lamps and offering up jeweled icons. Morgan realized with a sense of chagrin that she had no offering.

I don't see Narses, but I know that he's watching. If I don't leave something, he'll think me a heathen. Not the surest way to earn his trust.

She drew an arrow from her quiver. Several people gave

her an odd look. It wasn't quite the same as drawing a sword, but it still had a whiff of aggression. Carefully, she laid the arrow in one of the ceremonial bowls. It had a trilobe tip, with lovely barbs. It was one of her favorite arrows. Morgan arranged it in the bowl, as if it were a flower.

It's no pretty icon, but I'll bet you can find a use for it.

She walked down the nave to the altar, where a giant wheel had been erected. Water turned the wheel, and it seemed to whisper as it moved. Every gens was represented in the light and shadowed faces of the goddess. The dispassionate sicarius, who killed for profit. The sly trovador, who remembered the old ballads, and what they still meant. The masked meretrix, who offered sex and even love, for the right price. *Cold whores of the mind*, they were called. Six day gens to maintain the city by sunlight, and six night gens to betray it after sunset. Like guilds or families, they controlled commerce and offered unique masteries to their members. Every gens had a tower that rose above the tallest insulae, save for the tower of the Fur Queen, which hid beneath the ground like a blind root. The silenoi remained the wild gens, hunting at night for their own pleasure. Somehow, the wheel kept them all in balance. Or so everyone liked to think.

"A prickly offering." The spado's trilling voice emerged from the crowd. "I have a dagger, if you'd like to go all in."

"I've no interest in your little blade." She stared fixedly at the wheel.

"You're the first to express that sentiment. Most people quite enjoy it." He moved closer, until she could smell the sweet herbs on his breath. "Are we done jesting? I know that banter is essential, but someone is waiting for us."

Morgan looked at him strangely. "You're different here."

"Everything is different here." Narses gestured to the crowd. The lamplight made his red hair gleam. "Welcome to Egressus."

"This city makes me nervous."

"It should. You have no reputation here. You're practically a nemo."

Her expression hardened. "I belong to a gens."

"You'll find that your family ties, such as they are, don't really extend to this part of the world. Nobody cares whether you live or die. Nobody but myself, of course."

"Why so unctuous? You're a general, not a courtier."

"Here, I am many things. And you must be the same. You'll learn soon enough." He offered his arm. "Come. Time grows short."

"If I had a gold maravedi for every time someone said that—" She looked up, but he wasn't smiling. After a beat, she took his arm. "Fine. I'm coming."

"Stay close. I'm not the only one here with a blade."

"I thought weapons were forbidden in a place like this."

"Forbidden?" Now it was his turn to smile. "They're essential."

He led her past the nave and through a corridor lined with reliquaries. Bones and ashes, belonging to forgotten heroes. One was shaped like golden hands in prayer, while another was a beautiful woman's face, rendered in wire and precious stones. As they walked, the air cooled, and the oil lamps grew more scarce. Long shadows moved across old tapestries. The mosaics were difficult to make out, smoothed by the wear of countless footsteps. Morgan felt as if she were moving along fate's path. Something was guiding her through this dim place, as it had guided so many before her. Was it Fortuna? Did she stoop to concern herself with a fair-weather archer, a poor player living in two worlds? It seemed as though she must have more celestial concerns. Morgan tried to feel her in the dark, in the flashing tesserae, in murmured supplications rising on invisible currents to the oval of painted glass. In the end, she didn't know what she felt, precisely.

"I've heard Fortuna's voice," Morgan said quietly. "Perhaps I've even seen her outline, if only for a moment. Like heat haze on baking roof tiles. A shimmer, and nothing more. It happened, though. It wasn't a dream."

"Are you trying to convince me," Narses asked, "or yourself?"

"I'm not certain. Should we believe everything that we see?"

"I'm the wrong person to ask." He lifted the hem of his green robe so that it no longer trailed the marble. "Belief is expensive."

"You've picked an awfully inconvenient time for a crisis of faith."

"Faith lives within crisis. You can't have one without the other." He stopped in front of a small lararium, where a single lamp burned sentinel. "Besides, I didn't say that belief was impossible. Just costly."

"I've no money to leave at this shrine, if that's what you're getting at. I left all my coins with someone else."

"The lares don't need money." He laid a hand on the edge of the shrine. "Like any spirit, all they're looking for is a bit of attention."

He pressed a hidden lever. Morgan heard a soft click, then a grinding sound as the altar slid away from the wall. A narrow doorway greeted them. She saw the faint impression of carvings on the lintel, but time had worn them down to mysterious lines. The air coming from the doorway smelled slightly acrid.

"What is this?"

"A shortcut," Narses replied. "It was here before the hagia was built. Very few people know about it. Now that you've joined that select group, you'll be watched carefully."

"Thanks for that."

He shrugged. "You were already a person of interest. Now you've simply grown more interesting. Consider it a promotion."

"That should come with an increase in pay, don't you think?"

"Just follow me." He picked up the lamp, which was carved with vaguely threatening silenoi in the midst of a hunt. "The passage is too narrow for both of us to walk abreast. You'll have to keep close behind me, and follow the light."

"Perfect."

"Be thankful for the close quarters. The passage was designed to frustrate attack. This way, nobody can surround us."

"My bow is next to useless in here."

Narses stepped through the doorway. "Perhaps you should invest in a more practical weapon. Something that doesn't rattle like a box of bones whenever you move."

"You're full of great suggestions today."

He pressed the hidden lever again. The altar began to swing closed. "You'd best hurry. As I said before, we're on a bit of a tight schedule."

She followed him into the darkness. "You sound like a character from a story. Not mine, though. Something from her world."

"You mean your shadow."

All she could see was the back of his head, and patches of light against the narrow walls of the corridor. His voice was neutral, and it was impossible to read his expression. Spadones were the most skilled players. They gave away nothing.

"I think she knows more about me than I do about her. Is that normal?"

"A moment ago, you offered an arrow to a giant wheel. Since when are you concerned with what's normal?"

"I just want to understand how this works."

"You mean the game itself."

"I guess."

She had a dim memory of Narses telling her that it wasn't a game at all, that it was much more dangerous and seductive than any wager. But that was her shadow's memory. Hypnotized by the spado's wavering lamplight, she found it hard to keep everything separate. Morgan knew that she was in a chamber, stirring up dust and other unpleasant things. But a part of her remained elsewhere, behind a gauzy veil that moved with the same patterns of light, the same shifting mosaic. She had the faintest impression of watching herself, an indistinct shape that followed a bobbing light with peculiar trust.

"There are stories, of course." The spado's voice seemed to come from a long way off, even though he was only a few feet in front of her. "There have always been stories. Now they're full of holes, so we fill in the unknown with whatever makes sense at the time. But the stories are older than us. We worship them in our own way, like the lares, or Fortuna's wheel. In the end, we want them to save us. But that isn't their responsibility."

"Is this supposed to make things clearer?"

Narses stopped, and turned. The lamplight framed his face. His hair was vermillion in the glow, and for a moment, he seemed larger somehow. "Asking how it works is like asking how the worlds began. I don't simply carry that answer around, like an icon. The worlds are. They live, and struggle, and dance with each other. They've always been close. And if you know where the edges are, you can move between them. In the space between a great city and the greater wilds that surround it, there is always an edge. You've seen it. You've stepped sideways, into another life. But neither place is more real than the other."

He kept walking after that. Morgan followed him in silence. She kept thinking about her sister, the shadow. What remained of her life, when she ventured beyond the edge? And what about Morgan herself? After sunset, did she still exist? Or was she nothing but a sleeping reliquary, waiting for someone to lift the lid?

Narses knew more than he was saying, but she didn't want to press further. All he had to do was snuff the lamp, and she'd be at his mercy. Belief was expensive, and she didn't yet know how much he was willing to spend on her.

If she became too complicated, it would be easier to do away with her in a hidden passage, far from the hope of aid. Morgan was almost certain that she could see bones on the floor. The remains of other visitors.

Gradually, the air began to change. She could hear faint noises and smell something other than packed earth. They came to another doorway. Narses drew an L-shaped key from his belt. Morgan realized with a start that the door had six separate keyholes. Various images were painted around them. A boar stalked one keyhole, while a cockatrice writhed around another, its feathers painted with unblinking eyes.

"Is the door indecisive?" Morgan asked.

"Not quite." The spado sank to one knee and brushed away a panel near the bottom of the door. A seventh keyhole was hidden behind the piece of wood, which moved on a clever hinge. Narses fitted the key carefully and turned it clockwise. The door gave a shudder, then opened to reveal a well-lit chamber.

"The false keyholes activate a trap," he said. "You wouldn't want to see it in action."

"That's quite the precaution."

"You'll understand why in a moment."

She followed him down the new corridor. Light shone through glazed windows, and painted lares followed their progress. By force of habit, Morgan looked up, and saw a series of raised platforms above. Sagittarii stood with their bows at the ready, watching them below. One of them nodded to Morgan. She had no doubt that they were even higher up as well, concealed among the ornate stalactite patterns of the ceiling.

"We're in the arx," she whispered.

"Indeed. That was the point of the shortcut."

"What are you going to do? Sell me to Basilissa Pulcheria? Because I'd make a terrible bed-servant. I can barely walk in cork heels."

"Hush now," Narses said. "You're about to see something that few ever do."

He led her past a grand set of doors, flanked by two miles. The marble lintel was carved with names. Euphrosyne. Theodora. Irene. Pulcheria. They were all basilissae. The hereditary rulers of the city-states. They passed into a circular chamber whose walls were made of dark porphyry. It was like being enclosed by a mantle of deep purple. Sunlight lanced through an opening in the ceiling, dancing in waves across the jeweled walls. The chamber was empty, save for a carved chair with a purple cushion. Basilissa Pulcheria sat in the chair, absently reading a book with gilt covers. She wore a purple stola with red fringe, and her hair was caught up in a diadem of pearls and silver wire.

"Now is the part where you bend the knee," Narses whispered in her ear.

Morgan almost made a joke about curtseying, but it didn't seem appropriate. She sank to one knee on the cold floor, and the spado did the same.

Pulcheria looked up from her book. "That was quick."

"We took the shortcut, Your Grace," Narses replied. "I thought it best to avoid the crowds. Basilissa Latona is no doubt looking for us."

"My sweet sister." Pulcheria put down the book. "She's quite put out with you. The last time we saw each other, in fact, you were mucking about with her assassination attempt. That's like poking a beehive."

"An apt metaphor, Your Grace," Morgan said. "As I remember, a mechanical bee did figure quite prominently in the attempt on Your Grace's life."

"You can stop gracing me. I know my own worth." Her eyes were the same color as the walls. "As well as yours. Do you know what this chamber is, archer?"

Basilissa Latona had a grand reception chamber, called the oecus, complete with a hydraulic throne that could reach the ceiling. But this was something different. It was dark with accumulated memories. Older by far than her sister's throne room.

"Are these your private chambers?" Morgan asked.

Pulcheria laughed. "A bit too uncomfortable for that. Although it is a sanctum, known to very few. This is the purple chamber. The birthplace of basilissae for centuries. This is where the power to rule is transmitted, from grandmother, to mother, to daughter."

"Egressus was once the capital of the empire," Narses murmured. "Before it was split down the middle. The old ways are still respected here."

"You make us sound like a dusty scroll," Pulcheria said. "This city is the beating heart of the order that was. That's why my sister wants it so badly." Her eyes fell on Morgan. "That's also where you come in."

She frowned slightly. "I don't understand."

"Latona stole something from you. Now she wants to steal something from me. But we're not going to let her. The old ways die hard, and I have no intention of letting her usurp my position in what's to come. If the empire is to return, she won't be the one holding the reins. Not as long as I draw breath. She wants to wake the lares? Fine. Two can play at that game, don't you think?"

Morgan stared at the glittering walls. They were streaked with wine-dark veins and reminded her of something subcutaneous and alive. A beating heart. Gently, she placed her hand on the nearest wall. It was warm to the touch.

"What will become of the oculus?" she asked.

They'd been friends, once. In the days before he shed the red tunica of the auditor for the black of the oculus. Morgan didn't know if she could trust him anymore. She didn't even know who he was. Roldan? That shadow was long gone. Now he had another name. Aleo. In both worlds, she felt connected to him. Their shadows touched. She didn't want him harmed, though part of her feared that he was the true threat.

Narses and Pulcheria exchanged a look but said nothing.

3

SHELBY WATCHED THE COFFEEMAKER, WILLING
it to brew faster. She'd slept all of four hours last night, and
her body was still feeling the effects of the transition. Jet
lag between worlds. The drops of coffee reminded her of
sands in the hourglass. *These are the days of our grad student lives.* Her phone was already blinking, but she pushed
it away. Not yet. Her thoughts were still too disorganized.
She could barely remember a time when her phone hadn't
delivered pointless updates at seven in the morning, like a
breathless messenger who had absolutely nothing of conse-
quence to impart. *I got here as quick as I could, milady . . .
to tell you that you were tagged in a post about cats ignoring
vegetables.* She feared the encroachment of technology but
couldn't stop looking up facts on IMDb. Wondering about
television careers kept her up at night. That, and clandestine
meetings with rival basilissae who wanted her to be a double
agent. Shelby looked past the coffeemaker, at the stack of
Get Fuzzy comics that threatened to fall off the kitchen
table. Anxiety gnawed at her. Was she really up for this?

She could barely format her thesis. How was she supposed to foment a revolution? The light on the coffeemaker went off, and she poured herself a cup. This she could do. Even double agents needed something to keep them awake.

In the beginning, it was just a game. She'd always dreamed of falling into Narnia, or Middle Earth (not realizing for some time that the latter was simply another name for the medieval world—a rung on the ladder between angels and insects). The park had seemed like a dangerous diversion. Like anything worthwhile, it had risks, but they were acceptable. When Roldan died, everything changed. They weren't just casual players who fulfilled their fantasies at arm's length. The characters were real. They had lives, and secrets, and memories all their own. When they vanished, there was no way to recover them, no button to press or DM to argue with. Their loss diminished both worlds. And when Mardian appeared at the hospital, she'd realized that there was no real distance between Anfractus and Regina. Latona had charged across the Victoria Street bridge with a pack of silenoi behind her. What they did at night had finally begun to haunt them in the morning, and there was no escape from the consequences. Looking back, she should have known that it would be this way. But a part of her had thought: *Magic is easy.* As it turned out, magic was more of a relationship than a spell. It was beautiful, and devious, and surprising by turns, but never easy. And certainly not without a price. She'd signed the contract without reading the fine print.

Andrew had also signed a contract. Maybe he'd done it to save them, but now he was working for the other side. His wounded arm—clawed by a silenus—remained a silent witness to his change of fealty.

The coffee was beginning to work. Her body hurt, but her mind was wobbling to life. She checked her phone. There was a text from Ingrid and an e-mail announcing the two academic jobs in her field that would be available worldwide this year. She couldn't deal with either, so she texted Carl instead. Hopefully his phone wasn't buried. She brushed out the tangles in her hair, one foot on the toilet seat as she tried to maneuver within the tiny bathroom. She needed a full-length mirror but wasn't sure where to put it. The living room seemed like a perverse location, as if she were silently judging her guests. The bedroom had just enough space in one corner, but she was afraid of mirrors in the dark. There was something deeply unsettling about how they offered no reflection.

Shelby did the dishes. Washing up had always relaxed her. The smooth, repetitive motions lulled her into a pleasant trance, and she liked the idea of the plates slowly drying on a clean dish towel. As technologies went, it was flawless. It couldn't stop working or tell you that you had limited connectivity. Using a dishwasher was like asking a teenager to do your dishes for you. The activity was loud and prolonged, and afterward, everything had to be done over again. The thought made her slightly rueful. Even a few years ago, she never would have described "teenagers" as a shifty group, like some superannuated character from *Scooby Doo*. Now she caught herself thinking darkly about anyone who was younger. *They're loitering, officer. Texting loudly. One of them pointed at me.* Her own adolescence was still within spitting distance. All the epic frustrations and bewildering desires, along with the feeling that she would never be free. What precisely had she wanted to escape from? Now she regularly fell asleep on her mother's couch and loved waking up to the sound of her grandmother singing in Cree. The songs knew so much—far more than she ever would.

She locked the door and went downstairs, careful of the tricky step. She'd formerly lived above a vegetarian restaurant, but now it was a busy travel agency. The décor was all in red, and just looking at it made her feel tense. She couldn't imagine planning a vacation while staring at those angry walls. The cities on the board offered glimpses of parallel lives. London, Shanghai, Barcelona. For a reasonable price, she could reinvent herself for a weekend. A part of her wanted to grab the Sharpie next to the board and add two cities. *Anfractus. Egressus.* The ticket was free, but accommodations could prove difficult. So much depended on the grace of the wheel. Shelby walked past the bronze buffalo statue, which named the area *oskana ka-asasteki* in Plains Cree. *Pile of Bones.* What they now called Wascana Park (named after a grammatical error) had once been an ossuary for buffalo bones. She'd thought that the park itself was a strange miracle. But now it seemed that Wascana wasn't alone in its magic. Different parks could take you different places.

Shelby crossed Scarth Street and entered Victoria Park. The wind was picking up, and it licked the edges of the flyers posted nearby. Sunlight gleamed against the metal structures at the entrance to the park, which had been installed a few years ago. They were supposed to be art, but they looked like scrap metal. The park was an oasis in the heart of the city, though it turned a bit seedy at night. Some folding chairs had been placed near the entrance, where a woman was reading poetry before a small but attentive audience. Nearby, a student had fallen asleep, still holding her engineering textbook. A dog ran in ever-more-excited circles, waiting for his person to throw the Frisbee. A yoga group went through poses by the war monument, achieving a level of elasticity that made Shelby feel like a pile of bricks. She smelled coffee, roasting onions, and a faint miasma of pot.

It was hard to believe that this little park offered access to a strange city, where a queen ruled from a purple chamber. Aside from the folk festival, it was usually quiet. She could understand some secret power living in Wascana Park, which extended for miles and was girdled by its own lake. But this place was entirely unassuming. You might as well find an enchanted kingdom in a hotel mini fridge. Still. There were memories here. Dancing clumsily on the stage.

Watching the glowing monuments that they called light sabers changing color, until they cycled back to a shade of quicksilver that cut through the darkness. Watching Ingrid's shadow as it crisscrossed her own, and wondering if there was anything at all there. Most recently, she remembered the chill as she undressed before the war monument, like an acolyte performing a sacrifice. She supposed there was power in every place. Most people couldn't even pronounce Regina, but to her, it was home.

Carl was waiting for her beneath a tree. That was a surprise. She hadn't realized that he could move so quickly. In her mind, he was always on the verge of having a siesta. But over the past few months, he'd been more brittle. She guessed that he was sleeping less. As she approached, her suspicions were confirmed. He had dark circles under his eyes, and his beard looked more wild than usual.

"Hey." He offered her a paper bag, which smelled delicious. "Steamed bun."

"Are you communicating in a hundred and forty characters or less this morning?"

"My brain's still in sleep mode."

She took the bag. "Thanks. I haven't had breakfast yet."

"I figured."

"I thought the weed I smelled would be coming from your corner."

"Bit early for that."

The response confused her. "I once saw you drink vodka out of a mixing bowl. And it wasn't even your bowl. Why the sudden hesitation?"

"That was ages ago."

"It was last summer."

"I'm not always that guy."

She frowned slightly. "I happen to like that guy. I seem to remember a time when I was falling-down drunk, and he made sure that I got home safely. Even after I'd told him that he had a *cute assonance*."

He smiled at the memory, but it didn't reach his eyes. She ate her steamed bun in silence, while the park murmured around them. Carl stared at a patch of sunlight in the grass. He was somewhere else. Shelby realized that she would need to adjust her tactics. Carl had always been her sweet antagonist, but now it looked as if he'd been disassembled and put back together in a hurry. The seams were showing. Andrew was something else now. Perhaps he'd bargained for their lives, but something about it was wrong. She couldn't dispel the idea that he might have always wanted this. A whole new company. A new kind of power. Their group needed a leader, and Shelby was the closest thing that they had. Before Ingrid, she'd been the one with the most experience, the one with signing authority. It was time to step into that role again. Otherwise, they'd all sink beneath the weight of what was coming.

"It's not your fault," she said.

Carl blinked at her. "What?"

"All of this. The shit-show that we're currently in the middle of. Everything that's happened over the past few months. None of it is your fault."

"I get that."

"I don't think you do. Roldan didn't die because of you. He died because he made a choice. There was nothing you could do to stop it."

Carl looked at his hands. "I saw his expression. I knew what he was up to. I could have run faster, Shelby."

"No." She placed her hand on his. "You weren't even there. Roldan made the choice, and Babieca couldn't do anything about it. Not even if he was a fast runner. Which is impossible, because when he's sober, he can barely make it up a flight of stairs."

Carl chuckled softly. "What an asshole."

"The wheel turns. You can't predict where it's going to go."

"That's parking."

"We're *in* a park." She looked around. "Maybe we never left."

"What are we supposed to do?" He folded his arms. She could see a bit of his familiar waspishness coming back. "I don't even know who we're fighting anymore. Is Andrew the enemy? Does Latona want us dead? If so, she's playing the long game. Every time someone buzzes my apartment, I expect to see a homicidal eunuch, but it's always just the delivery guy."

"If you want to be absolutely sure, you could always just pick up the order."

"Spices of Punjab is too far away. I'd rather take my chances."

Now it was Shelby's turn to stare at the grass. She couldn't tell Ingrid. Not yet. But she had to tell Carl. Better to come clean now, before he pulled it out of her. Ingrid gave her the benefit of the doubt. Even if she sensed that something was wrong, she'd just put on another pot of coffee and refuse to ask questions. Carl was direct. If he saw a loose thread, he'd pull it until the tapestry was in shambles.

"I have to tell you something," she said.

"Are you quitting the program?"

She looked at him sharply. "No. Why would you think that?"

"Well, your supervisor might literally be a monster. And you haven't complained about your thesis in a while. I thought maybe you were teetering. The job placement rate is something like twenty-five percent. Nobody would blame you for leaving academia."

"This is your pep talk?"

"I'm only trying to be realistic. It's even harder to get a job as a historian. If I'm lucky, I'll end up as my mother's research assistant."

"Wow. The university should ask you to write their advertising copy."

"At least it would be honest."

"We don't know for sure that my supervisor is a monster."

"Ingrid hit a silenus with her car, and the very next day, Trish Marsden was in the hospital with a broken leg and multiple fractures."

"That doesn't make them one and the same! If you hit a coyote with your car, and the next day I ended up in the hospital, would you think that I was a shape-shifter?"

"I wouldn't rule it out."

She digested this for a moment in silence. Her subconscious certainly agreed with Carl, if dreams were anything to go by. The silenus haunted her. But there was absolutely no proof that the two were connected. For all she knew, Dr. Marsden had been hit by a drunk driver, and the silenus had crawled away at dawn. But when she'd visited her supervisor in the hospital, something had seemed not quite right. Then Dr. Laclos had shown up with coffee and pastries. It didn't seem plausible that a monster would eat a croissant. That didn't have quite the same effect as *I'll grind your bones to make my bread*. Though perhaps that was just ogres. There might be a whole cadre of civilized monsters who ate nothing but *pain au chocolat*.

Carl waved at her, and she realized that she'd been staring into space.

"Sorry."

"I said: if you're not quitting, then what do you need to tell me?"

That I'm falling in love with a single mom, and it scares the shit out of me. That I think we're all in way over our heads. That I don't know what my own mother wants from me. That I thought about quitting the program seconds before you mentioned it.

"Last night, I was in Egressus."

His eyes narrowed. "What do you mean?"

"I traveled there. With Narses. I mean, he showed me the way."

"Why are you talking to Narses all of a sudden?"

"He found me. Anyhow, that part isn't so important."

"It's important to me. If you're having secret meetings with Latona's former chamberlain, I think you ought to explain why."

"I told you. He approached me. It's not like I was stalking him."

"He just knocked on your door."

The problem with telling the truth is that there are no half measures. Either you're all in, or you're still lying. Shelby knew that Carl wouldn't let it go. She'd have to give him the whole story, even if the beginning was messier than the end.

Shelby sighed. "Fine. I was following Andrew."

"I know. I saw you getting out of your truck."

Her eyes widened. "You knew this whole time?"

"It was painful watching you deny it."

"Were you following him too?"

"No. I was at the paper store, and I saw you parked there, and wondered what was going on. When you didn't say anything at Ingrid's, I was even more curious."

"You could have just asked."

"And you'd have told me the truth?"

"Possibly."

"Well, now I'm completely won over."

They were silent for a beat. Shelby wished that she'd saved part of her steamed bun. It was a good excuse to stop talking. Finally, she said: "Andrew and the eunuch are working as some kind of team. I don't know if they're on Latona's payroll or not, but Narses seems to be having second thoughts. That's why he brought me to Egressus. I think"— she frowned—"he might actually be scared of Andrew. Of what he might do."

Carl took a moment to accept this. Then he looked at her strangely, as if seeing her for the first time. "Wait. You just followed a eunuch into a park, in the middle of the night, and then let him take you to a second location? Your mother would be so disappointed."

"That's her usual state," she murmured. "Look, I know it was sketchy. But I think he's on our side."

"You're that sure, huh?"

"He took me to see Basilissa Pulcheria."

Carl frowned. "He's some kind of double agent for her?"

"It stands to reason, doesn't it? Latona exiled him. Pulcheria's no friend of hers. They make perfect bedfellows."

"There's a little something missing, I believe."

She ignored this. "Pulcheria has been gathering strength for some time. She knows what Latona's planning, and she intends to stop it."

"So we get to be her pawns? That's a lateral promotion at best, Shel."

"We don't have a lot of options here. If she really intends to raise the lares as some sort of army, then we have to move quickly." Shelby didn't say *they*—she didn't quite want to believe that Andrew had a hand in this—but the doubt refused to vanish.

"How can you trust Pulcheria?"

"Because she owes us. We saved her life."

"She could still throw us under the wheel."

"It's not as if we've been doing a bang-up job lately as free agents. We're caught between rival queens, and if we don't choose one, they'll both end up crushing us."

Carl laughed. "Sometimes, I can't believe what we sound like." Then he stood up.

"Where are you going?"

"To get a hot dog. I can't hear any more of this until I've had a proper lunch."

"Hobbit."

He stuck his tongue out at her and walked toward the hot dog stand.

Shelby looked at the war monument again. She half expected to see a monster there, watching her from a patch of shadows. But the concrete was awash with light, and the only person nearby was a woman selling flowers.

SHE SAT IN THE DRIVEWAY, NOT QUITE ABLE to exit the car. It was strange. She wanted to be here more than anything. Her mother was away at a conference, and she'd suggested that Shelby check in on her grandmother, as if it were another errand. In fact, she relished the time alone with her. When her mother was around, they always ended up in the middle of a decades-long argument whose exact permutations eluded her. They knew all the lyrics by heart, while Shelby just hummed along, making sure that nothing sharp had been left on the kitchen counter. When her mother was gone, the tension dissipated. The house could breathe again. They'd order takeout and listen to opera on the radio, or *nokohm* would treat herself to a glass of prosecco and tell stories about the crazy uncles.

It wasn't that her mother created tension on purpose. Like most academics, she was an introvert who was paid to perform as an extrovert for several hours a day. She could spend hours in the garden, sparring with cucumbers, or lose herself for an entire day in a book about ancient phonology. But sometimes, it was as if some tightly wound spring within her suddenly burst from its mechanism. Shelby could almost sense it coming, a faint barometric change that signaled an oncoming fight. Her grandmother had no problem dealing with these tempests, but Shelby found them unsettling. Her response was generally to lock herself in the kitchen and wash every surface until it was reflective.

She wanted to see her grandmother, now more than ever, but something froze her to the seat of the car. Some feeling that she was going about everything wrong, that she'd missed a step and was screwing up the recipe for her life. The result would be tragic and inedible. She often felt this way. A therapist had once told her: *You're giving yourself too much power.* Then why did she feel so powerless? Or was this what mastery felt like? If so, it resembled a panic attack in nearly every significant way that she could think of. Her supervisor was always telling her to slow down, to reassess the problem. But that was equally impossible advice. It was like being told, *Well, don't get upset*, when you could feel the anger building inside you, a trembling firework on the verge of disaster.

Finally, she got out of the car and walked up the driveway. She'd brought flowers and a crossword. Her grandmother answered the door and gave her a hug. She smelled faintly of Oil of Olay. Her arms were surprisingly strong.

"*Tansi*, dear. How are you?"

"Good. How's your day been, *nokohm*?"

"You know me. Always the wild one. I've been catching up on *Judge Judy*." She saw the flowers. "Those are lovely."

"They're from Safeway," she admitted. "But I think they'll brighten the kitchen."

The kitchen was spotless and needed no brightening. Shelby arranged the flowers in a mason jar and immediately regretted buying them. The house was already in a perfect state of equilibrium, and her mother would only question their presence when she returned.

"Is that a crossword?"

"Oh yes. The weekend edition. Extra tough. None of that *Leader Post* nonsense."

"Just let me find a pencil."

They sat at the kitchen table for the next half hour, doing the crossword. Her grandmother's eyesight was failing, so Shelby read the clues aloud. She was held up for a moment by *penitents' antechamber*, but her grandmother pronounced "narthex" in an absent tone, as if she were merely recalling what day it was. They made short work of the puzzle and then watched *Jeopardy!* Shelby was embarrassed by her far-reaching ignorance of geography. Her grandmother second-guessed herself once, and when she realized that she'd been right all along, she swore. Shelby laughed and made them tea. Their rhythms were familiar and comforting. They sat on the couch pressed against each other, *nokohm* with her neck pillow, Shelby with her knees drawn up to her chest. They made fun of commercials. Once, her grandmother almost didn't make it to the bathroom, and they stumbled down the hallway arm in arm, laughing. In the end, she didn't need to change her pants, and a squeeze of perfume covered the momentary whiff of urine.

Her grandmother was still chuckling when she sank into her armchair. "That happened last week, when your mom and I were shopping. They only had one teeny washroom, and there was a lineup. Your mom was holding this froufrou handbag, the kind with the letters on it, and she kept trying to get to the front of the line. She was frantic. And I said, 'Daughter, if an old lady pees herself, it's not the end of the world.' She gets so riled up."

"She has a lot of responsibility at work." Shelby wasn't sure why she felt the need to defend her mother, especially here, in this intimate space. "I think she just gets overwhelmed and wants things to go smoothly."

Her grandmother was also famous for not complaining about anything until it necessitated a hospital visit. Bruises were *no great thing*. Falling could happen to anyone. She'd once baked a cake while suffering from kidney stones, her face bone-pale, and would only consent to visit Emergency once her skyrocketing blood pressure was confirmed. Shelby had inherited this stubbornness. She refused to take pain medication and would only visit the clinic if her phlegm turned neon.

"She's always been a frayed sort, your mother. She worries too much. Especially where you're concerned."

Shelby resisted the urge to roll her eyes. "She worries more about her course syllabi."

Her grandmother gave her a sharp look. "Don't you doubt for a second that she loves you more than life itself. You're everything to her."

"I know." It sounded unavoidably sullen, as if she were a child being told something that was patently obvious.

"She may not show it, but you're always on her mind, Shelby. She brags about you all the time. *My scholar daughter.* She wishes you'd visit more."

"Every time I come, we get into a fight."

She waved her hand dismissively. "That's just mothers and daughters. Why do you think we fight so much? It's a teakettle letting off steam. The better you know someone, the more you fight with 'em. You think you're mysterious, but there's always someone who's got your number, and they see all the silly things that are right in front of your face. But you can't be scared of a little fighting, my dear. It's part of life."

"Not my favorite part."

"Aren't you academic types supposed to love arguing?"

"Some of us prefer to write passive-aggressive footnotes instead."

Her grandmother laughed. "Where's the fun in that?"

Shelby made them cucumber sandwiches for lunch. It made her feel like they were characters in a drawing room comedy. After they'd eaten, she cleaned the kitchen while her grandmother did beadwork. Her fingers were still quick, and Shelby loved watching the beautiful patterns materialize. Her grandmother sang softly in Cree as she worked. It was a love song, but Shelby could recognize only a few words. She was just about to ask her for a translation when *nokohm*, without looking up from her work, asked: "So, are you ever going to bring the girl home, so I can meet her?"

She froze, the damp tea towel still in her hand. Water swirled in the sink. The entire kitchen seemed to be waiting for an answer. Shelby knew exactly what her grandmother was asking, but her instinct, as always, was to buy time.

"What girl, *nokohm*?" She stared out the window, unable to turn around. In the glass, she could see the faint impression of her grandmother, moving rhythmically, with the patience of a mosaicist. She would select a color, and then her hand would swoop, adding to the pattern that bloomed in her mind. Stitching a polychrome story.

"I'm old, not deaf," the woman replied, still concentrating on the work. "I've heard you talking about her with your mother. Ingrid. That's her name, right?"

Actually, she has two names. Shelby almost said it but managed to stop herself. Though some part of her suspected that her grandmother already knew this. That she'd known about the park and its secrets long before Shelby had.

"Yes," she replied finally.

"You've been spending a lot of time with her."

"I guess."

Why was she answering in monosyllables? *We're dating.* It was a simple response. Her grandmother obviously knew the truth. But the words eluded her. All she could do was keep washing the same plate, over and over. Even if her mind was frozen, her hands moved of their own volition, making circular patterns against the blue ceramic.

"Did you meet at school?"

We met in the Hippodrome, where she was fighting as a gladiatrix.

Shelby blinked. "In class. Yeah."

"And how long has this been going on?"

She wasn't sure what the question actually meant. How long had she been interested in women? How long had she been going to the club with Andrew and Carl, trying to work up the courage to take someone home? How long had she been sleeping in a house that smelled of coffee and fresh laundry, surrounded by unmarked papers and plastic dinosaurs? She could think of no satisfactory answer. It was like being asked, *What do you want?* She didn't know. But she could remember wanting it for a long time, in a thousand different guises.

"It's fine," her grandmother said. "I know that you don't tell me everything. Not like you used to, when you were little."

Shelby finally turned around. "*Nokohm*, I tell you things. I mean, maybe not everything, but I don't keep things from you."

"Oh?" This time she looked up from her work. "What about that picture that you stole from the mantel? I thought you would have replaced it by now, but the empty frame is still sitting in the drawer. Lucky that I'm the one who dusts, and not your mom."

The sudden change in topic was disorienting. It took Shelby a moment to realize what her grandmother was actually saying. Then her stomach began to roil. She'd taken the picture of her father a few months ago, with every intention of returning it, after making a copy. But it was still in her glove compartment. She could almost feel him watching her from the car, shaking his head in mild disappointment. If he'd ever felt that. She had no idea. She knew practically nothing about him, except that he was skinny, and that he was a terrible bowler.

"I'm sorry," she said. "It was stupid. I meant to return it, but—I don't know—in the end, I just couldn't."

"Come sit next to me."

Her grandmother's voice was soft, but also slightly imperious. There was no chance of disobeying. Shelby sat down at the kitchen table.

"It isn't just a long story. It's a shared one. Your mother, your father, and me—we've all got our own piece of it. And I know it's unfair to keep you in the dark, but there are things that only your mother knows, and questions that only he can answer. My piece is the smallest."

Shelby nodded. She was out of breath. The conversation about Ingrid felt like something that had happened ages ago. She thought about the photo, safe within the darkness of the glove compartment. The only thing she'd ever stolen.

"They loved each other. And they loved you. I remember him just staring at you, wonder in his eyes, like you were a constellation that he'd pulled from the sky. When you cried, he drove you in circles for hours, until you finally drifted off. Sometimes the only thing that'd put you to sleep was the sound of the vacuum cleaner, and he'd clean every inch of the house. Those carpets never looked better."

"Why'd he leave, then?" Shelby tried to keep the anger out of her voice, but she could feel it bubbling up.

"That's his piece of the story. I can't tell it for him."

She shook her head. "That's it? I get to hear about the vacuum, and nothing else? How's that supposed to help?"

Her grandmother started to say something sharp. Then her expression softened. She took Shelby's hand. "Darling, all I know is that he had to go. It wasn't because of any bad blood, and it certainly wasn't because of you. He had no choice."

"People ditch all the time. I'm sure they tell themselves that they have no choice, but it's a pretty weak argument."

Her grandmother stood up and touched her hair lightly. "Keep the photo. Your mom will never realize it's gone."

"Because she doesn't want to see him?"

"No. Because that kind of pain never goes away." She walked over to the cupboard. "Want some cheese and crackers?"

Shelby stared at the unfinished beadwork. It was a hummingbird.

"Sure," she replied. "I'll get the cutting board."

"I expect you to bring that girl around for dinner."

"She has a kid." Shelby blurted it out. Best to go all in.

Her grandmother was silent for a moment. Then she asked: "Is he a picky eater?"

She felt a strange fluttering. Had she mentioned Neil in front of her grandmother? If so, she didn't remember it. But the woman's prescience almost never surprised her. For all she knew, *nokohm* and Neil talked in dreams all the time, swapping stories with whispering death and his winged crew.

"He seems to like eggs," Shelby replied lamely.

"Good to know."

"Are you going to tell Mom?"

Her grandmother didn't turn from the cupboard, but Shelby could feel her smiling. "Let's surprise her, shall we? It's more fun that way."

4

THE BUS ROCKED LIKE A TOY ON A TRACK AS
it made its way down Albert Street. Through the window,
Shelby could see a layer of ominous clouds. They were still
making up their mind, but she was glad that she'd brought
her umbrella. She sat in the last row of seats, where she
could hear the engine growling. It was somehow comforting,
like a giant cat snoring behind her. The seats were just high
enough that her feet dangled an inch or two above the
ground. She resisted the urge to swing them back and forth.
Above her, a gently racist advertisement offered *sweet deals*
on smartphone plans, featuring a tiny wrestler as its mascot.
She tried to remember a time before commercials had
invaded every surface, but they seemed to have always been
there. She was just annoyed because her browser kept link-
ing her to strange weight-loss remedies. They were beginning to sound like the manuscripts that she read. *Secret
cordial cures all!* It was only a matter of time until doctors
began prescribing mercury pills again.

She'd forgotten to put gas in the truck, and it cost too

much anyway. This was her epic narrative. *Our heroine moves slowly toward her purpose, on public transit, with just enough change to buy a veggie plate from the canteen.* A part of her found it oddly satisfying. The universe got what it paid for. Employing grad students as heroes was sketchy at best, and if she was going to shoulder the responsibility, then fate would just have to pause a moment while the bus driver left for a smoke.

Shelby felt like a detective with no case files. Not a smooth rhetorician, like the Mentalist, but more of a second-rate sleuth who'd been put on warning. Even if she'd reduced their current conflict to a spreadsheet with dates and times, it still wouldn't make much sense. Latona was trying to raise an army of lares. She'd nearly succeeded, until Andrew had swapped out her mythic horn for a generic piano key. Now he was squarely in the middle of her plan, but Shelby couldn't figure out why the basilissa was moving so slowly. If she wanted the horn back, she could just torture him until he admitted where it was. Or she could tear up every piano and harpsichord at Plains University and bring back their mutilated keys. Instead, she was grooming Andrew for something. Letting him get close. Somehow, he'd become the Mary Sue. Was he sending out some kind of mating call that only dark monarchs could hear?

The bus pulled up near the university, which had recently invested in a giant chrome sign that was supposed to last for the next hundred years. Shelby checked her to-do list:

Discover if supervisor is monster.
Check for student tax credit.
Investigate army of elemental spirits.
Pay ~~half~~ one third of library fines.
Prepare for dinner with family and girlfriend that will
    bring relationship to screeching halt.
Divine reason for park's existence and our place in it.

If she hurried, she could cross out two items and still get stamps.

The Department of Literature and Cultural Studies was familiar and smelled of old coffee. The beige carpet reminded her of a movie theater floor, and she half-expected to see a strand of lights guiding her toward the exit. She saw Ingrid in the Writing Centre, marking up an essay in red pen. A student sat next to her, continuing to text. She'd forgotten that they were pulling grad students from different departments in order to keep the center open. Shelby wanted to talk to her, but the visit to Egressus weighed heavily on her conscience. First, she'd need to spin that.

She hurried down the hallway until Ingrid's profile was out of sight.

An idea occurred to her. It wasn't a very good one, but at the moment, it was all she had. She ducked into the general office. Tom, the departmental advisor, was gone for lunch, but he'd left the door open. She saw a paused episode of *Teen Mom* on his computer screen. He'd be back soon. Shelby walked behind the desk, where stacks of colored forms had been organized with loving care.

She pulled open a drawer and was met with the face of Garfield. More accurately, it was a stuffed Garfield keychain affixed to an office key. Tom called it the key of shame, because professors who'd forgotten their keys were forced to carry Garfield down the hallway, proclaiming their absentmindedness to everyone. She'd used it once to unlock the TA office after leaving her purse in the truck by accident. Now it felt heavy in her hand. A skeleton key that could open any office on the floor.

Shelby tried to stuff the key in her pocket, but Garfield's head wouldn't fit. This must be what it felt like to carry a dirty magazine home from the store, back when people still did that sort of thing. The hall was empty, but she was still convinced that everyone could see her, teetering on the brink of moral relativism. She stopped outside Dr. Marsden's office door. A pane of frosted glass obscured the inside. Various advertisements for conferences and calls for papers had been affixed to the door, as well as an image of Sarah Fielding.

She slipped into the office and shut the door as silently as possible. Light filtered in from the narrow window. Shelby touched the Victorian writing desk lightly. It may have just been her imagination, but the wood felt slightly warm. The desk was covered by stacks of books and articles, leaning into each other, like exhausted arches. A fountain pen lay next to a porcelain inkpot, positioned where you might normally expect to find a printer. The computer was old and practically nonfunctioning. Shelby had begged Trish to let her install a few updates, but her supervisor would merely look at the machine with disdain. *Let it die in peace,* she'd say. It had already become little more than a paperweight. Trish had a small laptop, but most of the time, she recorded her lecture notes in longhand. There was something magical about her cursive. Those graceful loops and twined letters reminded her of alchemical formulae. The occasional ink blotch was like a delicate cough, a hint of bodily presence.

She scanned the bookshelves, looking for anything out of the ordinary. One whole shelf was given over to Broadview editions of eighteenth-century texts. The weight of Samuel Johnson's biography had caused the shelf to bow slightly. There was Peakman's five-volume set of prostitute narratives, and Lady Mary Wortley Montagu's letters from Turkey, in which she expressed her own curiosity at watching Turkish women bathe in public. Montagu herself had been scarred by smallpox and endured the taunts of male poets with an inexhaustible supply of wit. The built-in shelves were resplendent with hardcovers, and for a moment, Shelby wanted to grab each of them, as if they were low-hanging fruit. She imagined Trish discovering her a few hours later, fingers black from old type, contented as a cat in a sunbeam. She had to focus.

After a moment of hesitation, she examined the drawers. Now she was committed. Mostly, they were filled with yellowing exams, old essays, and colorful handouts that had ceased to be relevant. Advertisements for courses and workshops that had come and gone. Some of them were at least five years old. There was a drawer that seemed to hold nothing but change, though all of it was meticulously counted and separated into piles. Another was full of books, which made Shelby grin. She'd run out of wall space and was using the drawers for excess book storage. She glanced at her phone. Tom would be back in a few moments. If she was going to find something, it would have to drop from the sky in the next sixty seconds.

She opened the filing cabinet. The first two drawers were filled with student reports and old correspondence. She was tempted to search for her own records but thought the better of it. Even if her supervisor's notes were complimentary, they'd only serve to give her anxiety nightmares for the rest of the year. Best to live in mystery. The top drawer was locked.

Now we're getting somewhere. If somewhere *means I have no idea where I am.*

She checked the top of the filing cabinet for the key, but there was nothing there. Trish probably had it with her. Shelby tried not to think about the ticking clock. *Focus.* A key like that was frustratingly small. The sort of thing that might slip off an ordinary key ring. Better to leave it in the office. She returned to the first set of drawers. They were clogged with papers and ephemera. That left the change drawer. She got down on her knees and reached into the depths of the coin vault. There was a sliding metal tray on the top of the drawer, which held pens and highlighters. She slid it forward and discovered a smaller tray that held a set of keys. The deduction may have been slightly obvious, but it still gave her a flush of confidence. *Eat your heart out, Mentalist.* She grabbed the keys and unlocked the top drawer.

The contents were unremarkable. More student records, along with some receipts from the British Library, and a leather agenda. Shelby felt as if she were rapidly approaching the conclusion to a poorly written essay. There was no way to tie her argument together, because it had never existed in the first place. What was she doing here? A clue might make sense in context, but she didn't even have a blurry outline of the larger puzzle. Would Trish casually discard evidence in her office? With nothing left to lose, Shelby opened the agenda. It was current and filled with neatly written notes about upcoming department meetings. She flipped through the pages, hoping to find anything mysterious. The thought reminded her that she knew nothing about this woman, her mentor. Aside from a few familiar names and dates, the agenda couldn't fail to be anything less than cryptic. The footnotes to another person's life. She was about to put it away when a folded piece of paper fluttered to the ground.

Shelby retrieved the paper, thinking that it was another receipt. But when she unfolded it, her breath caught. It was a prescription for anti-anxiety medication. She wondered if it had something to do with the hit-and-run. That would make sense. Shelby squinted, trying to read the small print. The prescription, she realized, was renewable. It had originally been issued two years ago, endorsed by a psychiatrist whose signature she couldn't make out. Shelby stared at the form. Trish had always been her rock. She could be severe at times, but Shelby had never seen her crack under pressure. Why would she be on anti-anxiety drugs? She supposed that it wasn't entirely uncommon. Academics could be fragile. Rumors were always circulating about faculty members who drank too much or relied on a heady cocktail of painkillers to numb their social phobias. But Trish had never struck her as that sort.

Shelby locked the drawer and replaced the keys. She was just about to leave when she heard footsteps in the hall. She froze. It might have been a student, looking for her supervisor. Then she heard the tinkling of keys. Her stomach did a flip. There was nowhere to hide. She could make up a story, but Trish would see right through it. For a moment, she thought about raising her hands, as if she'd just been arrested. Then she remembered the narrow balcony that ran the length of the third floor. It wasn't exactly scenic. Mostly, grad students used it to smoke and recharge their neurotic batteries. If Trish decided to glance out the window, she'd be discovered for sure. But the only other option was hiding behind the door, which hardly seemed viable, given the clutter. Shelby squeezed through the window and climbed onto the balcony. Too late, she realized that it was impossible to lock the window behind her.

Shelby heard the key in the office door. She shut the window as tightly as possible from the outside, then stepped away, just as the office door opened. The balcony was covered in gravel and old cigarette butts. A few rusty folding chairs had been positioned along its length, naked to the elements. The sky was the color of sleet. She knew that if she moved even an inch, the crunch of gravel would betray her. Inside the office, she could hear Trish set down her leather satchel on the desk. There was a brief silence. Was she staring at the window? Shelby had tried to close it tightly, but it remained ajar. The slightest breeze would blow it open again. She looked at the rain clouds.

Don't screw me, she thought. *Just this once. I know that you exist. I've seen you, lares of smoke and thunder. Caela. Just keep a lid on it, and I promise that when I get back to Anfractus, I'll give you a whole loaf of bread and a jug of oil. I'll trim the lamps on your shrine for a whole year.*

The clouds seemed to tremble for a moment, but the air remained still. Shelby tried to quiet her heartbeat, so that she could hear what was going on behind the window. She imagined Trish standing there, trying to figure out if she'd forgotten to lock it, or if some maintenance worker had left it open.

Both plausible solutions. Far more likely than the fact that your seditious graduate student might have broken into your office.

A phone rang. For a moment, Shelby thought it was her own. Her hands started to shake uncontrollably. This was it. Destroyed by her own carelessness. The only solution was to jump off the balcony. Perhaps then, in the general tumult, everyone would fail to realize that she was a petty criminal. She'd break something for sure, but there'd also be morphine.

Shelby put a hand to her mouth, to keep from giggling like a mad person.

Really, Carl? Now you call? You're going to get me kicked out of the program, and all because you couldn't decide on what flavor of dip to buy! It's always *the seven-layer! I shouldn't have to keep telling you!*

It took her a second to realize that her phone was silent. The ring tone sounded like Baroque chamber music and was coming from inside the office.

"Yes?" It was her supervisor's voice. "What do you mean, tonight? That's not what we agreed upon. No. This is moving too quickly."

Shelby frowned. Was she talking about the departmental colloquium? That was supposed to be tonight, but she couldn't imagine why Trish would be so hesitant about it. The program had been published weeks ago.

Dr. Marsden lowered her voice. "That was supposed to be tied up on the fifth floor. The provost made his position perfectly clear, and there was no way that—" She paused. "No. That's not what I'm saying. Don't put me in this position." She was silent for some time. Then she said: "Not all sacrifices are equal. Don't question my loyalty again. I'll be there."

Shelby heard some rustling of papers. Then another silence. She closed her eyes. All Trish had to do was open the window a crack. But she didn't. The office door closed, and she heard the key turn in the lock. She exhaled. Her mind was spinning. What was happening on the fifth floor? What was Trish involved in?

Not all sacrifices are equal.

Administration had its drama, but this sounded like something else. She thought about the prescription again. Her supervisor was unraveling. It remained to be seen what would be left once the dust settled.

Her phone buzzed. It was such a surprise that she nearly fell off the balcony. The message was from her mother.

Dinner at 6. Bring garlic bread. Grandma insists.

Shelby laughed. She felt a drop of rain on her cheek, then another. She looked up. The clouds were about to explode.

You owe us, they said.

"Right." She opened the window. "Tell me something I don't know."

NEIL ANSWERED THE DOOR. HE WAS WEARING a winged cape, and his hands were full of brightly colored stones. He'd already dropped several.

"Oh," he said, as if mildly surprised to see her. "You must be here for mine lecture."

Carl smiled at this. "What's the topic?"

"You will be learning about dragons and their eggs." He placed a pink stone in Carl's outstretched hand. "I give this lecture often."

"He really does," Ingrid called from the living room.

"You have forgotten your exercise books!" He patted Carl's hand in an avuncular way. "That is fine. I can lend you something to write in. You will need to take a lot of notes, because I speak so quickishly."

They stepped into the hallway. Neil's rain boots had a layer of fresh mud on them. He must have been puddle-jumping again, searching for the elusive changeling-dragon who lived beneath the merry-go-round.

Ingrid rose from the couch. "There's wine. I didn't know if you wanted red or white, so I opened up one of each."

"She's a ball of nerves," Paul confirmed from the kitchen.

"Not really." Ingrid smiled at Shelby. "I know it's just dinner."

It was and it wasn't. Shelby knew that she should say something comforting, but her mind had gone blank. Then Neil handed her a yellow stone, and she enthused about its various draconian properties. That was safer than discussing the fact that Ingrid was walking into a battlefield. She'd invited Carl as a buffer. He sensed this but was being surprisingly kind about it. Maybe he just wanted free food.

"It's not just dinner," Shelby said, immediately regretting it.

"It's not?" Ingrid's tone was light, but there were several competing questions beneath the one that she'd actually voiced.

Shelby took her hand. "Don't stress about it. Think of it as any other dinner, except for the fact that three generations of my family will be there."

"A *generation* is a very long time," Neil added. "Millions of years."

"Actually, bubs," Ingrid said, "it's closer to thirty years. Mummy and Paul are a part of the same generation. But you represent a whole new one."

"Ha!" Neil's expression was triumphant. "Mine own generation will be quite impressive. I can feel it."

"He's already sounding like a postmillennial," Carl said.

Ingrid touched Neil's cheek. "You're the apple of my eye."

"Oh, Mummy. You have a lot to learn about the human body."

Her look didn't waver. "Go get your easel. Uncle Paul was telling me that he wanted to see your latest drawing of King Cobra."

"I also drew snakish runes!" He ran for the stairs. "I'll go get it!"

As soon as his small form disappeared, Ingrid lunged for her shoes. "Transition time, everyone. I hid the easel underneath his Lego, so we've got thirty seconds to dash."

"More like twenty," Paul said. "He could find that thing in the dark."

"Thank you so much for watching him tonight. I won't be home too late."

"I've got practice tomorrow, so you can return the favor."

"You guys are like a well-oiled machine," Carl observed. "It's impressive."

Paul laughed. "You should have seen us during year one." He pointed at Ingrid with a wooden spoon. "This one had a penchant for nearly burning the house down."

"I barely did that twice," Ingrid replied. "Three times, tops. And Paul flooded the basement. He also—"

"—ten seconds!" He waved the spoon.

Ingrid ran out the door, with Shelby and Carl behind her. They didn't stop running until they were all in the truck. Shelby resisted the urge to peel out of the driveway, as if they were being pursued by a motorcycle gang.

"Sorry about the rush," Ingrid said, once they were on the road. "Our parenting style is all about the bait and switch."

Shelby smiled. "You seem to be doing a great job."

"It didn't feel that way during his meltdown at Canadian Tire, after we told him that he couldn't have a three-foot-tall garden gnome."

"I feel the little guy's pain," Carl said. "My mom told me that, when I was his age, I cried hysterically for three hours because she cut my pizza the wrong way."

"Every child is easy and difficult in their own way," Shelby added. She didn't mean it to sound quite so pedantic. Her mouth was clearly against her.

"That's a gem," Carl replied from the backseat. His voice

was neutral, but she could tell that he was struggling not to laugh. "Really puts the whole thing—"

"—fuck off."

"You're sort of right, though," Ingrid said kindly. "Some things go well, and some things are a constant battle. You can't tell in advance how it's going to turn out. I never thought I'd find myself staring at my child, asking him, *Aren't you even a little tired?* But I'm sure I'll end up doing just that when I get home tonight. When I was little, I used to love the ritual of going to sleep, with my toothbrush and water cup. It was sacred. Neil told me the other night that he *fears oblivion*. How could he even have a concept of that?"

Carl was staring out the window. He looked suddenly vulnerable, like a child trapped on an unexpected car ride. "Of all the fears that I can think of," he murmured, "that one makes the most sense. Kids have no proof that they'll wake up the next morning. You can hardly blame him for wanting some kind of guarantee."

They were dancing around the more obvious topic. Shelby had come to think of herself as something of an expert in this area. She was always dancing around a bonfire. Carl seemed to be doing it more by accident. He was just along for the ride and could really go either way.

Shelby looked at Ingrid, who appeared to be reading the safety instructions on the visor above her head. Stress reading. Did she suspect that anything was wrong? Ingrid had once told her that lying had gotten easier over time, which was precisely what scared her. The simplicity with which you could fold the truth like a cocktail napkin and use it to create a pleasant distraction. Now she was doing the same thing, and the ache in her chest would surely fade. Soon it would just feel like writing a bullshit thesis.

The rest of the drive was silent. When they arrived, Shelby willed herself to unbuckle the seat belt, as if this were any other visit. Ingrid tried to straighten her hair, then realized that everyone was watching and put her hands at her sides. Shelby knew that she should say something reassuring, but it was taking everything she had just to remain upright. Her grandmother answered the door. She winked at Shelby, and suddenly it was possible that everything might work out.

"You must be Ingrid."

"Yes," she replied, a tad uncertainly.

Shelby hoped that she wasn't slipping into some kind of fugue state.

Her grandmother squinted at the car. "I thought your little one was coming."

Ingrid appeared visibly relieved at the opportunity to talk about Neil. "He's staying with his uncle tonight. I'm sure he'd love to visit, though."

"He's currently on a lecture tour," Carl said.

"Well, he must take after his mom, then. We're an academic family too. Except for me. They can't teach me anything."

"I'm sure that's not true."

She shrugged. "When they try, I just go into another room. I find that works quite well. Now come inside. Granddaughter, did you pick up dessert?"

"It's in the trunk."

Her grandmother frowned. "That sounds a little ominous."

"It's neopolitan ice cream," Carl said. "Almost new."

"Be still my heart."

Ingrid followed them inside. Her hands were clasped together, like a medieval saint. Shelby was just about to say something about it when her mother walked into the living room.

She looked first at Ingrid, then at Shelby. Her expression was written in Sanskrit. Shelby wanted to put an arm protectively around Ingrid but found that she couldn't quite move.

"I'm Mel." She shook Ingrid's hand. "It's lovely to meet you."

She didn't say *finally*. Maybe her grandmother hadn't said anything. She needed the ability to stop time, so that she could interrogate both of them individually. Was a little chronomancy too much to ask in this kind of situation?

"Thank you so much for inviting me," Ingrid said.

"It's a pleasure having you."

Just say what you really mean! Stop communicating in mom semaphore! Shelby ignored the urge to scream.

"We're all pleased," Shelby said. "Let's eat."

Her mother frowned. "Are we keeping you from writing a conference paper?"

"No," she mumbled.

"You must be hungry." Mel turned to Ingrid. "She always gets a little fussy when she's hungry. Isn't there a slang term for that, now?"

"I believe it's"—Ingrid's tone was apologetic—"hangry?"

"What a perfect word."

"Leave them alone," her grandmother said. "Come help me with the gravy."

"I could also help with that," Carl exclaimed. "I'll be your gravy copilot."

She gave him a long look. "You'll stay out of the kitchen. Understood, grabby?"

His expression fell. "Yes."

Shelby and Ingrid set the table while Carl tried to think of reasons for sneaking into the kitchen. Ingrid turned the napkins into animals, which Shelby thought was a neat trick. Now they were dancing around the table in warm silence, but it wasn't a tactic. It felt careworn and domestic, as if they'd been doing exactly this for years. Shelby imagined a future in which Ingrid was a part of her family. It seemed within reach. She could picture Neil listening spellbound to one of her grandmother's stories, or delivering a lesson on snakish runes. She could see the delight in her grandmother's eyes as she followed along. She'd always wanted a full house, brimming with conversation, and a busy kitchen at the heart of it all. It was right there. All she had to do was . . . something. But what? How could she move from this peculiar limbo to the hovering dream, where everything was bright and finished?

They sat down to eat. Shelby almost hip-checked her mother as she rushed to claim the seat next to Ingrid. Carl sat next to her grandmother, who made a subtle gesture with her knife when she caught him eyeing her potatoes. They were silent for a while. Shelby reviewed and rejected topics in her mind until she was tripping over thesis statements.

"You have a son," Mel said. It was halfway between a statement and a question, as if she found the idea mildly curious.

"Yes. Neil. He's five." She seemed relieved to be talking about him, but the relief evaporated when nobody said anything else. "He's a dragonrider, currently."

Shelby's grandmother chuckled. "When Mel was five, she wanted to be a unicorn. Even taped a wobbly pencil to her forehead. I thought she might put someone's eye out."

Carl stared at his plate. Shelby could see that his head was exploding.

Her mother actually smiled. "That was my finest hour."

Shelby felt the unexpected need to rescue her. "Remember when I thought I was Spider-Man?"

"*Thought?* You were convinced." Mel turned to Ingrid. "She even made web shooters and ran through the house yelling *pew-pew*."

"Neil woke me up the other morning pretending to—" Shelby stopped in midsentence as her mother fixed her with an interested look. "On the couch, I mean. I was sleeping on the couch, and he woke me up. It was hilarious." Her voice fell on the last word, and she found herself staring at the cutlery.

"Ingrid, are you from Regina?" Her grandmother's voice was smooth.

"My . . . parents are from Alberta. I moved here for school."

Her hesitation over the word *parents* was like a car backfiring, but no one pursued it. Shelby felt as if they'd all been handed the wrong scripts for whatever this conversation was.

Her grandmother smiled. "Well. Family can be impossible, can't it?"

After dinner, she tried to help in the kitchen, but her grandmother shooed her away. Ingrid was lost in her mother's bookshelves. Carl ducked outside, and Shelby took the opportunity to follow him. The air was cool and felt strangely elastic. She could smell the roses in her mother's garden. They were more real than she was.

"So full," Carl groaned. "I needed some air."

"Me too."

"I think it's going pretty well. Your mom seems to like her."

Shelby rubbed her hands together ineffectually. "It seems that way. But the woman has no tell. I've never known what she was thinking."

"Your grandma's soft on her. That's the most important thing."

"She used to think that you and I were dating."

Carl laughed. "What a shit-show that would have been."

"Meh. I've always maintained that you're charming at first."

"Thanks."

Shelby stared at the fogged window. "I shouldn't have left her in there."

"She'll be fine."

"I wish I could hang a piece of sackcloth over my grade school pictures. I don't want her seeing them."

"We've all got those pictures. I had a fierce mullet."

"I could see you rocking that. I had glasses and headgear. Not flattering."

"She's into you. It's obvious. Don't stress yourself into a neurotic episode."

Shelby sighed. "How long can we keep her in the dark?"

"We may as well spill it. Secrets have a way of biting us in the ass."

"What am I supposed to say? That I went to the city of Egressus without her and met with Latona's rival? Then lied about it?"

He winced. "It doesn't sound great. Have you tried re-arranging the words?"

"She doesn't know that I've been trailing Andrew, either. Or that I met with Narses. Yesterday, I told her that nothing happened. My whole day was a non-event. What I should have said was: *A shifty spado dragged me to a purple chamber, where a queen basically scared the shit out of me.* I'm still dreaming about it, and not in a fun way."

"We need her help. If you come clean—"

"—then what? Everything will be okay?" Shelby stared at him. "I don't want to tell the truth. I want this." She gestured to the house. "Whatever this is. If it's a lie, then I don't care. I want it. And her. And nothing. I don't know. I can't do this anymore."

Carl's expression changed slightly. She turned and saw that Ingrid was standing in the open doorway. Her mouth was a thin line.

"There's ice cream," she said.

Then she walked back inside.

PART TWO

TROVADOR

1

NAKED AGAIN, BUT AT LEAST IT WASN'T RAIN-
ing. The cobblestones were warm against his bare toes, which
he flexed, as if to ensure that they still obeyed him. Shadow
played along the brickwork, making peaks and valleys. The
sun was a reassuring presence on his back. Like a familiar
hand, guiding him into a room. One of those small acts of
tenderness that only seem to happen when nobody is paying
attention. Babieca closed his eyes. If he stayed just like this,
the world would continue to revolve around him. Everything
would remain in its graven state, with his body in the middle, an insensate pin balancing a lock of impossible beauty.
It couldn't last. Julia was already on her way to the clepsydra. They had responsibilities, and she was still uncertain
of her place in all this. However had he become the more
certain one? He was no pack leader. Without Morgan and
Fel to keep him in line, he was little more than a wastrel with
a talent for strumming. Or a strumpet with a talent for wasting. He stared at his fingers, which were soft, unmarred by

the calluses of a real trovador. His whole body was out of practice. What did they expect him to do?

He could dimly recall a conversation with Morgan's shadow. *You've got this. She'll listen to you.* Because he had no gens, no honor. Because he was a disaster, and some people collected them. He would fit perfectly on her shelf.

Julia was the guide. Their cranky artifex. And if anything happened, she might have something with gears that could provide a distraction. Hopefully it wasn't just a pocket full of mechanical frogs. He couldn't remember if those were still popular with the aristocratic set. Judging from the mosaics that he'd seen in wealthy houses, they'd already moved on to ducks.

All we need to do is get our hands on some goslings.

He reached into the brick wall and withdrew his bundle. The lute case was covered in a fine layer of brick dust. He drew out the instrument and played a few notes. It was still in tune. For a moment, he forgot that he was naked and full of questions. The alley disappeared. There was only the staff of notes and the sweet sting against his fingertips. The yellow moss rustled, as if pricking up invisible ears. The sunlight riddled his eyelids, until the world was amber stillness and fire. He and the music were alone with each other. They stayed like that, dancing slow, for a stitch in time. Then he stopped and became aware, finally, of the sweat on his shoulders, the light cramp in his hand. The alley, his sole audience, kept its opinions to itself. He replaced the lute and slowly dressed. There was a pebble in his sandal, which he couldn't seem to dislodge, no matter how many times he shook it. His tunica was sour and needed mending in the worst way possible. The song was over.

He fastened the dagger to his belt, whose fake gemstones were chipped. The buckle was supposed to resemble a boar, but it looked more like a flattened-out dog. The chain that held the dagger was coming undone, and he had to keep checking to ensure that it was still attached. Not that the dagger was particularly useful. The cheap wire grip bit into his palm and was probably sharper than the blade itself. He hadn't used it in some time. He couldn't imagine plunging it into something that was actually alive. Mostly, its job was to cut apples (if he could manage to steal one) or to scratch graffiti on unguarded walls. Perhaps he wasn't a real trovador, but he did enjoy carving his name into various surfaces.

Babieca replaced the bricks in the wall. Now there was no trace of him left in the alley. It might have belonged to anyone. The moment that his life ended, this safe space would be given to someone else, some terrified nemo who was making the transition for the first time. After retching all over the cobblestones, they'd look up, trying to figure out what had happened. They'd see the moss on the bricks, the arterial shadows on the faded red wall, and wonder why it all felt so familiar. *Have I been here before? Did I ever leave?* Naked and disoriented, yes, but also on fire with hope. It was intoxicating: the realization that you'd shed your skin, that you could be anything in this reckless place. And they'd never stop to wonder if this lacuna—their alley, now—had once belonged to someone else.

He drew his knife and carved a capital *B* into the wall. The moss was slightly offended but made no visible protest.

Then he stepped out of the alley, joining the crowds as they merged onto Via Rumor. Brackish water flowed down the street, and he stepped onto the paving stones to keep from soiling his feet. A meretrix had done the same, and she regarded him for a moment. Her mask was carved with animals that blurred into one another, shadowed by foliage. He inclined his head. She gave him a half smile and then kept walking. The soles of her sandals had been carved with arrows, which she left imprinted in the dust of the street. *Follow me.*

He didn't, as much as he might have wanted to. There was no time, and the last thing he needed now was to run into Felix. The house father wasn't precisely an enemy, but whatever alliance they'd once shared was clearly a thing of the past. He was working with the oculus. Babieca didn't even know his name. He was just another mask. Someone he'd never really known in the first place.

The roar of the clepsydra brought him back to the world at hand. The giant water clock loomed over one half of the great piazza, thundering as it powered Fortuna's wheel. He watched her guises revolve. She danced, stole a loaf of bread, polished a knife against a whetstone. She was everything that they hoped and feared themselves to be. And she wanted them to change, to leap to another spoke, narrowly avoiding the crush of the wheel as it screamed past them. Day gens and night gens both held possibilities. Like peculiar families, they kept the city of Anfractus humming. The faces and blood ties were older than anyone could properly remember. Older perhaps than the imperium, which had either fractured or been broken, depending on the story that you heard. Some considered Fortuna to be an upstart goddess, while others maintained that she'd always existed, in one form or another, taking on whatever raiment they gave her.

Babieca liked the feel of the spray. He watched the ceramic vessels as they moved along a track, emptying themselves into the great tank. The wheel turned. For a moment, he thought he saw his own face, under shadow. But it was only a trick of the dance. When he blinked, the image was gone.

"I hope you aren't thinking of lifting anyone's purse." Julia materialized next to him, wearing a head scarf. A few orange curls were faintly visible around the edges. "I don't feel like starving to death in the carcer."

His expression hardened. "I'm no fur."

"Of course not. That's why you're being sent to the hidden tower. Because your morals are clearly impeccable."

"This wasn't my plan, in case you've forgotten. Pulcheria seems to think that we can enlist the aid of the Fur Queen, however impossible that might be. It's a pretty desperate throw, but I'm not going to argue with royalty."

"You were outvoted."

"Thanks awfully for reminding me. I enjoy reliving the moment."

She pulled him behind the shadow of an empty fountain. A few coins and wheel tokens gleamed in the gray water. "You may not be one of them," Julia said, "but you're the closest thing that we've got. You need to commit, or else it isn't going to work."

Julia had always stood at the edge of their company. It was her artifact that had propelled their first quest—a mechanical bee that had nearly killed Basilissa Pulcheria. The daughter of a master artifex, she'd always belonged more to Anfractus than any of them. As a result, she had the most to lose. For the first time, Babieca realized that some small, bleak part of him blamed Julia for Roldan's death. Her stupid device had started all of this. If they'd never met her, they still would have been haunting the Seven Sages taverna. Not a real company, but still, somehow, complete. Now they were broken, and still she refused to pick a side.

"Since when are you qualified to talk about commitment?"

"Listen, you arrogant shit. You may think that I'm not part of this, but you dragged me into it. Before I met you, I had a profession, a future. That's all gone, thanks to the dumbshow that you call a company."

Babieca shook his head. "You can only blame us for so long. You made a choice, artifex. It was a wild throw, but you made it, all on your own. And now you're a part of something. It may not be what you expected, but don't tell me that you aren't the tiniest bit satisfied with your decision. It sure as shit beats making mechanical frogs."

Julia started to say something sharp in reply. Then she sighed. "That was getting pretty dull. And the pay was awful."

"You're the daughter of a famous builder. This is where you belong."

"With a trovador who stinks?"

"It's the tunica."

She sat on the rim of the fountain. "You're not a fur. But Morgan's right. They aren't going to meet with someone who isn't at least slightly debauched. You're the best chance that we have." Julia blinked. "Now that I'm saying it aloud, it does sound bloody unlikely."

"That's a stirring speech."

"It's all I've got at the moment. Aside from a bomb in the shape of a pomegranate."

His eyes widened. "Really? Where is it?"

"I'm not telling you." She inched away. "And don't shake me, or this fool's errand will be over long before it begins."

"Does that mean you're ready?"

"It means I'm as daft as the rest of you."

He smiled. "That's what makes us special."

They headed toward the Subura. As they neared the infamous neighborhood, the ground began to slope downward, and they had to dance along the paving stones to avoid the dark effluvia below. Crumbling firewalls had been built around the entrance, to ensure that it could be cut off from the wealthier vici should disaster strike. Wolves and gamblers were considered acceptable losses, so long as the lavish homes on the hill remained untouched. They walked past the street popinae, which smelled of burning chickpeas. Every gens fought for space at the sun-warmed counters, while the exhausted owners ladled out bowls of questionable stew. Taverna were packed and spilling out crowds onto rickety patios, which made the street all the more congested. Through the shuttered windows, he could smell cheap wine, blackened mushrooms, and the reek of sweat. It was delicious. He spotted an unattended mug and plucked it from the counter. It was cheap terra-cotta, but the pornographic scene engraved upon it was still quite interesting.

"What are you doing?"

Babieca drained the cup and quickened his pace. "Just

getting into character. Would the furs really expect a sober singer to darken their door?"

"You're unbelievable."

He tossed the mug into an unsavory corner, where a young man in a wreath had already passed out and was snoring lightly. "You might want to loosen up as well. At best, they're going to think that you're a lupa."

"Do I look like a whore?"

"That question feels rhetorical."

They kept walking, until the black basia was in view. An indistinct figure was leaning over the second-floor balcony while a steady stream of people moved below. It might have been Felix, but he was too far away to tell. More likely, it was Drauca, the house mother, who often surveyed the vici from her crow's nest. Felix was probably in the tabularium, balancing the ledgers and avoiding confrontation.

The paving stones grew more uneven as they continued past the basia district. After a while, the road itself became theoretical, crumbling into mud and unsavory patches. Broken things glimmered in the dark water: a cracked amulet in the shape of a matrix, a legless doll, a bundle of rags better left undisturbed. A few wolves had set up shop in the long shadows, and they waited on stone beds, reading or patching their clothes. One boy played the flute, and his country song, though tremulous, was true. Babieca thought about stealing a few of the notes, but decided against it. Small betrayals were often the worst kind. He nearly tripped on a phallus carved into the disintegrating road. Fitting punishment. Julia snorted.

"They really are dangerous," he said.

"I don't know. I like the decorative ones that hang in doorways. I saw one the other day with lots of little bells, and it looked rather friendly."

"They're a relic of the old empire. Back when people still had a sense of humor."

"What do you know about the empire?"

He stepped over what looked like a nest of twigs or small bones. "Only what Felix used to tell me. When he felt like talking."

Julia made no response. The street gave up its battle and descended into marsh. They were close to the necropolis. He remembered gambling by the gravestones, while a few wolves attended to their offices. He could smell the decaying flowers and see the small speckled eggs left on the plots belonging to children.

"I'm missing something," Julia said finally.

"You've forgotten what happened the last time we visited this place? There was a silenus, and a good deal of running."

"Not that. I meant what happened between you and Felix."

"That's not a very exciting story."

"Morgan seems pretty annoyed by it, though she refuses to tell me anything."

"Well, it wouldn't be fun if it didn't annoy her."

Julia stopped walking. "Is that why the meretrix won't help us anymore?"

Babieca could feel himself growing angry. The wine wasn't helping. He didn't want to talk about any of his catastrophes. "I'm not the only reason."

"We're not going to get very far if you keep fucking us out of potential allies."

"I didn't—" He closed his eyes for a moment. "It wasn't that, all right? We may have collided once or twice, but it was just a bit of play. It meant nothing."

"To you? Or to him?"

He scowled. "This line of questioning may be why you have so few friends."

Julia smiled and made an expansive gesture. "I have a whole company."

They fell into silence again. Babieca tried to avoid the marsh, which hungered for his sandals. He thought of the baby bats, asleep in the crypt, and the still line of graves that resembled ivory dice. Each soul was a pip. He had no die to work with. Just the dagger, which might escape him at any moment. He thought of the fine blade that Felix had given Roldan, elegant and perfectly balanced. Was it somewhere in the ashes of the house by the wall? Latona had burned it down, to keep them from escaping, but they still found a way out. The bones of the house remembered, even as the flames devoured them. Not even a basilissa could prevent them from doing what they had to. *It's not my knife,* Felix had said. *It's yours.* The delicate incongruity of watching him lift the weapon, so carefully, as if it were hot and alive. It was probably melted now, a congealed pool of silver among the ruins.

"We were entangled," he said, after a time. "Briefly. I suppose we were both looking for something else. Though we forgot precisely what that was. It may not have existed."

"You sound like a tragic poet."

He shrugged. "A poet would craft a story. I don't really have one. I've never thought in terms of an epic narrative. I just crawl from line to line."

"That wine has turned you maudlin."

The anger broke free. Babieca turned on her. "What in Fortuna's name do you want from me? A song? Something you can dance to? It doesn't work that way. I'm an idiot. I ruin people. I've disappointed everyone who ever gave a shit about me. I've lied and stumbled and fucked my way through two lives, and neither of them is working out." He leaned against a brittle wall whose topmost part had fallen away, revealing a pulverized core. "The only person who ever truly saw me is gone. And before the body was even cold, I returned to the black basia for a bit of pointless trim. Even the sheets were judging me. How am I supposed to turn that disaster into music? Nobody would listen to it."

Julia was startled into silence for a moment. Then she began to laugh.

Her reaction threw him off-guard. "What's so amusing?"

"You talk like you're the first person who's ever been in

love. It's always a disaster. If it weren't, then you'd have nothing to sing about."

"I think you've missed the part of the story where everything I touch turns to shit."

Julia took his hand. For a moment, he expected her to squeeze it tenderly. Then she jerked it sharply, slapping him across the face with his own palm.

"You seem fine," she said.

"You're mad." He touched his cheek, wincing. "And *mean*."

"And you're acting like a spoiled puppy. Wake up, trovador. You're alive." She pointed at the necropolis. "Those poor bastards in there have no hold over you. They're nothing but a pile of grave goods. You can still change the world. Your song may be ridiculous, but it's far from finished. Snap out of it and start playing. Otherwise, I'll leave you here to commune with the dead. I could use an extra pair of sandals, and that lute will fetch a price, even if it is cracked."

Babieca grinned slowly. "You can be quite motivational when you're tearing a man's heart out. It reminds me that I hardly know you."

"I'm not that complicated. Neither are you." She started walking again. "Come along. This place is starting to stink."

They followed the crumbling wall that separated Anfractus from the forest beyond. Babieca could almost feel the silenoi on the other side, twitching their spears. They were always spoiling for a hunt. The basilissae had upheld the treaty that kept them from hunting during the day, but Latona wanted to change that. She seemed perfectly willing to trade the lives of her subjects for a chance at re-creating the imperium. Whatever that might mean. Shrines and frescoes were all that remained of the glorious empire, along with whatever agreements had been made to keep the hunters at bay.

He saw a flicker of something on the path ahead of them. Sunlight gleaming against metal. He grabbed Julia's arm, pulling her behind an anemic tree whose branches did little to conceal them.

"Someone's waiting for us," he whispered. "I just saw them."

"How many?"

"I don't know."

"How extraordinarily helpful."

"At least—" He bit down on his retort. "Never mind. I think it's a small patrol. Three at most. What's the range of your pomegranate?"

It took her a moment to register what he was asking. "It'll have to be close. And we'll need adequate cover."

He scanned the surface of the curtain wall. Large sections of it had crumbled away, revealing the original stonework. A bad patch job had resulted in an uneven section, which afforded a small niche where they might hide. At least, it appeared to be wide enough for two people. He couldn't be sure, and there was no time to measure the space.

Babieca pointed at the crumbling lacuna. "Get in there and wait for my signal. Then throw that thing as hard as you can."

"What's the signal?"

"My screaming."

Julia frowned. "Maybe you should hide. An artifex is more respectable than a trovador. They might let me pass."

"They're looking for a female artifex. They'll stop you for sure. But there's nothing unusual about a wandering singer. I can blend in."

"Babieca." Her voice wavered. "If they realize who you are, they'll crack you open like a lobster and nail your lungs to the wall. If Fortuna happens to be watching, you may already be dead when they do it. But there's no guarantee."

"That's a lovely image to put in my head. Thank you."

She grabbed his hand, this time in earnest. "You don't have to do this alone."

"Someone needs to reach the tower. You've got Pulcheria's token. If things go badly, wait for them to disperse, and then head for the cloaca."

He removed the lute from its case and kept walking. He

didn't look back. His instinct was to run or creep forward, but he willed himself to keep an even gait. He began to play an old song. "The Amber Tunica." He threw in some false notes. He could feel the slight weight of the dagger, still hanging from his belt. Would there be time to draw it? He tapped the surface of the lute, focusing on the tempo rather than the terror. As he neared the spot where he'd seen the flash of steel, he began to stumble and curse beneath his breath. He was a drunken singer who posed no threat. He repeated this to himself, until he believed it. Meanwhile, a silent, secretive part of his mind was constructing a more dangerous song.

A man and two women emerged from a bend in the city wall. He expected them to be wearing scale loricae, but they weren't miles. Instead, they wore gray tunicae with curious white embroidery around the sleeves. Their cloaks were fastened by silver fibulae, and as he drew closer, he realized that each of the pins had been carved with a pair of eyes. The pupils were winking garnets. They were speculatores. The spies of the basilissa. Not quite a gens, but invested with considerable power. In her mother's day, they'd been an oppressive force, hated throughout the city. This was the first time that he'd ever seen them up close. Two of them had daggers fastened to their belts, while the woman in front carried a gladius with a decorated scabbard. She also had a scroll case, fixed to her belt by a delicate chain. He wondered about the documents inside.

"Stop." The speculator leveled her blade. "Where are you going?"

Her black hair was tied back, revealing a neck crisscrossed with small, delicate scars. Babieca was so distracted that for a moment he forgot who he was supposed to be. Then he slouched slightly, letting the lute dangle from his right hand.

"Just coming from the necropolis." His speech was slow and heavy. "Played at a funeral. Sad affair. Now I'm looking to pay for some trim."

Her expression hovered between disinterest and revulsion. "You're going the wrong way. The basia district is behind you."

"It's kind of you, Domina, to think that I could afford a mask. There's a taverna by the wall that rents out rooms by the hour. Not that I'll need so long."

"I'm no domina," she said, though her tone had softened. "Where is this place of ill repute that you mentioned?"

"Begging your pardon, but, seeing as it's unlicensed, it doesn't have a name. Patrons simply call it the hole in the wall."

That last part was a bit much. He could see it in the way that her expression hardened again. But this was all part of the character. He had to be slightly repugnant. They were looking for a trovador who belonged to a company, not a pathetic scop who earned his keep by singing at funerals.

"You're awfully brazen about breaking the law."

He inclined his head. "Apologies, fair lady. I'm a bit in the cups already." He leaned against the wall. "If you'd prefer, I can turn right around and head back to a more reputable place of business. I promise to sing the whole way."

She grimaced slightly. "I've little desire to hear you, nor smell you. Be on your way."

He bowed, stumbling halfway through. "Fortuna smile on you."

Another speculator murmured something that he couldn't quite hear. The woman shook her head and made a dismissive gesture. Babieca kept walking. He made sure to lean slightly as he moved forward. He couldn't believe that it had worked.

"Wait."

He closed his eyes. *Damn the wheel. I was so close.*

Babieca kept his eyes on the ground and mumbled: "How can I be of service?"

"Show me your purse," the speculator said. "It's bad enough that you're charging mourners for folk songs. I want to see how much coin you made from their suffering. Hand it over so that I can count it."

"Beg pardon, but I really didn't make very much—"

"—*now*, piss-for-brains. If you're very lucky, I won't throw you in the carcer for petty extortion."

This was turning ugly. Babieca tried to hold on to the tune that he'd been crafting. If he could play a single staff of notes, they might just listen. The trick was getting them to stand still for that long. They were more likely to break his fingers. He made a show of searching through the inside of his tunica, adjusted his belt, then checked the lute case for good measure. Fel carried the company's coin. He didn't have a single maravedi to show them.

He was about to spread his hands in a defeated gesture, hoping that the speculator would think that he was damaged in the head. That might at least buy him some clemency. But then he heard footsteps, and cursing. Babieca turned, just in time to receive a blow to the face. He staggered backward, tasting blood. For a moment, everything turned upside down. Then he realized that Julia was standing over him, one hand still raised.

"You miserable son of a bitch!"

He spat out blood. "What's happening?" It came out as a sort of wheeze.

"Are you so drunk that you don't even recognize your own wife?" She shook her head in disgust. "We were married in the sight of Fortuna, and you promised to cherish me." She kicked him in the ribs, and he doubled over. "*Cherish.* Not leave me in that shithole of an insula, while you drink and whore your way across town!"

The speculator regarded her with mild interest. "He belongs to you?"

"Aye, Domina. This stinking pile of human refuse, I acknowledge as my own. My dear distracted husband." She gave him another kick, though it was slightly less vehement. "Any coin he makes, he gambles away."

"Apologies . . . lamb." Babieca struggled to rise. "I was thinking of you the whole time. I swear by the wheel."

"What cursed tavernae have you been haunting, wretch?"

He was impressed by her commitment to the role. "None, sweet wife. I was playing at a funeral. But I seem to have lost what meager coin I made there. This thrice-patched tunica is full of holes. It must have fallen out."

Her nostrils flared. "Now you're insulting my needle-work?"

Babieca could see that the speculator was growing annoyed. This new development had intrigued her for a moment, but now she was liable to arrest both of them. The others were absorbing the performance in stoic silence.

"I swear—" He gave Julia a sharp look. "I played sweetly for the mourners. The very song that I used to play for you."

"You're a liar and a whoremonger. Play it, then. I doubt you even remember how. Your fingers are as numb against the strings as they are in the bedroom."

The speculator rolled her eyes. "This has gone far enough—"

"Play, damn you." Julia moved as if to kick him again. "With these sober, goddess-fearing folk as your audience. Prove your worth."

Her eyes were full of hope. *You can do this.*

Before the speculator could protest, Babieca cradled the lute and began to play. It was an ancient reel—something that he'd heard once, in a smoke-filled taverna. More elegant by far than its surroundings. He'd snatched it that night and tucked it away, silently adding to it. Over time, held close in the dark, it had become his own composition. It was limned by his anxieties, his intensities and wild hopes. It was a summer storm, a kiss in secret, a whirling, unstoppable wheel. He felt it move through him, until every atom was spinning. His fingers danced along the strings. This was faster than he'd ever played before, and he could feel the cut of each note, but he wove that into the song. Blood in his mouth, ringing in his ears, spasms of pain and joy that made him tremble. The song was playing him now, turning him in its arms. He was the instrument whirling in the lathe, faster and faster, about to fly apart. It was love that kept him spinning, kept him together, soaking the strings in blood. He was alive and on fire. It was too much and everything that he wanted.

To be played. To be heard.

He opened his eyes (he didn't remember closing them) and saw the effects of the song. The speculatores were dancing. Not in jerky movements, like marionettes whose strings were being pulled. They had given themselves to the reel, and their movements were smooth, inevitable, as if they'd always been dancing. The women glided alongside each other. The subordinate officer spun her commander around, and she laughed richly. Her delight was high and trilling, a girl's laugh, startled by her own pleasure. The man danced by himself, turning and spinning to the beat, as if he had a ghostly partner. Their expressions were far away but also extraordinarily present, swept up in the song. What they were doing wasn't merely important. It was everything. They were dancing for their lives.

His fingers were bleeding now, and he could feel the pain. Sweat was getting in his eyes. His hand slipped, and he played a false note. The song shattered. The speculatores blinked and stared, as if they'd just woken from a long sleep.

"Throw the fruit!" Babieca cried.

Julia drew the mechanical pomegranate from her tunica. "Step back!"

"What are you doing?" The speculator reached for her blade, which she'd left on the ground while dancing. "In the name of—"

Julia threw the bomb at their feet. It detonated as she was running, and Babieca grabbed her by the arm, pushing her ahead of him. The artifact shuddered as it hit the ground, then exploded into a hundred buzzing pieces of metal. It took him a second to realize that they were mechanical bees. They swarmed in a cloud that enveloped the speculatores. Their roar was strangely metallic, and it made him shiver.

He saw flashes of blood and metal within the cloud. The speculatores were screaming, trying to get to their weapons. Then Julia was pulling him forward, and he could no longer see through the stinging cloud.

They ran until the road had almost disappeared. The marsh encroached on all sides. Nettles and osiers whipped him, but he kept running. He tried not to think of what they'd left behind. The song and the sting. His fingers ached. That was something to concentrate on.

He was gasping by the time they reached the entrance to the cloaca. Julia leaned against the crumbling wall. Neither of them seemed to register the smell.

"Are those things lethal?" Babieca asked.

"I don't think so." She was breathing hard. "They'll tire. Eventually."

"And then what? They'll attack some innocent bystander?"

"No. They only have a bit of life in them. It won't last."

He stared at the iron grate that led to the sewers. "Good for them. I suppose they're fulfilling their purpose."

"So are we." She withdrew an L-shaped key from her tunica. "This belonged to my mother. They used to call her the queen of the sewers."

"If you squint, it's nearly a compliment."

Julia unlocked the gate. "She engineered the great cloaca, along with the tunnels underneath. If her schemata are correct, then one of those tunnels should take us where we want to go."

"*Want* is a strong word."

"Stop dithering and get in here, before they find us."

He stepped through the open grate. Dark water poured across his sandals. Now his eyes were burning from the smell. Julia locked the grate behind them and pocketed the key. As they pushed forward, the ordure rose to his ankles.

"I'm so glad we decided to visit this place again," he murmured.

"We're safer down here than up there."

"Have you seen the size of the rats?"

"I'll protect you." She paused. "Though what you did back there was pretty great. The way you had them dancing? I've never seen anything like it."

His hands still ached. "It was something."

"Could you do it again?"

"What—make the rats dance?"

"I'd love to see that."

He rubbed his jaw. "You hit me pretty hard."

"Hush." She led him forward. "I knew you'd be fine all along."

2

"ARE WE INTERESTING?"

Julia paused in the middle of wiping something ominous from her sandal. She was leaning against the filthy wall of the cloaca, her balance precarious. "Excuse me?"

Babieca watched the river of ordure as it flowed past. Dark shapes were visible beneath the surface. Occasionally, something glimmered. A button, or a bit of colored glass. Detritus that was oddly beautiful in its state of decay.

"I mean, as characters." He took a step back from the edge. "Are we the sort of heroes that they write songs about?"

"You're the singer. I just tighten bolts." She replaced her sandal. "I suppose that armies have crept in through the sewer before. Cities have fallen. But those heroes probably weren't lost."

"Are we lost?"

"Not entirely. But all of these tunnels do look alike." She stared at a square of parchment. "My mother built this place, so she didn't need a map. Some of her notations look more like ink blotches."

"Characters in a real epic wouldn't be having these kinds of navigational problems."

She stared at him. "I don't know what tablets you've been reading in your spare time—or where you found any spare time at all—but we aren't exactly in the middle of a narrative poem." She gestured to the foul water. "This is as prosaic as it gets."

"Maybe prose heroes have their own set of problems."

"I don't understand what definition you're working from."

He shrugged. "People in songs are convincing. Shite at love, for certain, but at least they know what they're doing. I feel like one of your mother's inkblots."

"Your only problem is a crisis of confidence." Julia took him in with a glance. "That, and the fact that you can't fight."

"This coming from the woman who stabbed someone in the foot."

"It wasn't pretty, but it saved your life." Julia sighed. "Babs—"

"Never call me that."

She smiled in the dim light. "Just try not to lose your weapon. And keep your sandals out of the shit. That's all we can ask of any hero."

The lantern threw their hopeful shadows against the walls. Babieca read the occasional graffiti. *Diotima is a false friend. Felix belongs to every man.* He wondered if it was the same Felix. The name was probably common. Then he grew distracted by a drawing, which depicted a man wearing a cock helmet. There was no caption, which was a shame. Babieca wondered how many people had followed these tunnels. What had led them here, trying to outpace the filth at their feet? If Julia was right, then the furs took advantage of this underground nest. They were probably the artists in question.

"Do we even know that she exists?" Babieca's eyes watered, from both the smoke and what it was covering. "Has anyone seen her?"

"That's hardly relevant. Until recently, nobody had ever

seen a lar of the air. But I watched more than a few palace guards shit themselves at the sight of one. They're as real as a house fire. I imagine the Fur Queen is something like them."

"I hope not. There's no way that I'm riding another dragon."

"Well, strictly speaking, it was made of smoke."

"My bruised parts would beg to differ with you."

They followed the dark flow of refuse and memories. Babieca had to admit that the cloaca was something of a marvel. The founders had built these tunnels when the imperium was barely a spark, and they endured, stretching the length of Anfractus. They could take you anywhere, if you didn't mind rolling the dice. Furs, animals, and other things nested here. They were well out of their territory, and if Julia's plan didn't work, they might never leave. Blind and wet things, used to the darkness, would dispose of them.

"Maybe this is where the old basilissa's lampreys ended up," he observed, glancing leerily at the water. "I don't imagine they've grown friendlier."

"The furs have made nice pets out of them," Julia said. "Like tame dolphins, only with a lot more teeth."

"You're not helping."

She paused at a junction. The lamplight was inadequate. Both tunnels ended in blackness that might have signaled the end of the world. "The map isn't helping, either. My mother's notes resemble a broken mosaic. I'm not sure which way to go."

"Haven't we been following the aqueduct?"

She made a face. "Possibly."

Babieca closed his eyes for a moment. The chosen darkness was somehow more comforting than what waited for him in the tunnels. "This seemed easier when we were still a company. At least we knew what direction to take."

"Back then, we were simply looking for an entrance to the Patio of Lions. All roads lead to the arx—even these. But the furs don't want to be found."

"Do you think they're watching us?"

She held the lamp a bit higher. "I've no doubt. They're like cats, just waiting to see which hole we're going to scurry through."

"Did you ever think of becoming one?"

"A fur?" Julia looked thoughtful for a moment. "I suppose, on my darkest nights, I thought about giving it all up. Sometimes it felt as if the machines had betrayed me. That I'd been doomed from the start. On those nights, I peered down the blind alleys and thought about giving myself to the night gens."

"What stopped you?"

She reached into her tunica and withdrew a small device. It was a mechanical bee, a wonder of gears and graven silver, affixed to a small pedestal. Babieca almost reached out to touch it, his eyes widening in surprise. He remembered standing with her, in the undercroft of the artifices, digging through piles of rich debris and forgotten toys. Sulpicia, the sly-tongued fox, had shown her how to complete the mechanism. That little bee had quite nearly brought down the city of Egressus, when Basilissa Latona used it to draw the silenoi. Now it was still, but he'd watched it tear through the fading day, a scrap of quicksilver. He remembered the reckless joy they'd felt as they chased it through the streets. Nearly flying. A company dancing across the hot, uneven paving stones.

"Follow that bee," he murmured.

Julia smiled. "I remember."

"Why did you bring it?"

She shrugged. "I thought it might come in handy. It never would leave me alone. Kept buzzing outside my window, until I finally let it in."

"I guess he belongs to you."

"He?"

"Well, I'm no expert at sexing bees, but aren't men usually the ones who buzz outside your window? That sounds like a masculine strategy. All he needs is a tiny lute. He could sing to you about queens and honeycombs."

"Shut up."

"It's a perfectly serviceable metaphor."

"No—" She pushed him against the wall. "Shut up. Someone's coming."

He lowered his voice. "And where are we supposed to hide? Should I close my eyes and pretend that I can make myself invisible?"

"Shut your mouth, or I swear by the wheel—"

Something moved a few inches from his hand. At first, Babieca thought it was the living moss that clung to the alleys. The founders only knew where that came from or what its purpose was. But as his eyes adjusted to the flickering lamplight, he realized that it was a boy in a dun-colored tunica. He wore a cloak that looked as if it had been stitched from a dozen grimy shawls and scarves. Now it matched precisely the shade of the walls. Even his sandals were gray. It took him a moment to realize that the boy had always been there. He'd simply looked like one of the cloaca's shadows, still as the oozing stones. Two other figures resolved themselves in the dim glow, seeming to step from the walls, like ghosts. How long had they been there? Had they followed in silence the whole time, or had there been others, grim trees pressed close to the crumbling brick, listening to them as they fumbled through the dark? Babieca rather feared that it was the latter. The eyes of the cloaca had been following them from the very first moment.

"Well," he said, "I suppose it was foolish to think that we might sneak up on you." He inclined his head slightly. "Not that we mean any harm, mind you. I'm a poor singer, and this baggage next to me is an artifex. Mostly, she just tightens bolts. Her words."

The furs seemed to regard them as one presence. They were motionless. Babieca didn't feel the fear that he'd been expecting. After all, they weren't exactly menacing. The boy nearest him couldn't have been more than ten years old. No more than a grimy cherub, with calm gray eyes. Too calm, perhaps. A few feet away from him stood a woman with silver hair. It was difficult to tell how old she might be. Her face was smudged, and the lines on her forehead could have been the result of hard living, rather than age. Her eyes were uncommonly still, like the boy's. They weighed him piece by piece, until he felt naked. The third shadow was a girl, maybe thirteen, with close-cropped hair. She wore a boy's tunica praetexta, its red stripe now faded to rust. It looked as if her nose had been broken more than once. This was their welcoming party.

Julia drew herself up. Her voice was steady, though Babieca could detect a faint trill of fear humming around the edges. "We are emissaries of Basilissa Pulcheria. Her Grace has sent us to parlay with the Fur Queen."

The furs exchanged a look. Then the boy held out his hand wordlessly. Julia offered him Pulcheria's scroll. Neither had any idea what the basilissa had actually written in her neat, gliding hand. Perhaps it was their death warrant. He examined the seal critically. Then he slipped the scroll beneath his patchwork cloak and motioned for them to follow. The ledge was too narrow for them to walk abreast, so the boy led them in single file. The girl crossed to the other side of the tunnel, while the old woman followed behind. Babieca couldn't help noticing how effectively they'd been surrounded. Not even a spectacular diversion would buy them the chance of escape. All they could do was keep walking.

"I don't like this," he whispered.

"No?" Julia kept her voice down, but her eyes were bright with anger. "You don't think that walking into the furs' den with an escort is a brilliant plan? I rather thought that we'd outfoxed them, until this moment."

He eyed the girl, who seemed to regard them as slow-moving prey. "We're not exactly dealing with palace guards. They don't even have weapons."

She leaned in closer to whisper. "Did you see their eyes? They might be planning to eat us."

"You're a very soothing person. Has anyone ever told you that?"

The furs led them through a series of junctions and blind turns, until they were thoroughly disoriented. Their guides remained silent. He could hear the slow-moving river of refuse beneath them, as well as the dripping from above. Was there really a tower buried in all of this filth? People said that it grew like a blind root in the earth, a reversal whose defiance mocked the other gens. But why? There were shadowed corners on the surface that already belonged to the furs. They could have made their den in any number of hidden alleys, but they chose to gather here, in this place of forgetting, where dyes and piss and ruins mingled with water from the aqueduct. What worried him was how quickly he'd adjusted to the smell. Maybe he belonged here.

The passageway narrowed. The boy gestured to their lamp, as if he wanted to see it. Julia handed it over, and he snuffed out the light.

"Wait! How are we supposed to see?" The panic was hot in her voice. Babieca felt it coursing through his own body as well. A child's fear of the dark. He realized that they were being led by a child, and the thought made him laugh, before he could stop himself. The sound fractured as it struck the walls, which he could no longer see. For a long moment, nobody moved or said a word. *This must be what death feels like. No time or movement. No shape of things. No separation between you and the dark. Just one perfect pause that never ends.*

But gradually, as his eyes adjusted further, a gauzy outline began to appear. He couldn't quite see Julia, but he could make out the contours of her, as if an impatient artist had drawn an outline and then abandoned the project. He could smell the licorice on her breath. His heart was pounding in his ears. If he stared hard at the space next to Julia's shadow, he could see a slight separation, a contrast between her and the wall that he knew was there.

He felt fingers groping for his own. It was Julia's hand. She was sweating, even in the chill of the tunnel. He wrapped his fingers around her own, and there was a spark of contact, like two latches combining. Then cool, dry fingers slipped into his left hand. It was the woman with silver hair, standing behind him. She was barely an inch away, but he saw her as indistinct markings, rippling shadow. Her grip was surprisingly firm, and that calmed him, somewhat. Then the line began to move forward, slowly, but steadily. Their young guide must have known the place intimately, every stone, every turn, like a body grown familiar in the dark. Either that, or he had cat's eyes. For a brief moment, he wondered where the girl was. He imagined her watching them shuffling along from a distance, waiting for some silent order. Perhaps a whole army of cats was following them.

Babieca decided that this had not been their best plan.

They inched forward for what might have been hours. In the deep dark, there was no real sense of direction. Only the steady pull of Julia's hand told him that they were moving in a straight line. Sometimes he'd forget about the old woman, until he felt her body against his back, her cold grip on his other hand. Sometimes they were a shadow with three hearts, sharing the same shallow breath. His body was connected to theirs, had always been, faceless and silent beneath the earth. Inch by inch, they moved. The sound of the water began to recede. The quality of the air changed. Now it was cool and dry, like the woman's hand. Babieca could smell something metallic. Every once in a while, a spark flared that might have been a vein of quartz, or perhaps another set of eyes. He wanted to reach out and touch the walls, to see if they'd changed, but his arms were pinioned. They could only move as one, a machine with no choice but to go forward, gears turning. The smell reminded him of the undercroft beneath the black basia, where they'd first met Drauca. He remembered the beautiful stolae and winking gems, tools of the lover's trade. The tower of wigs and pots of precious tincture.

I once . . . knew a horse named Babieca.

He almost laughed again but thought better of it. The silence was somehow holy. They were in the heart of a tumulus, where old things slept. He could feel the memory of violence, the blood that had soaked into this earth, centuries ago. The ghosts were heavy like cobwebs, stirring against his mouth, and it took all of his concentration not to break contact and brush them away. Perhaps they meant no harm, though he couldn't be sure.

Suddenly, the path ended. He started to lurch forward, but the woman's grip pulled him back. They held steady for a moment. Then he felt Julia's hand moving, and he had no choice but to follow. There was nothing beneath his foot. Like a child learning to walk, he stepped into the void. Then there was stone. He felt it against his sandal. For a moment, he was torn in two directions. Then the woman gave him a gentle push, and his left foot joined his right. It was a step, he realized. Now that the vertigo had passed, he could feel that he was standing on a narrow step. He shuffled slightly and felt the step taper off as he moved to the left. Now his toes were dangling in empty space again, while his heel remained on solid ground. It was a spiral staircase, narrowing as it turned in a hidden gyre that could go on for miles beneath the surface. He had no way of knowing, and no chance to ponder it. For now the woman was gently pushing him again, while Julia's hand pulled him down.

It felt like a strange dance. At first, the movements were alien, but over time they grew familiar. Then there was only the dance, taking him farther beneath the surface. He'd spent his life descending these stairs, one inch at a time, inhaling the black scents of this stone bower. He'd been born in the dark. Nobody had told him about the sun, or the sound of voices. The stairs, he thought, must continue until they eventually reversed direction. His whole life was a dream of staircases that formed a perfect circle. He would dance with them, lifting and dipping, a line stretched blindly across some fathomless caesura.

Julia stopped, and he nearly ran into her. But again, the woman pulled him back slightly, anticipating the change in momentum. They were still for a breath. Then they stepped forward, on solid ground. Babieca could see something in the distance. At first, he thought that he was imagining some flicker of light. But then he saw the flash again. It was truly a lamp. Now he could see it dancing across Julia's face. Shadows resolved themselves. He could see the boy ahead of them, and the girl who paced them at a distance. They reached the lantern, which was affixed to the wall. It was carved in the shape of Fortuna, though time and the touch of damp had weathered her face. She was frozen in the act of cutting someone's purse strings.

"I think we've arrived," Julia whispered.

She pulled away from his grasp. The feeling of emptiness was indescribable. His fingers flexed, unsure of how to work on their own. The woman's dry grip was gone as well, and he realized that she was standing next to him. The path was now wide enough for them to walk abreast. Not a path, but a road. Its stones were uneven and had crumbled away in places, like the margins of a scroll. But it was solid.

The founders must have built this, when Anfractus was still young. In the summer of the imperium, before everything broke away.

Babieca couldn't imagine what a road was doing beneath the earth. Something must have buried it. Unless the stone had simply grown up around it over time, like some kind of ancient, questing weed. An undercity. If the skyways connected the buildings above, why couldn't there be secret roads below?

Their guide led them forward. It was no longer uncomfortable that neither of the furs had spoken a single word. Babieca had come to think of them as naturally silent. There was, in fact, something oddly comforting about their lack of speech. They didn't even require a gestural language. A glance was enough. He'd expected them to use a cipher, like the hand signs that were common among vendors in the Exchange, but that would have been too frenetic. This was closer to a serpent's tongue, rhythmic and silent, occasionally testing the air without making a mark. Footsteps in snow.

The thought struck out of nowhere, confusing him for a moment.

Snow.

What was that?

He recognized the word, could taste it even, but the precise meaning escaped him. In Anfractus, it was always summer. But some part of him—something that seemed much closer in the dark—remembered snow. The word was a creeping whiteness, covering him just as surely as night would, only in drifts of silver.

Smaller tunnels branched off from the path, each one flickering with its own light. Babieca caught glimpses of other rooms. In one, he saw a table full of daggers, gleaming in a circle of light. In another, he saw shadows moving. At first, they seemed to be sweeping across the floor. But they moved in unison, extending small hands, grasping at emptiness. *Again,* a voice said. They ghosted across the floor, hands outstretched. *Again.* The image was gone before he could decipher it. They kept walking. He peered down another tunnel and saw a room whose walls were covered in locks of every type. Some were shaped like human faces, while others were glaring lions, or plates with curling inscriptions. Heaps of keys covered the floor. A small girl— no more than nine—was squinting in concentration while she worked at one of the locks with a flexible bit of wire. The lock clicked open. She looked up at that moment, eyes flaring in triumph, and they met each other's gaze. Her joy leapt across the dark, and he felt it tear through him with burning paws. He grinned, and she did the same.

Finally, they came to a larger room. It might have been a hall, save for the lack of a hearth at its center. Instead, the space was lit by a sea-green glow that seemed to come from the walls itself. Babieca realized that it was patches of night-moss, which covered the stone like an iridescent tapestry. The feeling was akin to being underwater. The light moved because the moss was moving, just as it did in the alleys, but more insistently. Blind threads of it trembled in his direction. He wasn't sure if he should greet it politely or twist away from its peculiar, undulating grasp.

Benches lined the edges of what, he decided, he would have to call the great hall. There were rushes on the ground, which held bits of mystery, as well as meat. Furs talked quietly in groups, or ate in silence. Babieca nearly jumped out of his skin as something moved next to him. But it was only a thin dog, coughing on his foot. Its dark eyes resembled glass beneath the breathing glow of the night-moss. Everyone stopped talking and looked at them. Julia stood stock-still, hands at her sides. The boy was gone. Had he simply vanished? Babieca scanned the crowd but couldn't see him anywhere. The girl still lingered to their right but had moved a respectable distance away.

All eyes were on them. Babieca was about to say something when the woman with silver hair walked past him. For some reason, his mouth closed. A ripple passed through the gathered furs as she made her way to the center of the hall. She handed her cloak to a shadow nearby, and Babieca saw that underneath it, she'd been wearing a black stola. Gold bracelets flashed on her bare arms, and two brooches were pinned to the fabric of her dress, linked by a delicate silver chain. Now that she was beneath the light, he realized that her hair was a wave of silver, marked by a tortoiseshell comb. She washed her face in a basin, wiping away the smudged dirt. Then she sat in a leather chair—the only chair in the room.

"Welcome to my home," said the Fur Queen. "Not as impressive as the arx, but I like to think of it as a subterranean palace."

"Thank you—em—Your Majesty." Julia tried to execute a curtsey but only succeeded in tripping. Babieca steadied her. Did furs curtsey? He was unfamiliar with the rules of this buried court. Should he bow? The moment passed before he could move. He stood next to Julia, one hand on her shoulder, as if they were both a painted tableau. *Frozen intruders.*

"Let's have a look at your papers." The Fur Queen gestured with one hand. "Thorn, darling, give me the scroll."

The boy reappeared. He'd been standing behind her chair the whole time. Now his ragged cloak appeared to flicker beneath the light of the hall. First it was the color of the stained oak benches, and then the dark of the queen's gown. His hand, almost disembodied, was pale as milk against the shifting garment. She took the proffered scroll. For a moment, her eyes narrowed as she examined the wax seal. Then she broke it and scanned the contents. Nodding once in satisfaction, she handed the scroll back to Thorn, who receded into the shadows behind her.

The Fur Queen shook her head. "Basilissae. They're good at issuing proclamations, but not so expert at seeing the big picture. It's all a game to them. We're just stones on a board, and they'll sacrifice all of us, if it serves them." She looked up. "Are you stones?"

Julia frowned. "I'm not sure I understand the question, Your Majesty."

"It's simple. Pulcheria is using you. When your value fades, she'll discard you. Latona is doing the same thing with your friend—the oculus."

Babieca took a step forward. "You know about Roldan?"

He couldn't quite give up the name. They'd been close. Lashed together with a single belt, at one point. Now he was a different riddle entirely. He'd made a pact with Latona. He'd given her exactly what she wanted.

The Fur Queen's expression didn't waver. "I don't believe he goes by that name any longer. But yes. I see both sides of the board. We're all just stones in the end. But we can still surprise the hands that move us."

Babieca frowned. "But you're a queen. Doesn't that make you closer to the basilissae?"

Her mouth quirked slightly. "They only think that they're in control. I know that I'm not—which gives me a certain advantage."

"What does the scroll say?"

"Babieca—" Julia warned.

"What? I'm being hospitable." He inclined his head. "I just want to know what it says. If we're pawns, we might as well have a glimpse of the rules. In fact, I want out of this metaphor completely. No more talk of stones and strategy. What does she want from us?"

The Fur Queen looked thoughtful. Then she clapped her hands lightly. All of the furs rose silently from their tables and left the hall. Only the boy and the girl remained. Babieca could dimly make them out, positioned on either side of her chair.

"Thorn and Eth shall remain, if you don't mind. They attend me in all matters." She folded her hands and looked at Babieca. "What you're really asking is how it works. You want to know what the shadows mean."

"I don't understand."

"I think you do. Come here. Both of you."

Cautiously, they approached her. Thorn and Eth didn't move but watched them closely. Babieca wondered if the others had really left, or if they were still here, perfectly invisible. The Fur Queen gestured to the basin of water.

"Tell me what you see."

Babieca stared at her. "Is this another game?"

She said nothing. He leaned over, staring into the clear water. He could see Julia's reflection and his own. Beneath the glow of the night-moss, they both resembled ghosts. A young face looked back at him—though not quite as young as he'd expected. He had dark hair, and brown eyes that remained slightly guarded. His beard needed a trim. He had his mother's dark complexion, and his father's arrogant cheekbones. The face was one that he recognized, but also a stranger. That's who this must be. A face glimpsed in passing. Some part of him that he'd never chosen. Handsome after a fashion, charming at first, but not someone that you'd trust with your hopes and infirmities.

"Well?"

He looked up. "I see my reflection. That's all."

"That's everything." She smiled. "What is your reflection?"

"I'm no good with riddles."

"Then you're missing the point. What is your reflection, Babieca?"

He looked at Julia. Her expression said: *This is on you.*

"It's me," he said. "Or . . . a version of me."

The Fur Queen rose and stood next to him. Babieca was uncomfortably aware of her presence but didn't move.

"Our reflections are strangers," she said. "We need a looking glass to see them, or the eyes of another. Deep down, we're all two different people. There's the one looking out, and the one looking in. Neither is more real than the other. But what happens"—she brushed the water with her fingers—"if I disturb the view?"

His reflection scattered into points of light. Tesserae in a mosaic. For a moment, he saw not one face, but a crowd. A gathering of shadows moving across the surface of the water, each slightly different. In their dance, he saw an exquisite tension, a war of pain and promise, order and chaos, that formed wild islands in the water. He was all of those things, some savage archipelago of contraries and desires and beautiful mistakes. But what did they add up to? Who was really looking back at him?

"Light bends when it strikes water," the Fur Queen continued. "The earth bends when it strikes civilization, but it doesn't break. It changes. What you see in the water isn't simply a version of you. It's every choice that you didn't make. Every unspoken word. Every missed opportunity. We carry these shadows with us, and eventually, they take on a life of their own. A world of their own. And even now"—she looked around the hall, her expression somewhere between mischief and reverence—"they're watching us, from the other side. Watching us do what they never could, while we wonder if they're merely a dream."

"You're talking about the other world," Julia said. "Beyond Anfractus."

"They're the same," she replied. "Cities hemmed in by wilderness. Old territories, older spirits, captured but never conquered. Borders drawn in pen and ink, drawn in blood, which the land never agreed to. Our family trees are hopelessly entangled. Everything you do is another brick in the city of infinite alleys. Ripples on the surface of the water, spreading to the margins. Where your shadow hesitates, you will choose. What you forget, your shadow remembers. The worlds are parallel dreams. And if Latona raises her army, they'll both be in danger."

"How do you know all of this?" Babieca asked. "I thought that the longer you stayed in one place, the less you remembered of the other. That's the price of being a citizen."

"No. The real price is that you never forget." All three of their faces were framed in the water. Babieca couldn't help but feel as if he'd seen this woman before. He could see the outlines of someone else in her features, hear something in her voice.

"Pulcheria thinks that you can help us," he said. "Maybe we're pawns, and maybe she'll crush us beneath the wheel. It doesn't matter. All I care about is rescuing our friend."

"And saving the world," Julia added hastily. "That too."

"They're the same," the Fur Queen repeated. "Latona will offer him what he's always wanted. The power to transform things. He doesn't want to raise an army. But fate moves as it must. He thinks that he can outsmart her. That he sees what's coming. He doesn't. She'll turn everything against him." She looked at Babieca. "Absolutely everything."

He turned to face her. "Do you know him?"

"The oculus?" She ran a hand through her hair. "He was a stubborn child. Always trying to change the rules." The Fur Queen smiled a secret smile. "Fearless in his arguments, but scared of storms, and loud voices. My loveliest shadow. He never forgave me for leaving. He probably never will. But I've always kept him in my sight."

Julia shook her head slowly. "I don't understand. She knows Roldan?"

Babieca looked at her again. He saw the hint of a smile that played across her features, and the way that her eyes demurred slightly, even when she was watching them. He heard the regret in her voice but also the note of unwavering confidence. For a moment, he was a small boy looking up at her, trying to solve her. Then he knew.

"She's his mother," he said grimly.

Julia stared at her. "But that makes no sense."

"It's starting to," he murmured.

Thorn and Eth had drawn closer. Were they her children now? Babieca tried to grasp some connection between them, but they remained elusive. Maybe this strange night court was her family. A replacement for the one she'd given up.

"You understand," the Fur Queen said, "why it was necessary. I can see it in your face. You've worked it out already."

"You needed to hide him in plain sight. So that when the time came, there'd be no connection to you. No suspicion that he was also your pawn."

"This isn't just about him." She smiled again. "Though he surely thinks that it is. We all have moves to make. Latona has forgotten about me, but Pulcheria hasn't. She thinks that her sister won't expect this. Alliances among the night gens are practically unheard of. But her thinking isn't broad enough. She simply wants to maintain order, while Latona wants to burn down the world and start anew."

Babieca was suddenly aware of how cold the room was. How far underground they were. Nobody would miss them if they vanished. Pulcheria had known just how expendable they were from the beginning. He was tired of being another stone. Tired of being discarded, laughed at, forgotten about.

We can still surprise the hand that moves us.

Or bite the hand that feeds us. He thought of the painting they'd seen ages ago, in the villa where they'd met Felix. *Beware of dog.* Roldan's start of surprise upon seeing it, and then his own laughter. A painting couldn't hurt you. But perhaps that was wrong.

Perhaps he was the kind of dog to be feared.

"There's a third option," he said. "And that's whatever you want. Am I right?"

She nodded.

"Then tell us. But first, let's have something to eat."

3

THERE WAS SNOW IN THE DREAM, THOUGH HE wanted to call it something else. Some word from a dead language that meant more than it should. The cold seeped into his sandals. He recognized this garden, even ice-locked and silent. It was where they'd met the meretrix. He'd seen apple shavings devour themselves, and flame dancing on air. Now it was still. He held the lantern higher, and its flame made racing patterns along the white. Snow in Anfractus. It didn't seem possible, but his feet were numb from it. Babieca looked down. He had the sudden urge to cover his own tracks. He didn't want his pursuer to see them. But there was nothing to cover. He'd left no footprints. Just a long shadow, which grinned at him, unwilling to give any advice on the matter.

Beneath the peristyle, two figures sat at a small table, facing each other. Roldan fidgeted with the frayed hem of his tunica. It was no longer red, but black. It seemed too large for him. Felix spun a cracked mask like a wheel, glittering against the marble table. It moved in slow circles, catching the lamplight. His face was always in shadow.

"You missed summer," Roldan observed.

"I'm always late for the important things."

"I don't mind the snow." Roldan stuck out his tongue to catch a flake. "Sometimes I wish it would stop, but then I'm not so sure. Maybe it should cover everything."

Babieca took a small step back. He could feel the cold in his limbs for the first time. The lantern was broken and burning against the snow. He flexed his fingers, wondering what it would feel like to freeze. Maybe it would be like slipping into a bath, or letting your body surrender to perpetual night. It was no longer the cold that he feared.

"Whom do you serve?"

"That's like drawing lines on water."

Babieca grabbed his wrist. "I need to know."

Roldan looked at him for a moment but said nothing. Babieca relaxed his grip. Roldan touched his hand lightly.

"You're cold."

"That's how I know that I'm still alive."

"I think you've got that backward." Roldan cupped his hands, blowing on them. His breath was surprisingly warm. "You'd better go inside soon."

"Tell me first."

"Whom do I serve?" He considered it for a moment. "Ivory and ash."

Babieca thought he meant the lares of fire. "You'd truly raise an army of spirits for Latona?"

"I'm just the shepherd. Or spirit-herd. I'm not certain about the terminology."

"What does she really want?"

"To watch all the worlds burn."

Carl awoke in his bed, alone. His mouth tingled. For a moment, all he could do was stare at the ceiling. The blinds made abstract patterns against the stucco. He almost thought that he could see a face, the way you did sometimes when you stared into the knotted surface of a tree. Some uncanny correspondence. But it was nothing. He slowly attained a sitting position. The transition from yesterday had left him feeling slightly hungover. Real magic shouldn't do that, but maybe the park had always been something else. He rubbed his burning eyes. It was unusual to dream about Babieca. Or perhaps just unusual to remember. Even now, the details were melting as his mind roused itself. There was no sense holding on.

Ivory and ash.

It sounded like something from one of the Anglo-Saxon poems that Andrew studied. Carl had tried to read one, something about a wolf, but it was too enigmatic. He couldn't figure out who was speaking, or why. So he'd just mumbled that the imagery was creative, and Andrew had seemed satisfied by the response. He'd probably only been half-listening. Carl found history more comforting than literature. You could piece together a broken comb, reconstruct a shattered fortress. You could follow threads back to another time, whose trappings still survived, even if they were buried within a matrix of earth. Once, he'd held a Byzantine earring in his hand, surprised by the weight of it. The amber still gleamed. Centuries ago, it had formed part of a noblewoman's glittering network. People had seen it, winking from a cloud of incense. But poems were different animals.

Andrew had been revised somehow. The person that he remembered was that broken comb, that fortress whose bones waited in rainwater. Once, he'd forgotten who he was, and they'd lied to him easily, cleanly. Now it was his turn. His wounded arm pushed the wheel. All they could do was brace for impact.

Carl stumbled into the bathroom and stared at himself in the mirror. The stranger mugged for him, brushing the hair from his eyes. He stuck his tongue out, but the reflection merely looked unimpressed.

He had met Andrew's mother. The woman who'd been sending her son postcards since he was six. The settling silence in every conversation between Andrew and his father. They were very much alike. Both would float away in the middle of a sentence. At first it was imperceptible, but then Carl would realize that father and son were contemplating the full moon. There was nothing left, then, but to fix himself another drink and enjoy the space between them.

Carl surveyed the ruins of his apartment. Why couldn't he just clean it, like a normal person? He should *want* to clean it. Living in your own pile of academic detritus wasn't exactly hygienic. A discarded article had lain in the corner for two weeks now and was collecting a sheen of dust. He knew it was there, yet he felt no desire to pick it up. He was a lazy dragon, building his hoard from interlibrary loans, old bus passes, and clothes that no longer fit because he'd been living on coffee and the occasional cigarette. This was a dorm room, he decided, not an adult's parlor. And maybe that was his problem. Some part of him had peaked when he was still an undergraduate. Everything beyond that was just a thick layer of paint on an unsupportable canvas. He'd gone to university to learn something about himself, and what he'd learned was that he had no survival instinct.

Someone had messaged him using an online hookup app. It had the sort of one-word name that suggested enigma, but rarely delivered. Carl's profile was called *Justinian_88*, after the Byzantine emperor who'd ruled alongside his wife, Theodora, a former courtesan. She'd danced in pantomime plays as a girl, scarcely realizing that on the eve of the Nika Revolt, she would tell her husband: "Bury me in purple before I flee from this place." What had surprised him the most was that the simple *Justinian* was taken, which made him think that some doppelganger in Istanbul was logged on simultaneously. Perhaps they'd meet some night. This message was from *Electric_Cub*. It said: wanna pm? in the area, willing to host.

He deleted the message. Another popped up, and he deleted that one. The terminal encounters had become exhausting.

Carl loaded his profile and deleted all of the wry, leading answers. He replaced them with what he thought were honest responses:

What are you looking for?
Something challenging, like an open flame, or a pack of
   wolves.

What do you do in your spare time?
Mostly jerking off and converting footnotes to endnotes.

What can't you live without?
You. Just kidding. Coffee, Muppets, my mother's
   albóndigas.

What is your idea of a perfect date?
I get stoned and play old cartridge games all day. Shining
   Force, Wonder Boy in Monsterland, that whole oeuvre.
   My mom calls, and I listen to her read Borges. Then
   she listens to me eat pancakes. I stand by the fountain
   at Wascana Park and watch as the sunlight touches the
   gargoyles. I take a sweaty nap. I read about Greek fire
   on a patio. I pet my senses until I've dulled them. I
   decide to forgive myself for everything. I take a cold
   shower and drip-dry on the couch, watching the
   episode of *Mad Men* where Peggy stands on tiptoe to
   peek through Don Draper's office window. I eat a
   stack of saltine crackers with Nutella spread. I
   remember the wild heat of boyhood, the games and
   the dogs and the endless running. I remember when
   desire first took me, shaking my branches. I remember
   the first and the last and devouring the beautiful
   middle. Then I hear the buzzer.

How do you identify?
I take what I can get.

Are you looking for a long-term relationship?
Are you? Sweet algorithm, what are you looking for?
    What are you into? Where can I find you without your
    punctuation? If I wear the right color handkerchief,
    will you shock me in the park for everyone to see? Or
    are you more of a theater buff?

Submit.
Carl knew what he had to do. It wasn't a quest that would
end well, but he had no choice. Knowledge changed everything. It was the closest thing to power that they had, and
so they would use it. He would use it. On this side of the
park, he couldn't sing, but he was perfectly willing to dance.
    He pulled on an old pair of jeans with a staple in them.
Most of his shirts were dirty, because he kept spending his
Laundromat change on Popsicles. All he could find was an
Indigo Jones T-shirt with a tear in the shoulder. As soon as
he stepped into the hallway, he could hear music coming
from the sex shop below. Love Selection liked to play the
Baroque masters, as a sort of unexpected move to throw
their customers off-guard. He could see their cherry-red
awning from his patio, bright beneath the cloudless sky. He
walked past the entrance, reading a sign that politely
announced a BOGO offer on fetish DVDs.
    He followed Broad Street downtown, past the shimmer-
ing glass banks and the store that sold nothing but yoga
pants. It seemed like an odd extravagance for a prairie city,
but it was doing mad business. The furniture store was on
the edge of downtown—an edge that struck you with unexpected speed. The buildings gave way to dusty parking lots,
where signs pointed the way to a giant casino. He thought
about continuing down Osler Street, to the little park where

they'd smoked and watched the gophers. It would be nice to sit there again, watching the wild grass slowly deconstructing everything.

Instead, he crossed the parking lot and stepped into the air-conditioned furniture store. The contrast was shocking and raised gooseflesh on his arms. It took a moment to adjust to the fluorescent glow, which outlined small battalions of upholstered chairs and improbable bunk beds. A few customers milled about, sampling the merchandise. One couple looked embarrassed as they tested out a queen-sized bed. They left hand prints in the memory foam and bounced chastely to assess the springs. The unspoken question hung in the air: *Can we fuck on this?* But that wasn't included with the customer survey.

Andrew's father, Simon, managed the furniture store. He'd never seemed to have a particular opinion about this job. It was a natural extension of him, like a walking stick, worn smooth by the hand's pressure. Simon had raised Andrew in this store. They used to stage mock battles in the aisles. Carl looked for a part of Andrew in the face of this quiet, balding man whose fingers danced across an old keyboard. What did he know?

Simon looked up. The welcome script died on his tongue, and his expression became neutral. "Well, hey. We haven't seen you here in a while."

The *we* sounded promising. Perhaps he'd made the right choice. "I've been working on this article. You know the drill."

"I hear about it often enough. Wouldn't say I know it, though." His eyes flicked back to the computer. "You in the market for some new furniture? We just got in a shipment of chairs with cup holders. They've got a cooler built right in. Your choice of fabric."

"I doubt I could afford something like that."

"We offer a number of financing plans. There's one that I call the *grad student*. You only have to pay twenty-five cents a day for the next two centuries."

"Are you still pushing that store card?"

Simon spread his hands. "I know the interest rate is fatal, but my district manager wants us to rake in the new accounts. I think he's connected to them, like life support. Every time someone declines a rapid credit, his soul is in danger."

"I don't see why the furniture industry wouldn't use sympathetic magic." He shuffled a bit without meaning to. "Has Shelby been around?"

"Not as much as she used to." His eyes were on the computer again. "She brought coffee last week. Or maybe it was two weeks ago. I'm in this place so much that I forget about how time works. It's like being stuck in a sensory deprivation chamber."

Carl thought of a hundred ways to ask what he wanted to, but none of them seemed right. Had Andrew ever told his father about them? And what was there to tell, really? It didn't seem like the kind of thing that they'd talk about while watching an episode of *MythBusters*. He wondered sometimes if they only communicated for the benefit of other people. Maybe when they were alone with each other, in the semidarkness of the living room, they just settled into their hybrid chairs and said nothing.

"Is he here?" Carl asked finally.

Simon gave him a long look. He didn't know everything, but he did know something. Or, at the very least, he'd managed to connect some of the dots. In that look, Carl saw a father's protective instinct, a flash of annoyance, and something beneath it all that remained illegible. He considered the question, as if Carl were inquiring about a warranty.

"In back," he said simply. "Go check on him. The boy always forgets to eat lunch."

The boy made him imagine Andrew as a young spark, reading in secret or trying to stay invisible when it was past his bedtime. Simon had been mother and father, reading him stories about time travel and talking rabbits, pacifying him with a selection of night lights. Meanwhile, his mother had written to him from distant places. *Thinking of you in Lisbon, darling dove.* He thought about spilling everything. What was the proper way to tell someone that his ex-wife commanded a court of thieves? There wasn't an e-card for that. Most likely, he didn't want to hear about the past. Hers was a warranty that had expired long ago.

"I'll go remind him," Carl said. "Thanks."

"If you want to thank me, buy a Papasan chair. We can't seem to move any of them, and we need the floor space."

Carl grinned. "I'll consider it."

He crossed the length of the store. Furniture showrooms unnerved him. It was one thing to see chairs occupying a living room but quite another to see them arranged like identical troops, waiting to be leased. It was like wandering behind the curtain and seeing all of the stage props and costumes stacked neatly in rows. It made it more difficult to believe in living rooms, in spite of their lavish promises. He slipped into the back room. The land of misfit couches. Love seats and nesting tables were stacked on pallets. Some of the specimens were in pieces, like the harvest of a mad scientist's laboratory. In one corner, there was simply a stack of chair legs. Were they extras? Clone parts? Defective? He had no idea. Safety instructions were tacked to the wall, faded and crinkling at the edges. Carl smelled the tang of hot glue and the musty odor of disused fabric. It wasn't unpleasant. There was something warm and gently claustrophobic about it, as if he'd wandered into the world's workshop. Some cramped studio where an artist was patiently assembling continents and family trees.

Andrew sat cross-legged on the cement, frowning at a set of instructions. He was putting together a desk, and one of the parts seemed to be giving him trouble. Or all of them. He kept glancing from the paper to the pile of bolts, shaking his head slightly. He winced and massaged his arm, which must have tingled with familiar pain. The kiss of the silenus.

"Need some help?"

He didn't look up, which was unnerving in itself. "I think I've got it under control. Some of these instructions seem to be written in a variant of English, though. Maybe Northumbrian? I'm going to send them a strongly worded e-mail as soon as I manage to figure out how part C connects to"—he narrowed his eyes—"bridge F. Whatever that is. Should a desk have a bridge?"

"Maybe it's cosmopolitan."

Andrew made a sound. Somewhere between a chuckle and a cough. *Hmmph.* It might have meant anything. Carl blinked. Nothing about this was going to be simple.

"I could hand you things," he said. "Mop your brow and such. Or we could just smash the entire thing and call it postmodern."

"My dad sent you?"

"He thought you might need some assistance."

"He always thinks I'm lost." Andrew tapped two bolts together lightly. It was almost a meditative gesture. Then he looked up. "You can screw me."

Carl felt a lump in his throat. "What?"

Andrew pointed to the pile next to him. "Hand me screws. And such." He almost smiled as he said it. Maybe there were still some simple things.

Carl sat down next to him and began sorting through the parts. He eyed the instructions. Then, gently, he turned them to the right page.

"That might help."

Andrew looked down and laughed. "Huh. Maybe my dad's right to be worried."

"I blame the fumes."

"You may not be wrong about that. Sometimes I have glue visions, like Saint Hildegard. I always forget to write them down, though."

"I'll buy you a dream journal. Something with a wolf on it."

"Please don't."

"Wulf, min wulf."

Andrew looked up sharply. "Are you quoting *Wulf and Eadwacer?*"

"That's the only line that I remember." Carl handed him the hex key. "The Wulf-guy was carrying something. Or . . . was he an actual wolf? I guess they couldn't carry a bundle through the forest, unless they used their teeth."

Andrew balanced the top of the desk while Carl attached the base. "It's about two people who can never be together," he said, "and something that they make, between them. A child, maybe, or a riddle. Whatever *giedd* means. We don't know anymore. It's one of the most enigmatic stories in any language. Like a tapestry full of holes."

"Doesn't that frustrate you?"

Andrew shrugged. "I like riddles. Life is full of them." He tightened one side of the desk, while Carl steadied the other. "Can you drink soup, or do you need a spoon? Does every agreement end in a handshake? Why do the best shows always get canceled? How do you tell someone you love them?"

Carl looked at him cautiously. "You just say it."

"If that were true, there'd be no shows, or books, or songs."

They took a step back from the completed desk. Two screws remained on the ground. Carl picked them up.

"What do these belong to?"

"Best not to ask." He gave the desk an experimental nudge. "You'll make someone very happy, for a reasonable price."

Carl smirked. "Are you talking to me, or it?"

"Maybe both. Come on."

With that, he grabbed on to one of the large pallets and clambered on top. He used it as a stepping-stone to reach a higher pallet, then kept climbing, until he was eight feet off the ground. The stacked boxes formed a kind of ziggurat, with Andrew at its apex.

"Coming?"

"This is highly unsafe."

"Don't worry. I've been doing this since I was a kid."

Carl followed him, climbing up far less steadily. The boxes were solid, though a few shifted beneath his weight. Andrew was a weather vane compared to him. Carl reached the top and saw that there was a kind of nest there, complete with pillows and a few scattered books. Andrew passed him a pillow, and he sat down.

"I've always come up here to think. When I was little, my dad used to take me to this hardware store. I think it was called Lumber Land. Isn't that great? Practically Tolkienian." Andrew smiled distantly. "They had these cubes where they kept the precut wood, and they were stacked up so high. I loved to climb in them. My own private honeycomb. My dad used to yell at me: *Get down, monkey!* But I knew that it was a bluff. I'd wait for the moment when he opened his arms, and then I'd fall." He closed his eyes momentarily. "He always caught me. I don't think he'd do it now. Maybe I should try one of these days."

"Don't tell the district manager."

What he wanted to say was: *I met your mother.* The words danced on his tongue, but he couldn't let them go. He didn't know how to say it. That was another riddle, he supposed. Andrew was watching him from the corner of his eye. The space between them was barely a hand's breadth. Carl remembered the dream. If they kissed, maybe this would all be over. Black would fade to red. Heaven would swallow the smoke.

Carl swallowed. He meant to say several different things, and to mean all of them. What he managed, in the end, was a question: "Are you really working for Latona?"

He frowned. "Not for her, exactly. More adjacent."

"What game are you playing, Andrew? I want an honest answer."

The air grew cold between them. "Like all the honest

answers you gave me, when I thought I was going crazy? Is that the peace of mind that you're looking for?"

"That was different."

"Why?"

"Because you died!" Carl willed himself to stop shaking. "Roldan died."

"And you still haven't forgiven him."

"What are you talking about?"

Andrew's face hardened. "For a whole summer, I could see it in your eyes. This grief that you refused to explain. It was Felix who finally told me."

"Well, he's helpful that way. It's easy to lie when nobody has to see your face."

Andrew looked at him carefully. When he spoke, his voice was measured, as if he'd been saying the words to himself for a long time. "I'm not Roldan. I don't know who he was, or what he meant to you. But he's gone now."

"You remember him. You dreamed of salamanders. You told me that yourself!"

Andrew's expression wavered for a moment. Then he looked away. "Don't ignore the larger picture. Latona's on the move. Everything you fear is true, and if we keep wasting time, she'll get exactly what she wants."

"With your help."

His eyes were bleak. "Is that what you—" Andrew shook his head. "I'm not helping her. It may seem that way, but don't believe it. I'm trying to protect us all. She thinks that I can convince the lares to follow her. She needs to keep thinking that."

"Can you?"

"I'm not sure. Felix seems to think so."

Carl frowned. "Are you just playing each side against the other?"

"No. Our side is the resistance. And you're a part of that— you all are—but you need to wait until the right moment."

Suddenly, Carl wasn't sure what to tell him. There were three sides now. Three queens. Where did that leave the silenoi? He imagined a moment of reckoning. Three queens circling each other warily, swords in hand, while Narses and Mardian tore each other apart.

"Ivory and ash," he murmured.

Andrew stared at him. "What?"

"Nothing." Carl made his way down the mountain of pallets. He motioned to the desk. "At least we did one thing right."

"What about those missing screws?"

Carl shrugged. "It'll hold."

He left the store in a hurry. Simon was occupied with a couple buying a dining room set. He didn't look up to say good-bye. Carl crossed the parking lot and took the bus to campus. He had a feeling about something, though he couldn't quite put it into words. He stared out the grimy window as the bus rattled down Broad Street. His phone buzzed. It was Shelby.

What's the plan?

He pondered this for a moment but didn't respond. The bus pulled up in front of the Innovation Centre. A hot dog stand was parked by the entrance, and students lined up, drawn by the smell of grilled onions. A warm wind shook the trees. Gophers convened by the entrance to the university pub, exchanging secrets. Carl walked through the doors. The murmur of parallel conversations rose up around him. Everything was so familiar, yet he could feel something peculiar that he couldn't trace. He walked past the food court, down the climate-controlled hallway. Past the bookstore, which announced a sale on hardcovers, and the orange clock that had been stuck on the same time for years. Or maybe it was time that had stopped.

Carl took the elevator to the Department of Music. Posters advertised the Baroque chorus, as well as several visiting composers. The sound of strings drifted from one classroom. His fingers twitched. There was no music in them, and yet some part of him remembered what it felt like to dance along those frets. He felt the calluses hardening, the sweet pain of playing too long, as the world vanished. He rubbed his hands, but they were soft. He couldn't say precisely where the memory came from. It was as sudden and real as a match, untended, burning his fingers.

The equipment room was unlocked. He stepped in and flipped the light switch. Pianos and harpsichords faced him, blanketed like animals put to bed. There wasn't much time. If anyone happened to wander by, they'd want to know what he was doing. Quietly, he slipped off the covers. Some of the pianos were a brilliant white, others a burnished black. The oldest had been painted numerous times and now stood in the corner, peeling. That one must have been a donation from some elementary school classroom.

Where did you hide it?

Carl tried to reconstruct the events of that night, but they remained blurry. There had been a dragon made of smoke, and hunters, and the basilissa herself. Latona had offered Andrew something—or was it the other way around. They'd clasped hands. But the key. The *giedd*, the riddle. Where had he put it?

She can't find what's in plain sight. Ivory and ash.

He circled the pianos. They all looked the same. He briefly thought about bashing his head against the keys. Which one would he have chosen? Some were imposing, while others barely seemed to qualify as pianos at all. They were the sort of instrument that your parents would force you to learn scales on. He touched one key, then another, and another. He played every note that he could think of. But they added up to nothing.

The mark is what's important. What we leave behind.

He scanned the instruments again, looking for engravings. Maker's marks. Anything that might hold a clue. Many of them had embossed plates, or small characters etched into them, but he could barely read the stylized letters. And even if he'd been able to, what would they tell him? Andrew didn't know anything about music.

That thought brought him up short.

He wouldn't have chosen based on tone, or shape. It would have been something else.

The mark.

Carl got down on his hands and knees. He examined the keys from a different perspective. It wasn't a real key, after all. It was a horn. Some wild magic of crossing had diminished it, but it was only hiding in plain sight.

He would have moved quickly. Where was he standing?

Carl studied the room again. Then he saw the harpsichord, pushed against the wall. It was unremarkable but somehow dignified. Still on his knees, he crawled over to the instrument. Anyone looking through the door would have thought that he was paying homage to the genius of music. He gently ran his fingers along the keys. All of them *plinked*. He tugged on them experimentally. Some had yellowed slightly, and a few were sticky. He pressed one of the sharps and saw something that he'd missed before. His breath caught. He pressed it again. There was a spot of dried blood on the white key. It was small, and almost entirely obscured by the facing key. But it was there. Like a bit of rust.

Andrew's blood.

Carl could hear someone in the hallway. He reached into his pocket and withdrew the flat wrench that he'd taken from the furniture store. He used it to pry off the false key. It offered little resistance. It wasn't supposed to be there, after all.

He pocketed the key and slipped out of the room. A custodian gave him an odd look but said nothing. He was listening to a set of headphones. Carl kept walking. The key was burning his hand, just as the imaginary strings had done. It was the horn that summoned the lares, and this world could no longer contain it.

He had to keep it safe from everyone.

4

ANFRACTUS WAS A DIFFERENT PLACE AT NIGHT. Smoke from countless fires mingled with the dark clouds, but there was still moonlight. Thin and miraculous, it gilded the red roof tiles. Most of the botteghi were shuttered and sleeping behind locked gates. The tavernae and street-side cauponae were in full swing, though he noticed an increase in the miles who patrolled Via Rumor. They would be watching for hunters. The silenoi mostly kept to the alleys and skyways above the city, but they'd grown bolder since making the pact with Latona. One or two might be dealt with beneath the lamplight, but a pack of them in the dark was another matter entirely. They wouldn't retreat, even if they were outnumbered. Babieca patted the sword at his belt. It was heavy and useless, like some monster's limb that he'd convinced himself to carry. A talisman that couldn't possibly save him. The real weapon was the lute case strapped to his shoulder. He'd have more luck conjuring a reel than swinging his stubby gladius. At least he remained invisible, for now. The hunters tended to prefer aristocrats, who had a sweeter taste.

He stepped over the body of an unconscious reveler, snoring against one of the white paving stones. Best to avoid too much drink. The silenoi considered passive prey to be a bit dull, but if they were hungry enough, they'd drag away the sleeping bodies. He needed to stay alert. He was alone. The night gens would offer him no protection, and even the city guards would simply avert their eyes if something attacked him. Letting nature take its course. He was the very reason that the silenoi hunted at night. Fools who wanted a taste of the dark city. He wouldn't know that he was being followed until his back was against a reeking wall. He couldn't even hire a link-boy to light his way, since they only served the wealthy. He had to make do with a cracked lantern and the flickering lights of the Subura. The district of pleasures and rude endings. This neighborhood had made him what he was. Tuneful, wary, and just mad enough to think that this plan would work.

There were other options. He could prostrate himself before Basilissa Latona, hoping that he wouldn't be fed to her lampreys. He could pay a visit to Felix. The house father of the black basia was seldom under guard. He could creep into the tabularium and lay the edge of the sword against Felix's unprotected throat. That would provide him with answers. But these were suicidal moves on a board that cared nothing for him. The long game was the only solution. If he wanted to stay alive, he needed to increase his value as a player.

The wilds were the thing. He'd been pondering it ever since he'd first discovered the ingress that led between worlds. There was a soft space between city and wilderness, a line of old power that kept them a hand's breadth apart. That moment between waking and sleep, full of dawn-cares, when your body floated in a strange pool of knowledge. The cracks themselves were like alleys, where the city's drama faded to a distant murmur, both dead and alive. Latona wanted to control them. *She wants to watch all the worlds burn*. Babieca wasn't certain of that. When they'd heard her speaking with Mardian on the Patio of Lions, fire seemed far from her mind. It was power that she'd wanted. The power to resurrect an empire. Unlike her mother, who'd seen reform glimmering along the edge of a blade, Latona fought with contracts. She'd sell her own city to the hunters, if it meant gaining an advantage.

But she couldn't buy the lares, the spirits that had gathered to watch in fascination as settlers built the first shrines. They'd remained beyond her grasp, until now. His hope was that she would reach too far. He had other hopes, but they seemed less likely, rattling around like the few spare coins in his pouch. Trust. Desire. Escape. In the dark, they seemed less real, but somehow more possible. Lunacy at its finest.

He followed the ancient wall that circled the city. It gleamed with bits of quartz and porphyry, no doubt broken from some older monument. It was in everyone's nature, he supposed, to build walls around things. *This is mine.* And desire nudged us to climb over, to break through, no matter the cost. The city was alive with betrayals, misplaced bricks, moonlit repairs. The web of skyways above was silent, though he knew that people gathered there, out of sight. The great insulae rose everywhere, teeming with bloody stories and gabled windows lined with flowers. He could hear the *cucurrucucu* of the rooftop doves, a gentle staccato to the sounds of love and fighting within. He couldn't tell if the hunters wanted to destroy this, or if they were drawn to it, like crowds to a harp.

He paused at the crossroads of Via Rumor and Aditus Papallona. The Avenue of Butterflies. If he climbed uphill, he'd reach the wealthier vici, giving way to arcades fragrant with lemon trees. Eventually, he'd come to the Arx of Violets, where death waited for him on swift sandals. If he turned in the opposite direction, allowing himself to descend past the low firewalls that separated rich from poor, he'd come to the necropolis. There, among the tall osiers and marsh fires, the silenoi would embrace him. It might be comforting to fall soundlessly in the mud, to join the slow spread of decay. The hunters would hold him still as they unlocked his bones, like a sacred cabinet, prying open the delicate hasps. They would lay him red and simple, solved at last. There was something to that. He imagined some brightness spinning away, tumbling grief over game, to join the smoke.

Instead, he chose the middle way. The path led him to the southernmost corner of Anfractus, where two great walls brushed among a scattering of houses. It was an unfinished place, neither rich nor poor. Garments soaked in tubs of acrid dye. People leaned out of windows, breathing in the warm air. If he listened closely, he could almost hear the wild sounds beyond the high walls. The greening unknown beyond the city, where imperial roads had surrendered to the dominion of moss and small forest lives. The twin rivers thundered, Clamores and Iacto, locked in their perpetual game of Hazard. And somewhere to the south, Pulcheria stood at the heart of her city, Egressus, weaving threads. The rival queens were inevitabilities, like the lares themselves. They had always been fighting, above and below, fingers on the ivory. Latona in her anger, Pulcheria in her cold grace, and the inscrutable queen of the catacombs. Warriors one and all, whose shield-dance would sweep everyone away. Fortuna watched them with indrawn breath. Her instruments of wrack and wonder.

The trick was to move beyond their sight. To mean something while seeming nothing. That he could do.

The fire had faded, but its marks were still there. Much of the house had crumbled to blackened timbers. The roof had partially collapsed, offering up the bones of the place. But some of the rooms had also survived. He wasn't sure why Latona hadn't razed it to the ground. Most likely, she wanted to remember it. Another sort of trick. If you knew how to use it, you could move between, at a price. Babieca could remember the dizzying feeling of transit, the confusion that followed. This was a dangerous ingress. Lean too heavily on it, and you could end up lost to yourself, unable to recall either place. After a time, only the fault line would become real. At least, that had been Felix's warning. But he'd never really trusted the mask and wasn't about to start now.

He couldn't quite trace the roots of his mistrust. Perhaps it was dull jealousy. Felix had wealth and status. He may have been a lupo, but he was Latona's favorite wolf. And Roldan—or Aleo, as he was known now—seemed eager to follow him. Maybe it was bitterness. Felix had danced with him for a while, but only as a diversion. That was all they really were to the mask. Distractions of different orders, meant to entertain for a while. Still, he dimly remembered that Felix, in another guise, had come to their aid. In some distant tabularium, filled with bright boxes and blinding lamps, the wolf-shadow had led them to a barrow full of weapons and strange armor. Had he also taken the middle path? Or was he the enemy that had circled them from the very beginning?

Babieca picked his way carefully among the debris. The front of the house had crumbled, and the floor was heavily scarred. The walls were covered in soot, though he could still make out some of the frescoes. They'd all been naked in this room, politely ignoring each other. The house had seemed impregnable. Some relic of old magic that would survive long after they'd gone. But now it was bone and ash. He walked to the corner of the atrium, whose walls remained mostly intact. A breeze slipped in through the shattered window. Fire had fused the cheap glass to the floor in long rivulets that reminded him of candle wax. He nudged the flagstones with his sandal until he found the loose one. Then he knelt down, prying it free with the hilt of his sword.

Everything was as they'd left it, including the red tunica. He reached underneath and carefully withdrew the blade. It had slept untroubled. The whorl-patterned guard seemed traced with fire. It was light, but not insubstantial. He cut the air with it experimentally. In the right hands, it would be truly dangerous. But not in his.

Babieca slipped the dagger into its sheath and fastened it to his belt. He no longer felt lopsided. *All I need is a helmet,* he thought, *and I could be a musical miles.*

He slipped the lute case from his shoulder and opened it. Gently, he laid the instrument against the floor. The horn was underneath. It was carved with the likeness of Fortuna, and as he stared at it, as the goddess looked back. The carvings around her uncoiled. He heard the scrape of metal and the hum of something terrible. He wasn't sure if it was coming from the ivory, or if the house itself was rumbling in sympathy.

Latona had described it as a forgotten heirloom. Something discarded beneath cobwebs in the royal undercroft. *This old thing? We're practically giving it away.* But if such a weapon had always belonged to her, why hadn't she used it before? And why hadn't she come looking for it? She'd been content to leave it on the other side of the veil, where anyone might find it by accident. Maybe the horn itself was no longer important. It had done its work, after all. The lares of smoke were awake. But he had the feeling that its task wasn't over. They would have need of it in the coming days. If he buried all of the sleeping relics in a hoard, it might just be enough to save them.

He wrapped the horn in Roldan's tunica and replaced the stone. He covered the spot with debris. By the time he was finished, his hands were dark with soot, and his tunica smelled like a pyre. The broken house seemed to regard him with curiosity. Was its power still intact? It seemed reduced to cinders and blackened paint. He tried to think about some place far away, whose possibilities remained undiminished. But there was no sting of vertigo, no force dissolving the world beneath his feet. Just the weight of Felix's dagger, and half-moons of ash beneath his fingernails.

Babieca sat down among the cinders. He picked up the lute. His hands were dirty, but he couldn't help himself. The strings yielded as he began to play a song of his own invention. His voice was thin as it assailed the blackened timbers, but it gained power with each word. The horn growled beneath the stone. His sole audience.

Memory's a minor coin
Discarded in the street
A thing of smoke and sentiment
Exhausted from the heat
Keening like a house on fire
Resplendent in its grief
A song of ash and ivory
Undressing at your feet.

There was no more. He put away the lute and was just about to rise when he heard something stir. He scrambled to his feet. Before he could draw the dagger, a shadow unlaced itself from the wreck of the atrium. Babieca felt himself relax, but only slightly. He picked up the lute case and slung it over his shoulder.

"Did you follow me?"

"It wasn't hard." Aleo stepped over a bit of rubble. "You stick out like a sore thumb after sunset around here."

"And I suppose you've adjusted completely to the night gens—a true oculus now?"

"It's a different perspective. That's all."

Babieca moved to the side. It wasn't quite a retreat. More of a shift. He wanted to put some distance between them and the buried horn. "When did you arrive?"

He surveyed the skeleton of the house. "Maybe I never left."

"That's cryptic even for you."

Aleo smiled slightly. "I just got here."

Did you hear the song? He couldn't ask. He didn't want to know. The horn was whispering things too, but he tried not to listen. Could the oculus hear? Their power resided in sight, or so he'd been told. Perhaps he could see through the stone. Babieca didn't want to chance finding out whether this was possible.

Aleo looked at him. "I make you nervous." Roldan would have turned the statement into a question, but this was not Roldan. He saw it now. It wasn't just the black. His voice was different. His hands were still, his gaze steady. No flutter of uncertainty. No squinting as he searched for the right word. He could see the shadow of those familiar things, but they were little more than an afterimage. The man he'd known had wintered into the one before him, and Babieca felt strangely lost. They were strangers after all.

"What does it mean?"

"What?"

"Your new name."

Aleo cocked his head. "Wild throw."

"That's appropriate. I suppose you have a die, now."

He reached beneath his tunica, revealing an obsidian die with gold pips. Babieca touched it lightly and drew his hand away. "It's like ice."

"You're surprised?"

"I guess not."

"What were you expecting? A miracle? Your friend preserved in amber? That was never going to happen. You must have known."

"You bear no resemblance to him."

"Untrue." Aleo took a step forward. "Would you be here, otherwise?"

He placed his hand on the dagger's hilt. "I won't help you. And I won't serve her."

Aleo looked at his hand. "Go ahead. A weapon like that deserves to be used."

"This is your brilliant plan? Convincing me to kill you?"

"There's a salamander behind you, and another watching from the rafters. Try it, and you'll surely burn."

Babieca drew the knife. "Show me."

Aleo made a low, whistling sound. Babieca felt the heat on his bare legs. Twin tendrils of smoke were rising from a spot next to his feet. He thought he saw two coals, winking at him from the dark of the debris. Another cloud of smoke formed lazily in the topmost corner of the atrium, beneath the shattered roof.

"Are they dogs to you now? Pets to be controlled?"

Aleo shook his head. "They do as they please. But they like to be noticed. They're a bit vain, in that sense. And they enjoy showing off. I wouldn't test that, if I were you. A salamander's purpose is to burn. If I dare them to, they'll melt the very stones."

Babieca started to say something. Then he put away the dagger. The smoke gradually diminished, though he could feel something invisible twining at his feet.

Aleo watched him sheathe the blade. "That's wise."

"I don't need it."

He struck Aleo. It was a glancing blow, but it had a definite effect. The oculus stumbled backward. He touched his face in astonishment. Blood flecked the corner of his mouth. Babieca felt the heat return. The salamanders were curious at this unexpected turn of the wheel. Aleo stared at him.

"Why did you do that?"

"Because you're acting like a cock."

He wiped his mouth. "You still think this is all about you. That I've done this solely to hurt you, as if you were at the center of it all. You're a drunken bard with no prospects and no power. This could never be about you."

Babieca stepped forward. He could feel himself redden and hoped that it wasn't obvious in the dim light. "At least I'm not a traitor. You sold us out to kiss that woman's ring. You think she'll give you power, but she's played you like a cheap cistrum. Maybe you see spirits now, but you're blind to what's in front of you."

"And what's that?"

"You can't control them. He knew that. You'll kill your-self trying, and that's exactly what Latona wants. To watch the worlds burn."

Aleo narrowed his eyes. "I can't imagine where you get your information from. Purple scrolls and ridiculous stories."

"Actually, your mother told me."

He let that sink in for a moment. Aleo seemed on the verge of replying. Then he paled slightly. He seemed to look straight ahead for a moment, without seeing anything. Babieca felt the surprise go through him like a bolt.

"You—" He turned slightly. His voice, when it emerged, was barely a murmur. "You've seen her?"

"We had an illuminating conversation. Your name came up. Both names, in fact."

"What did she say about me?"

"She said—" He watched Aleo's face fall. He'd finally discovered what linked the oculus to the auditor. Their com-mon longing. The triumph was bitter in his mouth. All of his anger melted away. "—that she misses you. That she's always loved you. That it wasn't your fault, and soon she'll see you again."

Aleo's voice broke. "Is she safe?"

"I'd say so. She has an army of furs at her command."

"She—" He frowned. Then it clicked into place. Slowly, as if he were half-asleep, Aleo sat upon a blackened timber. He said nothing for a long while. Then he laughed.

Babieca sat next to him. "I'm not sure what your plan is," he said, "but we have plans of our own. We could use your help. It's not too late for a change of perspective."

Aleo shook his head. "I've already gone too far. I need to see it through. You may not believe it, but we're on the same side."

"I've heard that before."

"It's the truth." He looked at the floor. "You're not a minor coin."

The flush returned to his cheeks. "Heard that, did you?"

"Perhaps."

Babieca shifted in place. "That's what it feels like, most of the time. I can't see spirits or build fabulous machines. I'm shite with a sword. But I know who I am. I've felt power at my fingertips. The glory of the old songs. All I have are my blisters and my pride, but I'm not afraid anymore. I'll fight to keep this all from going up in flames."

Aleo gestured to the debris. "I think you're too late."

"Not yet." He took Aleo's hand. "Come look at this."

The oculus said nothing. He simply followed. Babieca stopped before a fresco. Much of it had been obliterated by the fire, but patches remained. He pointed to a blue smudge in the heart of a melted panel.

"Do you see that?"

Aleo squinted. "There's not much to see."

"It's been here forever. No fire can destroy it. I thought it was a dolphin, but you saw what it truly was. Do you remember?"

Aleo stared at the wall for some time. He reached out, brushing it lightly. The soot stained his hand. He looked at the stubborn mark, and his eyes softened.

"I do."

Aleo kissed him. Babieca felt the warmth travel down his spine, until it reached his sandals. Though it may have been the salamanders, pressing at their feet. It wasn't a desperate kiss. It was strangely careworn, patient as the cinders and the relic that slept beneath them. It was a long game whose rules had gone up in smoke. They'd done this before, in a stone cell with a mechanical fox hiding beneath the bed. Different people in a different room, trying to prove that they were alive. The stones were the same, the dark thrill of fear, the heat at the center of things. Aleo pulled him deeper into the wreckage. Now his back was against the wall. He felt dizzy, like a prisoner tied to Fortuna's wheel. His limbs were liquid. Aleo kissed his neck, and he murmured something, but it wasn't a word. It wasn't anything.

His hands shook as he unfastened Aleo's tunica. He kissed the line of moles on his breast. His fingers left sooty prints.

The narrow window cast moonlit stripes along their bodies, wrapping them in uncanny bands. They were side to side now, two stones that fit together. Babieca smelled the ashes in his hair. They were a hall joined by bone and timber, warmed by innumerable fires. Aleo squeezed his hand, as if he might break it, and Babieca growled in delight. Now they turned on desire's lathe, chipping away at each other, sweat and sawdust. Now it was the scent of rain, thunder moving wise and slow from crown to slender foot. The charm in his mouth that tasted of long-buried gold, and Aleo sighing against him, caught in the spin. The wild throw in his arms, the cold die that burned him, even as he sought its pitiless edge.

Take it all. Fortuna knows it's not enough, but it's yours. My imposter song. My falling down. All that I've wrecked. My semiprecious cares, and the blistered fingers that would die to play you once, only once. I loved you like a house on fire, and this is the very last room. The beams are laughing in the blaze. Take that too, though I scarcely understand it. Every damned scrap of me is yours to raze.

The sweat was in his eyes, the dirt in his hair, and Aleo's hands everywhere. They kissed, forming a brooch that writhed with animals and grinning lapidary. Babieca tasted until his mouth was slick with spit. Aleo's smaller body held him, searching the edges of the map. Now he was shredding his parchment skin. His nails dug into Aleo's shoulders. The shadow's hands moved down his legs, smoothing the pelt, burnishing bare steel. He climbed the walls, burst through the fallen roof and into the gathering clouds. He felt himself unravel beneath Aleo's hand. The blow went through him, and he shuddered as the heat covered his chest. Aleo cried out, though it may have been the house itself, or something far away.

They drifted in the flood, half-conscious. Aleo was shivering, and Babieca held him, stroking his hair. He wrapped the black tunica around them, noticing for the first time that a bloodred swan had been woven into it. His fingers traced the embroidery, then moved across Aleo's back, drumming softly. They fell asleep in the ashes, locked tight.

It was deep night when they awoke. At first, Babieca couldn't remember where he was. It felt as if he'd been dreaming for ages. There was a fierce warmth against him, fluttering but somehow steady. He realized that Roldan's head was nestled in the crook of his chest. The auditor was snoring lightly, and Babieca could feel the tickle of his breath. No. Not Roldan. He remembered, then. He felt the pins and needles as circulation returned painfully to his limbs. Groaning, he shifted position, and Aleo woke. For a moment, his eyes were a blank slate. He looked bemused and sleep-heavy. Then he too remembered, and Babieca watched his face change. They looked at each other without saying anything. He thought that the oculus might kill him then. He couldn't say why. There was a wildness in his expression that he'd never seen before.

But he didn't pull away or reach for any of the weapons that remained close by. Instead, he curled back into his original position, head against Babieca's chest. He could only imagine what his heartbeat sounded like, thready and panicked. But gradually, the blood stopped pounding in his ears. They were quiet and careful with each other. He smoothed Aleo's hair, listening to the sound of night birds, the rustle of wind as it picked up flashes of dust among the alleys.

"Are they still here?"

Aleo shifted, wrapping an arm around him. "Who?"

"The salamanders."

"Of course. We were their own private hypocaust."

He chuckled. "I'm surprised they didn't join in."

"They're lizards, not libertines."

Babieca looked at him for a long time. "What does this mean?"

"It means we're quite lucky that nobody stole our belongings. We fell asleep in the middle of an abandoned house."

"You know what I'm asking."

Aleo cocked his head. "I can't say for sure. But I've always been on your side. Even when you couldn't see it."

"You're with her."

"More adjacent to her."

Babieca pinched him lightly. "Don't play with terms."

Aleo kissed his eyebrows, a dark benediction. "My fealty is my own secret to keep. But you have to trust me."

"How can I? You keep riddling me."

He tongued Babieca's ear. "You didn't mind earlier."

"I need to know that I can trust you."

Aleo ran a fingertip down his chest. "Don't lose faith. I promise that things are about to change. But I need you in this fight."

"I'm essential, am I?"

"You're the song that begins it all."

He kissed Babieca, drowsy and slow. Then they struggled to their feet and dressed. Babieca was starting to feel the cuts and bruises now. He grimaced slightly as he slipped the belt on, tipped by the weight of sword and dagger.

He was about to say something when he saw the woman standing in the blasted doorway. She was flanked by half a dozen miles. Moonlight silvered the pearls in her hair, gleaming against the embroidered stola. She stepped across the threshold, and her smile chilled him, as the die had.

"Brilliant," Latona said.

He stared at Aleo. He must have looked so stupid in that moment, like a fish gasping for air. He couldn't say anything. There was grit in his mouth, and a spreading terror in his chest that nearly made him fall.

The miles strode across the room, swords drawn. One of them grabbed him by the arm, but he offered no resistance. He tried not to look at the spot where he'd buried the horn. Had the oculus seen him do it? *Maybe I never left,* he'd said. Babieca tried not to think about it, humming beneath the earth. He felt a distant pain in his arm, but mostly, he was numb. One of the miles unbuckled his belt, taking the dagger from him.

Latona examined the blade. "This belonged to a friend of mine," she said. "Well, a former friend."

"What do you want?" Babieca asked finally.

It was a ridiculous question, but the words came unbidden. He met her gaze. The basilissa considered him, as a storm might consider an island before tearing through it.

Her eyes surveyed the little cuts, the soot prints that still marked his bare arms. She looked at Aleo briefly, then back to him.

"A happy ending," she said.

Aleo stared at the ashes.

PART THREE

MILES

1

INGRID DIDN'T EXPECT TO FIND HERSELF IN the dragon's lair. She was barefoot and had to walk carefully to avoid stepping on anything precious. She picked her way among the gilded harps and chalices, trying to be soft, like a real burglar. Her foot snagged on an embroidered pennant, but she managed to extricate herself. Smoke curled from the worm, asleep on his pile of treasure. In fact, the worm was made of smoke, and his rippling form stretched from one end of the barrow to the other. Ingrid crept near. Gemstones glittered within the transparent body. She'd forgotten her sword and feared that the dragon might be sleeping on top of it. She squinted but couldn't make out anything for certain within the dim light. It was her fault. Leaving a sword behind was one thing, but you should never invite dragons into your life. The smoke parted slightly, and she saw a glimpse of the blade. All she had to do was reach in and snatch it back. The hoard itself seemed to be waiting for this. The harps watched her in hushed amazement. The dragon slept on.

She waited for the smoke to part again.

Don't bother. It was her foster mother's voice. *You'll only botch the job. Go make some more coffee. That's what you're good for.*

Ingrid hesitated. The hoard sighed, or maybe it was the dragon. They were inseparable. For the first time, she noticed that Paul was perched on a collection of gleaming breastplates. He was six years old and wearing stegosaurus pajamas. His knees were drawn up to his chest. He saw her and put a finger to his lips.

"Get down from there," she whispered. "Safety first. *Always.* Don't you remember?"

Now he was trying on the armor. He fumbled with the clasps, and she wanted to show him the right way, but the dragon was turning again. This was her last chance.

She could see the chipped hilt of her gladius. Her hand darted forth, grasping it. Triumph made her smile. But then the smoke closed over her arm. It was impossibly cold. Ingrid shivered violently as the dragon regarded her with countless winking eyes.

Too slow.

It opened its jaws, and for a moment, she saw through the smoke. She saw the monster's heart, a summer berry ripe with blood. Her eyes widened.

"I know you."

Then it rushed in, and the weight of the hoard was on top of her, the gold crushing her as the dragon unfolded, unfolded.

Ingrid woke to find Neil's nose pressed an inch away from her own. He was lying on her stomach, and one of his small hands kneaded her forehead, like it was a dough. When she opened her eyes, a brilliant smile spread across his face.

"Mummy! You have waked up, and next to your son!"

She shifted position. "You're actually on top of me, bubs."

He rolled onto his side. "I have brought you something."

Ingrid stroked his hair. "Precious. What is it?"

Neil handed her a painted rock, closed in his left fist. It was yellow and green. She remembered decorating it yesterday. That was before the science experiment involving propulsion, but after the dragon egg scavenger hunt in the backyard. It had been a busy day. All she'd been able to think about was how pitiful the shrubbery looked, battered first by snow, then by dry heat. They needed to buy some potting soil.

He placed the rock in her hand. "This is the last of the high loves, Mummy. It is mine very special present to you."

She gathered him in her arms. "Sweetness. Thank you for this." Then she sniffed the air, frowning. "Do you smell that?"

"Paul has made a small fire in the kitchen," he murmured into her chest.

"Let's just see what that's about, shall we?" Ingrid set him down. She slipped on her bathrobe and padded down the hallway on bare feet. One of her toes had a surprisingly painful bruise. She couldn't remember the reason. Wounds were common in her line of work, and sometimes their origins remained obscure. Neil chirped behind her. The extra hour of sleep had been Paul's gift, but now she had to catch up with her son's ebullience. When she entered the kitchen, she found Paul standing on a chair, waving a towel at the smoke alarm. The air was heavy, though it smelled delicious.

Paul grinned. "Sorry. I was making tamale pie, and it got away from me."

"That happens to the best of us."

"Coffee's on." He stepped down. "I mean, it's always on. There's no real sense in turning off the machine. But at the moment, it's semifresh."

Ingrid poured herself a cup. It took a certain amount of restraint not to finish it in a single gulp. The last visit to the doctor had provided a graphic description of what excess coffee was doing to her insides, but Ingrid couldn't imagine drinking less. It was her only vice, except for the very occasional cigarette, consumed in secret as if it were stolen Easter candy. She held the cup in her hands, trying to absorb its properties through osmosis. Neil was climbing on her, but she set him on his own chair. Before he could protest, there was a plate of garlic toast and rolled-up ham before him. Sometimes Paul had a dancer's timing in the kitchen. The boy frowned at it for a moment, then popped the ham in his mouth.

Touchdown.

Ingrid drank her coffee in delicious silence, allowing herself to stare fuzzily out the window. Her mind was still pulling itself together, but she liked these hazy moments. They reminded her of drifting on the surface of a pool in summer, eyes closed, letting the sun make shapes against her eyelids. Nothing was terribly essential. Neil's feet drummed rhythmically against the table. Paul walked in circles with a tiny fan. Birds gathered at the feeder outside, and she could hear splinters of laughter in the distance. Now her mind was rumbling through its latest checklist, but she told it to hush. The last of the high loves. She'd better enjoy it.

Paul gave Neil a glass of juice. "Remember that you're going to Erica's birthday party," he said. "You'll have to get dressed as soon as you finish your breakfast."

This was a fatal miscalculation. Neil put down his fork and began contemplating the food distantly. If he refused to eat, he could stave off getting dressed indefinitely.

Paul knelt beside him, whispering: "I hid a pudding cup in your closet. Once you finish eating and get dressed, you can search for it."

He wolfed down the food and ran to his room.

"That was sheer poetry," Ingrid observed.

Paul shrugged in mock deference. "I hid the pudding cup under his clean outfit. We'll call it a dragon prophecy—that should be enough to convince him to wear the khaki shorts."

"I think he's on the verge of seeing through this prophecy business."

"We can still milk it." He grimaced. "Milking dragons. That must be a dangerous business, and an image that I'd rather not think about."

She laughed, nearly spitting out her coffee. "Like having sex with a porcupine. Something that needs to be done very carefully."

Ingrid said nothing about the dragon of smoke in her dream. Nor did she mention Paul's six-year-old self, fiddling with the armor. She supposed he was a warrior after all, even if his battles were fought with utensils and permission forms. Her brother. Where would she be without his help? They'd be living on a diet of buttered noodles and potato salad. The fridge door would be a chaos of forgotten bills and progress reports, instead of the orderly triumph of charts and stickers that it was today.

"I couldn't do this without you," she said.

Paul blinked at her from the kitchen. "What?"

"All of this. The breakfasts, and the birthday parties, and the sleepless nights. And the Lego. My God. All those pieces. And the cartoons, the apps, the everything. You're a bloody super-dad, and I love you for it. Because I'd be lost without you." She could feel her voice breaking now. "And you didn't have to do any of it."

Paul walked over and gently took the cup from her hand. He sat down next to her.

"I wanted to," he said quietly. "I've always wanted to. Don't ever think it was a tough choice, because it wasn't. Neither of us planned on any of this, but I love that sweet whelp with every atom of my being. It's an honor to be his uncle. Or whatever I am to him."

"He calls you *mine Paul*."

Her brother snorted. "A bit too Germanic for comfort, but I'll take it." His eyes narrowed slightly. "Are you going to tell me what's going on?"

At that moment, Neil burst into the hallway, naked from the waist down. He held the pudding cup with an archaeologist's expression of wild discovery.

"It fell into mine grasp!"

"Pants first, buddy," Paul said. "Then you can have it."

Neil mumbled something darkly, then went back into his room.

"At least we don't have company over," Ingrid said. "That's generally when he decides to forgo wearing pants."

Paul gave her a long look. She knew precisely what it meant but feigned confusion to buy herself a few more seconds. "What?"

"You know what. You said it yourself. We haven't had company in a while."

"We've been busy."

"Uh-huh."

"Don't *uh-huh* me."

He sighed. "Where's Shelby?"

Ingrid stood. Too late, she realized how dramatic the gesture seemed. "She's working on school stuff. Comprehensive exams."

Paul laughed bitterly. "You think I don't know what *working on comps* really means? You've used that one too many times."

She was stricken for a moment. She'd always suspected that Paul could see through her lame excuses, but he'd never confirmed it until now. He didn't seem angry. In fact, there was something eerily parental about his tone that made her recall the "super-dad" title that she'd given him seconds ago. Was he also raising her? The thought was slightly mortifying, but she couldn't immediately discount it. Throughout their childhood, she'd been the older sister, the nervous steward, keeping him out of harm's way. But when Neil arrived, Paul had proven himself to be unexpectedly capable. Over time, it seemed that he'd crept into her former role, while she drifted further into slippery chaos.

"We had a fight," she admitted. "One of those silent ones that are way worse than the yelling kind. I guess I've been avoiding her."

"What about Carl and Andrew?"

"They're sort of a package. Or they used to be, at any

rate. Andrew's more of a variable now. Without Shelby, they don't really have a reason to spend time with us."

He frowned. "They're not a single organism. They do have lives apart from her."

"It's hard to explain. Grad students tend to cluster. They were her friends before they were mine. Now I'm on the outside. But I put myself there."

"There's more to it than that."

She pretended to concentrate on the bird feeder. "What do you mean?"

"Andrew stopped coming over a few months ago, but that didn't stop Carl and Shelby from setting up camp in our living room. The last time the two of them came over, they were both acting strangely. Did something happen?"

"It's just friendship politics. I barely understand it myself."

He physically turned her chair around, as if he were talking to Neil. "That's not going to fly. What happened?"

He always saw more than he let on. She'd known that one day, concealing all of this from him would prove impossible. She'd prepared dozens of counterstories, but he was too close now. Only a touch of honesty could defuse him.

"Andrew"—she hesitated—"was going through some things. He was seeing a psychiatrist, but I don't think he was happy about it. That put some strain on the group. Carl has his own stuff, which is no less dark. I know I'm not much older than them, but our lives are so different. I think it's their instinct to stick together."

The reality was that Andrew had changed. Quiet before, he was like a ghost now. She wanted to talk to him sometimes, but they'd never really been close. She remembered him standing before the basilissa, stretching out his arm. He'd switched sides for them. Unless he'd always been intending to turn.

Paul nodded. "Fine. That doesn't explain the fight, though."

Neil ran into the kitchen. Now he was completely dressed. He'd chosen sweatpants instead of the neatly pressed shorts, but Ingrid couldn't complain. She'd let him wear a cape if it meant getting him out of the house. And for once, his timing was perfect.

"You look very presentable." She kissed him on the cheek. "Put your shoes on."

He made a face. "My feet will be awfully hot!"

"Sandals, then."

"No! They bite mine toes!"

"Gum boots," Paul said.

Neil brightened. Then he went to the door and slipped on his boots.

Really? Ingrid mouthed.

Paul shrugged. "The heart wants what it wants."

His expression said that their conversation wasn't over, but for now, he was satisfied with what she'd told him. It was better than *comps*. She made a mental note to discard that excuse, which had outgrown its usefulness. Had she finally reached the end of her rope? Maybe it was time to tell the entire truth. She imagined how it might sound. *We discovered a park that leads us to another world. Andrew died, and now he's different. Not in a good way. I used to guard a brothel, but now I spend most of my time hunting dragons, which is something that my son would actually understand quite well.*

She could test the explanation out on Neil. He'd be all too happy to accept a world in which his mother had access to edged weapons. Currently, he was dancing in his gum boots. She looked at the painted rock, which he'd left on the table.

"I should go to campus," Ingrid said. "I'll try to be back early. But you can have the house to yourself while I'm gone."

"Uh-huh," Paul replied.

THE FIFTH FLOOR OF THE WILSON LIBRARY was reserved for print journals, though much of it had given ground to computers. The library's digital collections were far more expansive than its fading repository of bound journals. Over the years, the periodicals floor had become a kind of attic for superannuated electronics. All of the oldest copiers and desktop units found their way here, plastic covers yellowed by smoke and age. There were giant mechanized staplers, hole punches that could only manage to inflict two puncture wounds, and microfiche readers, propped against the wall like cars abandoned by the side of the road. The furniture was mismatched, and some of the couches looked like they belonged in a museum. There was also something called an Integrated Reading Room, which appeared to be a kind of media cave with leather chairs. It was empty. Outside, clouds had begun to gather. She could hear the wind howling through the ducts, but it seemed far away.

Ingrid walked among the stacks. She lightly touched the neglected journals, the copies of *Yale Review* from the fifties, typewritten and bound between uniform covers. Everything that she published—if she ever published anything—would someday end up here, housed on vertical shelves. A graduate student would spin the crank, like Fortuna's wheel, that moved the shelves apart. She would run her thumb along the bindings until she found that obscure article, written by a student from another time. Everything about it would be quaint, from the typesetting to the cheesy graphic on the cover. But perhaps, like Ingrid, she would open the journal and smell the pages, enchanted by the subtle reek of binding glue. She would test the journal's heft in her hand and feel somehow comforted by this object, demanding to take up space in an otherwise weightless environment.

She found Shelby looking at the Renaissance periodicals. No doubt, they'd both arrived at the same time, only to be drawn in by the siren shelves. Ingrid's original blueprint for a library was the one that she'd gone to as a child, with plush blue couches and nooks where she could lose herself in *The Tombs of Atuan* or *The Weirdstone of Brisingamen*. When the community library had a book sale, it was like every holiday rolled into one. She could scarcely believe the worlds that her allowance would afford. She wondered if Shelby had been the same. The six years between them were just enough to create a gulf. Shelby liked to text, while Ingrid preferred the burn of the phone against her cheek. As Ingrid watched her, scanning the table of contents, she seemed to be nothing but possibilities. An ideal candidate for anything that life might offer. She could do a postdoc in Vienna, or take over a research center at one of those universities that was always bathed in sun. Eventually, this place wouldn't be enough for her. And what could pull her back? Reading bedtime stories must pale in comparison to teaching graduate seminars in Santa Barbara.

Ingrid could do with some sun herself. And Neil would fall in love with the ocean. She realized that life wasn't an episode of *House Hunters International*. Ordinary people didn't move to San Juan because they wanted "something different." It couldn't be that simple. Then again, nothing about her life was ordinary.

Shelby saw her and put down the journal. "Thanks for coming."

"I was going to anyway, even if you hadn't texted." Ingrid felt as if a ruthless editor were combing through all of her responses, crossing out every second line. "I thought that we should talk. Not in a scary way. Just—you know—after what happened."

"You mean the part where I lied to you, and then subjected you to painful small talk with the matriarchs of my family?"

Ingrid smiled. "It wasn't painful. I really liked your grandmother. She's lived a dozen lives, it seems. And your mother was nice."

"Don't ever call her that to her face. She thinks *mother* is a weak noun."

"I'll try to be stoic when I'm around her."

Shelby drew closer. "My grandmother liked you. I could

tell. She didn't kick me under the table or fake an attack of angina to get away. That means she had a good time."

"And your mother?"

"Don't even try to solve that puzzle."

"Have you—" Ingrid ran through a dozen ways to phrase the question, but none of them made it any less leading. "I mean, I'm sure you've brought girls home before. And boys. Maybe even at the same time. I'm not judging."

Shelby cracked a smile. "Clearly you are. A little bit."

"I'm no gold star lesbian myself."

"You have a son—I kind of assumed that."

She reddened slightly. "Right. Well, that's a story."

"No adjective?"

"What do you mean?"

"Normally, people say that it's a long story, or a weird one. Not that sleeping with a guy is weird. I mean, they smell different, but not weird. Kind of like cookies."

Ingrid laughed helplessly. "I lost you there."

"My high school boyfriend never washed his jeans, and they always smelled like cookies. I have no idea why." Shelby took a breath. "What I'm trying to say is that I'm sure the story has a lot of adjectives, but you don't have to tell me. It's not like I've been completely honest with you. I took a road trip to Egressus without telling you."

Ingrid nearly said *Parking*, but she knew that the fifth floor was empty. Instead, she sat down by the window. The clouds were darkening. She could almost feel them rattling the glass, trying to get in. Shelby sat down next to her. Ingrid could smell her conditioner. The proximity was making her consider a number of adjectives. *We could kiss right here, in the stacks. It would be the most action they'd seen in years.*

She was on a roll, though, as far as honesty was concerned. Better to keep moving forward than risk getting mired in secrets. They weren't helping anymore. The lie had too many moving parts. But for the first time, she could see the dim outlines of an exit, glowing in the dark. All she had to do was step through. Shelby put a hand on her knee. The contact made her a little dizzy. She was embarrassed to realize that the library was acting as an aphrodisiac. It thrilled her a thousand times more than a hotel room. A part of her had always wanted this, long before she could articulate what it might be. Shelby's thumb on her spine. The unbreakable silence of this place, which had felt like home when home was something else.

"When I first came to Anfractus," she said, "I was naked and terrified. I didn't know what had happened. Everything was so bright and sharp. But I also wanted it. The first time I held a sword, it was like swimming"—she smiled—"or climbing a tree to the very top, and seeing butterflies. It wasn't just a weapon. It reminded me of everything good, everything that made sense. And I didn't want to lose that. So I kept coming back."

"It doesn't mean that you're a violent person," Shelby said gently.

"But I am." Ingrid looked at her. "I was made for it. The dance. The blood arc. The sound a body makes when it unravels. It was everything. And I was *good* at it. That's how I became a miles." Shelby's hand was still there, but her expression had changed. Ingrid swallowed and kept going. "The night that I killed for the first time—the night that I won my die—I walked the streets in a haze. I ended up at the black basia. I didn't know what I was looking for. I didn't even have a token. I walked past the revelers, and down a long hallway, with beautiful murals on the wall. I came to an unexpected room. And he was there. Without his mask. I saw his face in the lamplight."

Shelby looked confused for a moment. Then she paled. Her hand pulled away, squeezed into a small fist. "You're not talking about—"

"—Felix." Ingrid nodded. "Neil's father."

Shelby stood. "Oh? So he's not your 'supervisor,' then? Man, you had all of us fooled with that brilliant lie."

"Shelby—"

She shook her head. "What an idiot I've been. When he came to your doorstep, calling himself Oliver, I knew that there was something between you. I could feel it. And later, in the tabularium, the way he looked at you—" Her body seemed to be closing in on itself. "How could you keep this from us? From *Neil*? Christ, Ingrid, you've got Paul running around like super-dad, trying to keep all the plates spinning, while Neil's actual father is"—she began to laugh helplessly—"a whore. In a mask. Wow. This is some messed-up, *Game of Parks* bullshit, and we're right in the middle of it."

Ingrid wasn't sure if the laughter meant that Shelby was still on her side, or if she should be running out of the library. She took another breath. "He had his reasons for leaving. And I have mine for not telling Neil. At least not this second."

"I thought my lies were tangled. But what you're doing is in a totally different class. I'm actually a little in awe."

"I have a son to protect." Ingrid's voice was close to a growl. "Do you know how scared I was—the day that Oliver came knocking at my door? Of course we concocted a story. It was the only thing that made sense at the time. If Neil ever—" She looked away. "Sometimes I want him to see Anfractus. But most of the time, I pray that he never does, even if he was born there. Because I can't protect him from what's beyond the park."

Shelby's face softened. She took out her phone. "Here. This is why I asked you to meet in the first place. Read this text from Carl."

Ingrid took the phone from her. The text was short and simple:

Went on a dig. If not back tomorrow, don't look for me.

She frowned. "Is he on some kind of archaeological trip? It seems like a pretty weird time to leave town."

"Of course he's not on a trip. Carl never works on his thesis."

"You think it's a code."

"I think he's done something stupid. And by that, I mean stupid even for him. But he's left us this clue."

"*Went on a dig*. What could that mean, if not the obvious?"

"If I'm right, it means that we're up to our neck in badness. With both of them gone, there's only two of us. We're barely half a company."

"We've got Sam," she said, after a moment. "That's three."

"Sam doesn't deserve to get involved in this. She may not be an innocent bystander, but she's not an accomplice, either."

"Maybe we should stop underestimating her. If she wanted out, we've given her all kinds of chances. But she still returns our calls."

"Texts." Shelby smiled a little. "Nobody calls anymore." She checked the messages on her phone as she spoke. Her expression was difficult to read.

"Did Carl send another text?" Ingrid sighed. "Of course he didn't. He's probably on the other side of the park, and that was a stupid question."

"Not Carl." Shelby looked up. "I invited someone else to this meeting. I'm sorry I didn't tell you earlier, but—well—not feeling too bad about that, all of a sudden."

"You invited someone to our"—she couldn't quite say *date*—"archive?"

"We need help. And more than just Sam. I made an executive decision to expand our company. After all, we need a fourth."

"A fourth what, exactly?"

The elevator chimed. Ingrid heard footsteps, and then a tall man with red hair stepped into the reading room. It took her a moment to recognize him.

"Narses," she said. "Don't you own a club, on this side?"

He was Latona's former chamberlain, a spado. Ingrid hadn't really thought about him since that night at the club, when he'd threatened to tell her brother everything. The park did something to you. It replaced your family with its ancient roots. Whoever he really was—eunuch or entrepreneur—he wouldn't hesitate to destroy their lives.

She imagined becoming a spado. Had he endured the cut? Or did it happen in the dark interval between the park and the city beyond? Maybe it was like losing a rib in your sleep. It was possible, she saw, to give up one sort of power for another. To leave a piece of yourself behind, in exchange for a weapon on the other side.

He inclined his head. "Actually, my name is Glen."

Ingrid tried not to smile. "It's quite fitting."

Shelby turned to him. "Glen's going to help us breach the Arx of Violets."

Ingrid was no longer amused. "Why would we do that?"

"Because that's where she's keeping him."

"If you're right," Glen said, "she won't kill him. Not yet. First, she'll try to extract as much as she possibly can— while he's still able to talk."

Shelby rubbed her shoulders. "I've been in that dungeon. I know what goes on."

"I still have connections with the palace spadones. I can get you in. But this is not what Pulcheria had in mind."

"She's calling the shots now?"

Glen stiffened slightly. "She's a nobler patroness than Latona. Less unhinged. You'd do well to follow her instructions."

"But we won't," Shelby said. "And neither will you."

"Why do you say that?"

"Because you're a general. At least, you used to be. You thrive in battle." She gave Ingrid an odd look. "And we're about to give you one. Deep down, I don't think you can resist the opportunity to make things messy. Am I right?"

Glen looked at her. "You've changed since last we spoke."

"There's a lot of that going around. Are you in?"

"If this is to work, we'll need a larger company than four."

Shelby scanned through the contacts on her phone. "Way ahead of you."

Ingrid felt a bit sick to her stomach. But also strangely hopeful.

She'd been waiting for a fight like this.

2

THE CAMPUS WAS A GHOST TOWN. INGRID
could hear the climate control whirring, and the sound of a
vending machine dispensing something high in calories.
Athena's Pub was open, but most of the tables were empty.
Students tended to scatter on the weekends. The ones who
stayed were usually living on campus, and they would go
on occasional quests for food, trying to keep their energy
up as they studied for the next test.

In a survey class, Ingrid had encountered the phrase *wintered into wisdom*. Most of the time, she felt as if she'd
summered into exhaustion. Once, Neil had led her to the
bedroom. It was 1:30 in the morning, and he'd managed to
outlast her again. His small hand guided her to the bed, and
he tucked her in, saying, *Hush, Mummy. Hush, tired old
Mummy. There you go*.

"This way," Shelby said, taking her through the doors
that led outside. "It's faster if we cut across the green. I'm
not sure how long she's going to wait, so we'd best be quick."

Ingrid followed her silently. The campus green was

touched by sunset. Burnt orange light moved across the dry grass. Two students were kicking a ball around. They looked up in surprise as the women passed them, as if they'd taken their solitude for granted. Someone had spray-painted Andy Warhol's image on an upright pillar, and art lay scattered around the edges of the grassy swath. There was something that looked like a metal hamster ball, and concrete mushrooms painted various colors. The ground sloped as they crossed the open space. In the distance, she could see the communal garden. It was curious, this in-between green. Everyone had access to it, but no one had time to enjoy it. That was its curse. Bees gathered in a lazy cloud, humming around the crocuses and gardenias. Someone had planted peppers and drawn a small sign next to them with a stylized sombrero. She couldn't tell if it was ill-advised or tender in some way. *Let sleeping peppers lie.*

Ingrid stopped in front of the garden.

Shelby gave her a look. "What? Is there a rock in your shoe? Just shake it out."

"There's a rock in my life."

"That sounds like the opening line to a bad Christian musical."

Ingrid watched the ball as it dazzled its way across the green. She thought of how Fortuna was sometimes called *ball-player.* She'd wait for you to draw near, then toss the sphaira in your direction. Most of the time, the love-ball hit you square between the eyes, and you went down like a ton of bricks, spitting blood. That was how she liked it.

"The plan almost makes sense," Ingrid replied slowly. "It's not our worst plan, that's for sure. But what then? Even if it works, and we manage to rescue Carl, I don't see what we're supposed to do after that." She looked at Shelby. "She's got us on the run. All we do is react to her every move, and then she watches us scatter. I don't think we can keep this up."

"We? Or you?"

Ingrid frowned. "I'm in this as much as you are."

"Right. No argument there." She put a cautionary hand on Ingrid's shoulder. It was the first time that Shelby had touched her since their fight at the library. "But you're in a different position than us. You've got your whole family to think of."

"You're my family too. All of you. It's not like we're a separate unit anymore."

Shelby's expression softened. "I know. But ultimately, you've got a lot more to lose than we do. I'd understand if you wanted to back out."

Ingrid could feel that curious shift in her gut, the moment when anger suddenly overwhelms stasis. "Why are you always telling me to run? It's like you're building this equation around me, and whenever I try to help, you push me away."

There was a flash of anger in her eyes. But it faded. The sunlight was in her hair, and for a moment, she looked otherworldly. A falling star, crackling in the long, dry grass. Ingrid wanted to touch her face, to keep her from going out. Would she stay? Had it ever been possible, or was she just fooling herself?

"I don't want you to run," Shelby said. "In case you haven't noticed, I'm kind of lost without you. I just don't want you to get hurt."

Ingrid reached out to smooth her hair. It was impossible not to. "It all hurts," she said. "You can't stop that. Luckily, I've got a full medicine cabinet at home."

Shelby chuckled. "We're going to need some aloe. Maybe some splints."

"It's a really big cabinet," Ingrid murmured. Then she kissed Shelby. Two bright spots on the green. Their shadows danced in the weeds. Ingrid pulled away, just in time to see the ball whizzing toward them. She caught it smoothly, without thinking. Her hands burned from the impact, but she held it, redolent with grass and new plastic. One of the guys came jogging over with a sheepish grin.

"I'm really sorry about that," he said, cheeks reddened. "The sun was in our eyes, and we didn't notice you there."

"Not a problem." Ingrid tossed him the ball. "We were distracted."

"Nice catch, by the way."

"I have a child who likes to throw things. I'm kind of an unofficial goalie."

He smiled at them both, then ran back to the green.

Shelby seemed about to say something. Then she shrugged helplessly and kept walking. Bees droned among the petals. Ingrid tried to remember what she'd been about to say, but the argument was gone. She made a mental foot-note to return to it, adding to the long list of errata that she'd promised to deal with, if she ever had the time.

They entered the transitional hallway that connected the science and humanities wings of the campus. Ingrid smelled fresh paint. There was a sheet of drywall, standing abandoned and confused in the middle of the hall. Tools were scattered around it, as if some cosmic event had swept away the people who'd begun the repairs. They passed the shuttered café, and Ingrid noticed that Shelby was shivering.

"I've got a sweater in my bag." She began to rummage through it. "And a Kinder egg, if you need that. Some jelly beans. A tape measure, for some reason. This might actually be a black hole that leads to another universe."

"No, I'm not—" She managed to look slightly uncomfortable. "I had this dream, a while ago. The campus was covered in snow. There were monsters chasing me, and I couldn't register for any of my classes."

"Was I there?"

"Yeah."

Ingrid smiled slightly. "What was I doing?"

"Being cryptic."

The elevator rose. Shelby remained distracted. An age seemed to pass as they moved between floors. Ingrid remembered her own dream. Paul's curious expression as he put a finger to his lips. The dragon made of smoke, devouring her hand as she reached for the sword that might have been a trick all along. She flexed her fingers experimentally, as if she could still feel the bite of the dark. All that treasure. What was it doing there? Heroes were always looking for treasure, but what did they actually need it for? She couldn't imagine a fantasy realm that had embraced the gold standard. She could still see the gleaming armor, the spray of gemstones like shells on a beach. Dragons didn't know the worth of their own hoard. Maybe her sword was just as pointless. Still, she could have used it right about now. If something attacked them, her only weapon was a bag full of oddments.

They stepped onto the third floor. The Department of Literature and Cultural Studies was a honeycomb of silent offices. Rumor had it that they'd soon be merging with the Faculty of Fine Arts, in order to create something even more far-reaching and complicated. A grand unified theory to solve the university's budget crisis. They'd need to print larger posters, if that was the case. It would be hard to fit *Department of Literature, Culture, Writing, Cinema, Communications, Sculpture, and Everything You Ever Wanted to Know but Were Afraid to Ask* on a standard sheet. Maybe a banner of some sort.

"I don't see any snow," Ingrid said. "That's a good sign, right?"

"I'm not sure. Weather changes on a dime around here."

Ingrid paused in the corridor. "Tell me again how you managed to get both of them here on a weekday?"

"With Dr. Marsden, it was easy. I just told her I was having a thesis crisis, and that I might want to switch to liberal studies. She e-mailed me back right away. Dr. Laclos was a bit trickier, since he's not even on my committee. I may have e-mailed him from Andrew's account and pretended to be having an academic meltdown."

Ingrid frowned. "You hacked into his e-mail?"

"*Hacked* is a violent term for it. I used my giant brain to guess Andrew's password, which wasn't all that hard. He uses *Serenity* for everything, even his bank account."

"Please don't hack into that."

"Not a chance—he has the worst finances of us all."

Ingrid gave her a long look. "Are you sure that you're right about this?"

"No. But if there's another option, I'm all ears."

"You're really going to tell your supervisor that you hit her with a car."

"*Sam* hit her. And it was a truck."

"And you don't hear how crazy this sounds."

Shelby flashed her a smile. "I didn't say it was a great plan. But if I'm right, they may be our only chance of rescuing Carl."

"How do you plan on beginning this conversation? *So, Dr. Marsden, have you been experiencing any monstrous symptoms lately? Do you happen to remember chasing us through the park like a wild animal?*"

Shelby squared her shoulders. "She's an academic. She appreciates logic. I'll make a strong argument and call on some secondary sources. That's you, by the way. You're my secondary source."

"I want out of this assignment."

"Too late. You're in—you said so yourself."

"I'd like to change my topic."

"Come on."

Trish Marsden's office was everything that she'd pictured. The built-in shelves were lined with eighteenth-century volumes. Ingrid wasn't much for that period, but she still wanted to run her fingers along their spines. The desk was covered in loose papers, as if to deliberately spite the neglected file folder in the corner. A narrow window overlooked a cement balcony that wrapped its way around the arts building. Mostly, this was the realm of neurotic students, burning through a pack a day while they waited for inspiration to strike. Of course, this never happened. All you could do was read until your brain melted, and then hope that you remembered how to write when the moment arrived. Before Neil was born, she pulled all-nighters with an explosion of junk food on her kitchen table, mainlining Twizzlers while struggling to decode her own sticky-note system. After he arrived, the process was much the same, only with more nighttime interruptions. It was hard to craft a footnote when your child would emerge from his bedroom, rubbing his eyes blearily and asking if you'd like to play One Thousand and One Hugs and Kisses.

Dr. Marsden sat behind the desk, her fingers steepled, as if she were about to offer a benediction. At first, Ingrid thought that she was talking to a student. But it was Dr. Laclos who sat across from her. Rumor had it that he was gunning for tenure, and the circles under his eyes were darker than usual. He wore a rumpled polo shirt with a lopsided collar, and Ingrid had to hold herself back to keep from fixing it. She had the same issue with Paul's collars. She couldn't stand to send him into the world looking uneven. He reminded her a bit of Paul, in fact. He had a faint beard, which was the result of neglect rather than design. His right hand was attached to a dangerously large cup of coffee, while the fingers of his left hand played with a red pen. He spun it absently, over and over again, until it was a flickering wheel.

Shelby knocked lightly on the door.

Dr. Marsden looked up. "Oh, hello. Dr. Laclos and I were just discussing the results of the last budget meeting." Her expression darkened. "There were, of course, no results. There never are. Budget meetings are actually stitches in time that produce nothing, save for a lingering, existential headache."

Ingrid had the feeling that her statement was both true and false. There had been a budget meeting, but that wasn't the topic of her conversation with Dr. Laclos. The two of them exchanged a brief look. Shelby's theory was that they were dating, but if that were the case, Ingrid couldn't see why they weren't more obvious about it. Trish was a bit older, but that often seemed the case in academic relationships, where people met each other at disparate career stages. There was no hint of a scandal. What was the point in being subtle?

"Thanks for agreeing to meet with me on such short notice."

"Supervisors are always on call," Dr. Laclos said, still spinning the pen. It was the first time that Ingrid had heard him speak. His voice was deeper than she'd expected. She could imagine him singing baritone in a choir.

"Funny you should say that," Shelby began.

Both professors suddenly turned to regard Ingrid, as if they'd just now detected the presence of an interloper. *Not an English person.* That was how she often introduced herself to Shelby's friends. They tended to have a whole constellation of weird prejudices about the Faculty of Education, so it was safer to just describe herself as *not English*, as if the language was somehow foreign to her.

"I'm Ingrid," she said. "Pleased to meet you both. I'm—"

"—in education," Dr. Marsden said. "Yes, Shelby's told me about you."

This brought her up short. What had Shelby told her? Ingrid couldn't imagine her name coming up in a supervisory meeting. Did Dr. Marsden know that they were . . . whatever they happened to be? Had Shelby simply mentioned her name in passing? Ingrid was surprised by how quickly the paranoia bubbled up within her, like one of Neil's science experiments involving vinegar and baking soda.

Dr. Laclos stood up. "I should probably be going. I also have an unexpected meeting."

"Actually," Shelby said, "you might want to sit down."

Ingrid closed the door. The move was instinctual, but as soon as she did it, everyone stared at her. The door shut with a loud click. She froze with her hand on the knob.

"Sorry. Should I leave it open?"

"Nope," Shelby said. "Closed is good."

"What's going on?" Dr. Marsden asked. "Why do I have

the feeling that I've just walked into something that could involve litigation?"

"Nobody's suing anyone," Shelby clarified. "Andrew's going to be furious at me for using his e-mail account, but I don't think he'd commit to pressing charges. That would really eat into his gaming time."

Dr. Laclos frowned. "Wait—did you e-mail me, pretending to be my graduate student?" He seemed to be seeing her for the first time. "Whatever for?"

"The better question," Dr. Marsden said, "is why have you brought Ingrid? Are you supposed to be some kind of witness?"

It took Ingrid a moment to realize that the question was directed at her. "Ah—not exactly. I'm more of a . . . secondary source?"

Dr. Marsden's tone was flat. "I don't follow."

This was spinning out of control. Andrew's supervisor hadn't moved an inch, but something had shifted around him. Ingrid could feel his anger rising. The room was beginning to turn. The books seemed to lean in, curious about what he might do. Dr. Laclos made a small sound in his throat. It resembled a cough but might have been a growl.

Shelby was poised to deliver her speech. But it wasn't coming. She just stood there, mouth open slightly, ready for the explanation that couldn't quite emerge. For a moment, the office was quiet as a grave. Shelby wasn't saying anything. She was frozen on the edge of some impossible thesis. Ingrid sighed inwardly.

"I'm the one who hit you," she told Dr. Marsden. "With my car. The first two times, I mean. The third time wasn't me."

The look that Dr. Marsden gave Ingrid was nothing short of astonishing. It was the same look you might give a stuffed bear that suddenly began talking about the economy. Ingrid saw the realization dawn coldly in her eyes. *This one knows. She isn't just part of the scenery.* And that look confirmed everything that Shelby had suspected. Trish Marsden had been at the park that night. Only not Trish Marsden. A monster with her memories.

"I was hit by a drunk driver," Dr. Marsden said slowly. "Shelby tells me that you have a little boy. I'd hardly peg you as the type to cut a swath of destruction through the park."

"I can be destructive when I put my mind to it," Ingrid replied. "But I didn't want to hit you that night. You . . . weren't yourself. But you knew that already."

Dr. Laclos was holding the pen tightly now. Ingrid wondered how fast he could move in this form. Was part of him always a silenus, or was it a kind of shadow, the way she experienced Fel? She didn't want to test this hypothesis. Marsden was able to maintain her composure, but Laclos had stiffened and was looking at her with eyes that no longer belonged to a shy academic. In fact, she'd seen those eyes before.

"What are you suggesting?" Dr. Marsden asked finally. "Come out with it. I've no patience for this."

In reality, she was stalling. She was watching Dr. Laclos with an expression of barely contained anxiety. He hadn't said anything yet. He was drawing spirals against the desk with the red pen. Slow, deliberate spirals. The way that a hunter might track its prey in ever-tightening circles, until there was nowhere left to run.

"We need your help," Shelby said finally.

Shelby's voice broke the trance. Ingrid looked up from the desk and saw that Shelby had moved. Now she was standing directly in front of Laclos. Her hand was a light pressure on Ingrid's shoulder, pushing her gently to the side. Ingrid didn't move. Another part of her mind was scanning the office for something to use as a weapon. Lots of hardcovers but none big enough to do permanent damage. A stapler. That might do in a pinch. Her eyes fell on a letter opener. There. But would she be quick enough to grab it? She had to keep it in her line of sight.

"You may need a lawyer, at this point," Dr. Marsden said.

"Or a psychiatrist. Possibly both. Either way, you should go." She glanced at Laclos. "Now, Shelby."

There was a peculiar trill to the way that she said Shelby's name. She was afraid for her. For both of them. Ingrid tried to watch Laclos from the corner of her eye. Why was he so familiar? If Marsden deferred to him, then the silenus they'd faced in the park—Marsden's shadow—must be middling in her power. Laclos was the true threat. Her self-control wasn't the result of experience. It was fear.

Those eyes. They fixed on her, and his growl was unmistakable. The memory hit her like a rock. Darkness. Dried flowers. Sparks on stone. And that same trill of fear, in the voice of a mother. Ingrid tasted bile in her throat.

"Septimus," she murmured.

He was the right hand of the princeps of the silenoi. A pitiless general who loved a game called latrinculi, which involved circles and stones. The last time Ingrid had seen him, Septimus had been standing next to Basilissa Latona. Hooves striking sparks against the floor. Even in this form, there was something primordial about him. An intelligence rooted in darkness and rain-cut groves. The monster uncurled in his eyes.

Laclos stood. A force seemed to be pushing down on him, distending his features. Ingrid shivered. Looking down, she saw frost beginning to form on the desk. She could see her breath now. Shelby's hand clutched her shoulder.

"The dream's coming true," she whispered. "Only I was wrong about the monster. She wasn't the one chasing me. It was him."

"You left that part out," Ingrid said through clenched teeth.

"I may have been editorializing."

Laclos took a step forward. His eyes were headlights. The letter opener was too far away, and beautifully pointless. They had no weapons. But that didn't mean that they couldn't still fight. Ingrid drew herself up. If she was going to face a nightmare, she'd do it with her eyes open and her feet on the ground.

"What is the sacrifice?" Shelby asked.

Laclos paused. "What do you know about that?" His voice was somewhere between human and animal, an unearthly rumble.

Shelby looked at Dr. Marsden. "I heard you on the phone. I may have broken into your office. I'm sorry! But it sort of pales in comparison with"—she gestured to Laclos—"whatever's happening here."

Dr. Marsden rose stiffly. She walked to the other side of the desk and placed her hand lightly on his arm.

"They really do need our help."

"And why should we trust them?"

"Because we know where the horn is," Shelby said. "And we'll let you have it."

Laclos stared at her. "You're prepared for the consequences."

"We don't have much to lose at this point. The spadones can get us into the arx, but we need a diversion. Can you help?"

Laclos considered this. Then he looked at Ingrid.

"She'd kill for you," he said. "That much you can trust."

3

THEY CAME TO THE HOUSE WHEN THE LIGHT
was red and rippling across the sky. The sun fired the roofs
and spires of the city, until they seemed to be baking in a
clay oven. Fel washed her hands in the disused fountain
outside. She was already sweating and covered in dust.
Water sluiced from the mouth of a stone silenoi, and she
filled her leather flask. It was warmish and metallic but
better than nothing. The straps of her lorica were chafing,
and she felt like some overcooked animal beneath the bronze
plates. Her sandals slipped against the wet stone. In the
distance, she could hear fighting, or possibly loving. It was
hard to tell in this vici, where the insulae were thick, and
the air reeked of tanning hide. *Things come out of this
neighborhood,* she thought. *The bolts and threads that hold
us together.* And things remained. The spine of a place that
used to be their own.

Fel smiled without meaning to.

Morgan shifted next to her, digging a rock out of her
sandal. "What?"

"I was just remembering when I showed you this place. We had to undress in front of each other. I sneaked a peek."

"Bad miles. You ought to know better."

"And you?"

Morgan feigned shock. "I averted my eyes, like a woman who fears Fortuna."

"I think you're confusing her with someone else."

"Things were simpler then. Felix was our ally. The house was ours to use as we pleased. I suppose we'd warmed to being heroes, at that point. Or whatever we were." Morgan surveyed the blackened entrance. "It seemed like she couldn't touch us."

"That was never true."

They were silent for some time. Music drifted down the street. Fel spotted a fur, watching them from the nearest alley. Just a smudge looking darkly at them. Now they had a retinue of sorts.

"Will she come?"

Morgan scanned the empty street. "If I were her, I'd stay far away."

"She knows the risks. She'll do what she must."

"And the wheel turns." There was a bit of iron in Morgan's voice. "And the bullshit platitudes begin. All this is happening because some bitch in the sky likes games."

Fel gave her a look. "Do you think that's her only motive?"

"I don't know what to think." Morgan ran her fingers along the scorched wood. "I heard her voice once, but it didn't fill me with dread, or awe. Maybe it was just Latona, talking through one of those trick fountains. Maybe it was my own voice."

"There are crueler gods. Like the ones the silenoi serve."

Morgan shrugged. "They're blood-soaked, but I appreciate their honesty."

"Perhaps you should join the wild gens."

"You're angry that we're working with them."

"Not angry. Just cautious. I seem to be the only one who remembers that the silenoi have been hunting us from the beginning."

"They're not the only thing."

Fel bit down on her reply. She knew that Septimus would tear them apart, if given the chance. That was his nature. Morgan wanted to believe that some kind of truce was possible, but she was entirely focused on saving Babieca. She'd do anything to keep him from harm. That left Fel with the task of watching. When the hunters turned on them, it would happen quickly. She needed to be ready, even if Morgan wasn't.

She was about to say something to this effect, when she noticed a woman in a head scarf making her way down the street. She was carrying a sack. Fel hoped that it was teeming with weapons, or something that they could trade for weapons.

"It stinks here," Julia said. "I never noticed that before."

Fel handed her the water flask. "Have some of this. It's no treat, but it will keep you from getting light-headed."

Julia wrinkled her nose as she uncorked the flask. "Did something die in here?"

"Just drink."

She obeyed, and handed back the flask. "Thank you."

"What's in the bag?"

Her smile grew slightly impish. "You'll see."

"You always bring presents. That's one of your best qualities."

"That, and my poor memory. I keep forgetting how dangerous it is to hang out with you lot. So here I am again."

"Thank you for coming," Morgan said. "We couldn't manage this without you."

"We'll get him back. Don't worry."

Morgan smiled in return, but it didn't quite reach her eyes. Fel wanted to touch her, but there were too many layers separating them. It would have to wait for later. Morgan led them into the remains of the house. The atrium had collapsed. The air was thick with soot. Light from a broken window filtered in, making patterns against the ruined floor. They picked their way carefully through the debris. Fel saw what used to be a table, and melted lumps that could have been acedrex pieces. The murals had mostly been destroyed, but she could still see the remnants of one. Yellow and red angles framed a mysterious landscape whose particulars were burned away. She wondered who had painted them. Had this place ever been a home? Or was it all part of the basilissa's engine?

They knew so little about Latona. Her desires were a mystery, her fears even more so. She wanted to restore the imperium, but what then? Did she really presume to rule over it all? And what would be left? Fel knew that she had a chill grace, that she was masterful at playing stones, and that she loved her daughter. Everything else remained as incoherent as the mural, covered in soot. That was their real weakness. It wasn't simply that they'd become bedfellows with the silenoi, or that they were risking everything to save a trovador. It wasn't even Morgan's stubborn loyalty to the one called Aleo, who resembled the friend that she'd known but was an entirely different puzzle now. Much worse than this was the fact that they'd never truly seen their enemy, not as a person. Latona was a blank tablet. You couldn't fight someone about whom you knew virtually nothing. You might as well go to battle in pitch darkness.

"Are you sure it's here?" Fel asked.

"My shadow seems to think so. The memory's hazy, but I think this is where we have to look. It's an ideal hiding place."

Julia kicked one of the beams. "It's not exactly secure. Anyone could rifle through what's left of this place."

"But they wouldn't. Because it no longer exists." She grabbed a fallen plank. "Help me lift this, will you?"

Fel took up one end. Together, they dragged it to one side. Morgan knelt down and drew her knife. She worked the blade along the edge of one of the flagstones. When she applied enough pressure, it came loose.

She smiled. "Clever boy."

The horn was wrapped in cloth. She withdrew it carefully, studying the patterns engraved within the ivory. The air grew still. Fel thought she could hear the sun going down, sizzling as it slipped below the horizon.

"Beautiful things are always so much trouble," Morgan said.

There was noise at the door. Fel placed a hand on the hilt of her blade. Morgan gave her a long look, but her hand stayed where it was.

Two silenoi walked into the broken atrium. Their cloven feet stirred the dust. They must be walking very softly, to prevent cracking the stone floor. Septimus entered first. He was covered in coarse black hair from the waist down. His upper body was marked by intricate scars, which formed a tracery along his chest and muscular arms. The failing light revealed the outline of his horns. Fel's hand tightened on the hilt. Amber eyes held her, until she was the fly, trapped inside for millennia.

He was joined by a female silenus, a bit smaller, though no less fearsome. She spoke in a low growl, a dark throatsong, and Septimus replied in the same language. It was hard to tell if they were quarrelling or simply agreeing with each other. Every movement, every rumbled, enigmatic word, seemed to augur the threat of violence. It was heavy on them. Fel could sense it as a kind of dramatic vibration. But neither made any move to attack. They all stared at each other in calculated silence.

"This is awkward," Julia said finally. "Are you going to eat us?"

"Not unless we have to," Septimus replied.

It might have been a joke, but his intonation was difficult to read. Fel decided to take him at his word. She half-drew her blade.

Septimus looked at her. "Think it through, miles. They'd both be dead before you could stick me with that."

"I wouldn't be so sure," Fel replied. "She's a pretty good shot. And the artifex has a sack full of"—she frowned—"something. I'm assuming it will hurt."

"Let's not place bets on that," Julia said.

Morgan stepped between them. "This is simple. We have something that you want. They have something that we want. It's an exchange."

"How do we know that they won't rip our throats out, once they've got the horn?" Fel tapped the hilt of her blade. "There's nothing stopping them."

"We made a promise." The female silenus spoke for the first time. "We will honor the agreement. Will you?"

"I don't even know your name," Morgan said. "I just realized that."

The silenus inclined her head slightly. "Skadi."

Morgan studied her scarred face, as if trying to find someone else. Then, with a deliberate motion, she gave the horn to Skadi.

"This belongs to you," she said. "Use it, destroy it—I don't care. As long as you help us rescue our friend."

"They're not going to destroy a priceless artifact," Julia said. Her eyes widened. "Are you? Because, if that's the case, then my gens would be very interested in—"

"—no more offers," Septimus said. "We will help spring your singer, in return for this."

"But why?" Fel asked.

His yellow eyes narrowed. "What do you mean?"

"You could just take it. You don't owe us anything."

"Stop helping, Fel," Julia snapped.

"Just tell me why," Fel persisted. "You've spent centuries hunting us like prey. Why are you helping us now?"

"We share a common enemy," Septimus replied. "Someone who no longer respects the hunt. We have seen the end of things, and she is the scream at its center. The one who will cause everything to sink into darkness." He gave her a search-ing look. "It was not a game to us, this hunt. You were never prey. Now you will hunt alongside us. As it might have been ages ago, had your wheel turned in a different direction."

"And your princeps? What does he say about all of this?"

Septimus and Skadi exchanged a look.

"He doesn't know," Morgan said. "You're acting without his sanction."

"Something must be done," Skadi replied. "Something unexpected."

Morgan straightened. "Good. That's kind of our spe-cialty."

"And you, miles?" Septimus glanced at her sword.

Fel sheathed the weapon. "I'll try anything once," she said. "Even if it's the craziest thing I've ever heard of."

"That's the spirit," Morgan said.

They made their way uphill toward the arx, relying on the alleys to provide cover. For all their size, both Skadi and Septimus could move in complete silence. They kept to the shadows, and when Fel did catch a glimpse of the pair loping behind, their movements were unexpectedly graceful. The same hooves that shattered stone seemed to glide across the uneven ground, barely raising dust. Her hand still strayed to the sword hilt. These were not allies. They were monsters who'd decided to make a compromise, but the turn was on its way. Morgan would never see it coming. In spite of her bluster about Fortuna, the sagittarius still wanted to believe in miraculous change. Fel knew better. The silenoi were predators. They couldn't shed centuries of instinct like a soiled tunica. They would fight alongside their prey until the moment was right, and then they would turn to strike.

Violets flamed on the road that lead to the arx. Their fragrance settled over everything, reminding her of a warm bath, the temptation of sleep. Miles stood like thorns among the flowers, watching their procession as it stumbled along. Their clothing concealed the armor beneath. They might have simply been hired help, but the miles watched them all the same. If they noticed the silenoi, all chaos would break loose. Fel glanced backward, to see if she could spot them, but there was only the still road and a few scattered wagons.

They came to a sheltered spot beneath a lemon tree and stopped. It was close enough to the wall that the growing shade was thick. Fel saw the eyes of the silenoi before the rest of their bodies materialized. They hovered like marshlights, poised to lead them in any direction but home. Julia seemed on the verge of saying something but held back. Fel knew what was on her mind. Even Skadi and Septimus were working without a net, uncertain of how this would end. *The basilissa wins all.* You couldn't beat the queen at her own game. Not unless Fel was right, and Fortuna really did have a sense of humor.

Morgan scanned the line of trees. "This is the spot that Narses told us about. Fourth lemon tree from the bench in shadow. It should be in plain sight."

"There," Septimus replied. "Between the tree and the wall."

He stood some distance away, but his vision was the keenest. Fel would have to remember that. He would spot any uncanny movements on her part, unless she kept a generous space between them.

Morgan retrieved the small iron-bound chest and opened it. She drew out a pair of green tunicae, along with a set of keys.

"These won't get us into the carcer, but they should open some doors along the way." Morgan handed Julia one of the tunicae. "Put this on."

"You think I can pass for a spado?"

"You're tall and gangly," Fel said. "As long as you keep your hair covered, nobody will think to look beneath your cowl."

"Thanks for that," she said, slipping on the tunica. She made a face. "It smells like a bloody apothecary. How much perfume do they wear?"

"Chamberlains are supposed to smell nice," Morgan said,

putting on the second tunica. "It distracts you from the knife in their belt."

Fel turned to Septimus. "You never answered our question about this sacrifice."

The silenoi exchanged a look.

It was Skadi who answered. "We can't say for certain. But we believe that Latona means to forge a blood pact. The sacrifice will unite her with the lares. It's an old sort of power—unpleasant even for us. But it works. If the lares believe that she'll provide them with blood, they may follow her to the plain of battle. Even without your oculus."

I'm not sure he still belongs to us, Fel thought. She didn't say it aloud, though.

"Who does she plan to sacrifice?"

Skadi frowned—if a silenus could actually frown. "We can't say—"

"—for certain, I know. You keep saying that, but it's not making me believe you."

"Fel." Morgan put a hand on her arm. "We have to work with them."

"She's only trying to protect you," Septimus said. "She doesn't trust us. And she shouldn't. I suppose we share the same instincts."

Fel let this pass. "Surely you have a theory," she ventured.

Septimus considered this for a moment. "The girl," he said. "Her daughter. That is who we believe the sacrifice to be."

Morgan's eyes widened. "Eumachia? That's impossible. You were there when Latona found her in the crypt. She was terrified that something might happen to her."

Something meaning Septimus. The silenus made a strange gesture that might have been a grand shrug. "Was it fear? Or a performance? She tricked me into playing her game. She's manipulated you from every angle. If the ritual is to work, the sacrifice must be a potent one. A true loss. What could be worse than losing a child?"

Morgan turned to Fel. "Do you think she's capable of it?"

The miles felt a coldness settling in the pit of her stomach. "I don't know. But I'm not willing to risk it. We'll have to divide our forces. The girl trusts you. Go to her usual haunts, and try to find her. Enlist the foxes if necessary. I think they're more loyal to her than they are to their mistress. Bring her to the undercroft, where we escaped last time."

"What about me?" Julia asked. She tried to square her shoulders, making the question something of a challenge, but Fel saw how nervous she was. A builder with a bag of tricks. Not the shield-maiden that she would have asked for at a time like this. And yet she'd followed them this far, with no weapons or fabled sight or songs to protect her. In a way, that made her the bravest among them.

"You'll stay with me," Fel said. "I can use some of your machines."

"We will shadow you both," Septimus said.

I'm sure you will.

"Thank you," was all she said. "There are furs in the palace as well, loyal to their queen. They can help us in a pinch. The spadones that serve Narses will keep the miles occupied as best they can."

"What of the spadones who serve Latona?" Skadi asked. "Surely they will suspect something. And their mistress can be highly persuasive."

"That's the part where I sort of hate this plan," Julia said.

"Hopefully," Fel replied, "this will be over before they have the chance to realize that anything is amiss. We need to throw the die and get out as quickly as possible."

Septimus nodded. "Lead the way."

Fel didn't relish the thought of exposing her back to them. But she had little choice. Morgan was used to guarding the battlements in solitude, and Julia, while she had a sharp eye for detail, was unfamiliar with the rhythms of the palace. She was the leader by default.

They slipped in through the postern gate, which was open

to receive supplies for Latona's celebration. *Thank Fortuna she has so many parties,* Fel thought. The miles at the gate watched them coldly, but Julia and Morgan kept their heads down. Fel had donned a helmet with bronze neck guards that concealed much of her face. The miles to the left wrinkled her nose when Morgan drew closer. The fragrance was familiar enough. She waved them past, fixing Fel with a curious gaze. Trying to remember where she'd seen those eyes before. Fel inclined her head and ushered her spadones through the gate.

Giant amphorae full of wine were stacked against the red pillars of the room beyond. Vaulted arches turned the ceiling into a painted illusion. Deeper in the arx, there would be archers waiting on hidden platforms, swords behind every tapestry. But the service quarters were relatively unguarded.

Fel turned to Morgan. "This is where we split up. Julia and I will head for the carcer. Nobody's going in that direction, so we shouldn't encounter too much resistance. The undercroft is below this floor. When you find Eumachia, bring her back there. And be careful. We'll need your bow if we're going to get out of this den of vipers." She hesitated. Then she kissed Morgan lightly, placing a hand on the small of her back. They shared a breath, and then pulled away.

Morgan's eyes danced. "Be careful yourself."

"Septimus—" Fel began. But both silenoi had already disappeared. "I suppose they're already playing the part of shadows."

"Maybe they're scouting ahead." Julia tried to sound cheerful.

Fel smiled at Morgan. "We'll see you soon."

Then they were descending. The air cooled as they neared the lower levels of the arx, where things were left and forgotten. Weapons and relics, amphorae and souls. The realm of torture used to be quite extensive when Latona's mother ruled the city, or so Fel had heard. She hoped that the singer was still in good condition. He had information, and Latona would need to extract it before disposing of him. It all came down to how much he could endure. Trovadores weren't known for their resilience.

"What are they going to do with that horn?" Julia asked.

"I don't know." Fel took the stairs slowly, listening for activity below.

"Do you think he's still alive?"

She swallowed. "I don't know."

"Is there any chance that—" Julia stopped in midsentence. "You don't know. Sorry. Just trying to make demi-hysterical conversation."

"We'll be fine," Fel said, though she didn't quite believe it. "Just stay behind me. If I tell you to run, don't hesitate."

Julia stared at her. "And where would I go?"

Fel didn't answer. They moved slowly down the corridor, cleaving to the wall. Lanterns cast their shadows against the floor, which had shifted from pale travertine marble to scuffed stone. These lower levels were the root system of the palace, and aesthetics were not a priority. The lights grew more sporadic. Fel caught the scent of stagnant water and packed earth. They were near the carcer.

"Have a distraction ready," she told Julia.

The artifex nodded. "It won't last for long."

"I only need a few seconds." Fel inched around the corner, then grabbed Julia's arm, holding her in place. "Six guards," she whispered. "They don't want Babieca going anywhere. Two of them are busy playing mora. That could work in our favor."

"Six?" Julia's eyes blazed. "Fuck the wheel, are you insane? That might as well be an army. Only one of us is even armed."

Ingrid handed her a knife. "This is my favorite, so don't lose it." Then she smiled wanly. "You don't have to be afraid. This time, the monsters are on our side. Plus, if we die, it will be very quick. You won't even feel it."

"You shouldn't use words," Julia muttered.

Fel stepped around the corner, shedding the cloak that concealed her armor. She drew her second-favorite dagger and threw it at the miles who was sitting down, flickering through mora shapes like shadow puppets. He didn't have time to look up. The dagger pinned his free hand to the table, and he made a sound like an astonished grunt. She could feel the mist flowing over her eyes but willed it to stay back. She wouldn't take a life unless—

The nearest guard leapt at her, gladius already drawn. Fel threw the cloak around his head, dragging him to the ground. She reversed her sword and brought the pommel down on his temple, dazing him. Then she took his blade. The remaining guards advanced upon her slowly, like a pack of wolves. The element of surprise was gone, and there were still four of them to contend with. The one that she'd wounded remained on the margins, clutching his punctured hand to his chest. Still a threat.

Anytime, Septimus, she thought.

They danced around her. A woman in a bronze lorica made the first move—a downward slash meant to expose her. Fel parried with one blade and kept the other high. She felt, more than heard, the second guard approaching from behind. She feinted at the woman in bronze, then turned and dropped to one knee. The other miles had drawn herself up to strike but found herself staring at empty air. Fel aimed for the gap between greave and scalloped mail. She missed the very satisfying artery but still managed to bite into a half-moon of exposed flesh. The miles cried out, giving ground. Fel kicked her in the stomach, then rolled to the side as the first guard's blade came down like a cleaver. Pain blossomed in her shoulder as she hit the floor. They were already moving in. She used the wall to launch herself forward, ducking as the swords groped for her.

Ignore the shoulder. You're not a body. You're a weapon.

One of them caught her in the arm, ripping through a

clasp on her lorica. She smelled copper and sweat. *Not your blood. You don't have blood.* Fel drove her helmet into the chest of the nearest miles, who was also bleeding. She pushed with all her might, ignoring the wave of dizziness. The guard lost her balance, staggering. Fel turned and swung the borrowed blade like a scythe. One of them grabbed her wounded arm, and then the mist was there. She struck the woman in the face with the hilt of her blade. The blow dislodged her helmet, and Fel grabbed a clump of her exposed hair, pulling her down. She kneed her in the throat and flung her to the ground. They knocked her second blade from nerveless fingers, but she still had her bright nail. Fel heard a sandal scrape behind her, and then light exploded as the blow caught her in the side of the head. A second later, and it would have bitten through her neck. It shattered the guard on her helmet and left her ears ringing as she fell to one knee.

She was sick from the pain, and everything was humming. For a moment, she heard something like cold laughter, the sound of a fountain bubbling. Fel saw the unearthly shine of the blades. Her left arm was numb. She tasted bile. Not fear, though.

Run, she tried to say. *Julia, run now.* But the words stuck in her throat. There was nothing left but a dark current rushing through her. Fel tightened her grip on the blade.

Then she saw the frog.

It hopped across the stones, approaching the band of miles. It was joined by another, and then two more. They were made of bronze, and Fel could see their black eyes swiveling, as if in consideration. One of them had a spot of blood on its gleaming head. Was it hers?

Frogs. She nearly laughed.

Then she heard a click. And something told her to get down.

The first frog leapt. In midair, it blazed like a star and exploded. Shards and wheels and red-hot springs dazzled the air. The miles in front went down like a toppled barrel, screaming and covering his eyes. Then all the frogs were leaping and dying, brilliant and deadly as they fulfilled their maker's purpose. They were grisly fireworks, popping and flashing as they exploded in a spray of sharp parts. There were dozens of them, springing into balls of flame, impossibly beautiful in their death dance. It was raining hot shrapnel. Fel had managed to crawl away, shielding her face with the broken helmet, but the others weren't quick enough. The dazzling bursts caught them in the face, blinding them, biting exposed flesh, setting fire to hair and cloth.

As the grim fireworks faded, Fel rose stiffly, breathing through the pain. She swept through their ranks like a misericord, ensuring that they stayed down. It wasn't hard. Most of them were half-blind and astonished. Frogs. Of all the vicious inevitabilities that Fortuna might throw at them, frogs were not what they'd expected.

Julia emerged from around the corner. She saw Fel's arm. "That will need some care."

Fel wrapped a bit of ragged cloth around it. "Fine for now."

"It doesn't look fine. Nor do you."

She was breathing heavily. "I'm alive. Thanks to you."

"Babieca was actually the one who gave me the idea. He said that a frog army might be entertaining." She surveyed the fallen miles. "I used one of my mother's recipes. I didn't realize how effective it would be."

Fel smiled painfully. "I'll never see a lily pad the same way again." She gestured toward the unconscious miles. "Look for the key. I'll find him."

Julia knelt down, gently searching the bodies. Her care seemed strange after seeing her unlikely weapons explode. Fel made her way down the corridor that led to the cells. Most were empty, though ragged bundles lay in a few, unmoving. Sharp things were bolted to the walls. A pair of tongs lay upon a brazier, glowing from the heat. She spied a pile of long bronze nails and tried not to think about their function.

She heard him before she saw him. A clear voice singing in the dark.

The prize of night deceived him
When it sidled in so sweet
A song of ire and icicles
Too old to be discreet
A kenning to unravel him . . .

He paused.

"If you're not careful," Fel said, "you'll run out of rhymes."

Babieca peered at her from the darkness. "Fel?"

She approached the bars. His eyes widened when he saw the bandage on her arm and the remains of her helmet.

"Turns out," she said, "we're lost without your bloody music."

He smiled. "I knew you'd come."

Julia emerged from the entrance, carrying a lamp. "They're waking up. We have to hurry if we're going to make it back."

"We can't go," Babieca said.

Julia stared at him. "Did someone fracture your skull? We're getting you out of here."

"The sacrifice," he said. "I heard them talking about it. I think that she's going to kill someone."

"It's a certainty," Fel replied.

"Do you know who it will be?"

"Eumachia. We think."

Babieca shook his head. "Not even Latona would do that."

"Are you so certain?"

"Yes. No." He leaned against the bars. "It could be her. But what if you're wrong? Someone will die by her hand, if this ritual goes off."

"We have the horn," Fel said.

He relaxed slightly. "I knew Morgan would find it. That's something."

Julia opened the cell door. "I suppose we couldn't talk you into a hasty retreat?"

"We have to stop her. Or at least try." Babieca reached out, gently pulling something from Julia's hair. "Is that a gear?"

"Exploding frogs," she said.

He laughed, and the sound of his glee filled the carcer. "I told you it was a good idea!"

4

FEL TIGHTENED THE BANDAGE AROUND HER
arm, trying to keep her face like glass. The company didn't
need to know that she felt tired and broken in several places.
There could be no blood trail leading the rest of the guards
to them. *You are not a body. You have no blood.* She bit her
tongue and kept walking. The wound would heal and leave
her with a ragged scar. It was nothing like the mark on her
leg, the one that had nearly ended her. The shoulder would
need to be looked at. No matter, since it didn't belong to her.
Not at the moment. The body was a crumbling villa with
many rooms, and when one became unusable, you simply
stepped into another, trying not to notice the dust and creak-
ing foundations. Even in pain, she could still use two blades,
if she had to. The arc would be clumsy and short, but it could
still kiss an exposed bit of flesh, bite into the line of beauty
that separated armor from nerves.

Fel looked back at the slow-moving company behind her.
Now that the light was better, she could see that the guards
had gone to work on Babieca's face. He had a deep bruise

on his cheek and an ugly mark on his jawline, and his left
eye was shot through with blood like a trickster god's. He
walked with a slight limp, favoring one leg. It wasn't permanent damage, but Julia had noticed as well, and her
expression was difficult to read.

It was the artifex, oddly, who seemed the most composed.
She scanned the corridor, marking each shadow and flicker
of movement. Her sack was still half-full, and Fel wondered
what else she had in there. She'd already produced bees and
frogs. Maybe next time, it would be something from the
canid family. An incendiary puppy would be an excellent
distraction. The thought made her realize that she might be
slightly delirious.

"Puppies," she murmured.

Julia turned. "Did you say something?"

Fel shook her head. "Only to myself."

The artifex frowned at her. "Let me see your arm."

"It's nothing. We have to keep going."

"Fel—"

"I said it's nothing." Babieca was looking at her now. She
kept walking, as if she were merely entering another room
and not dancing on the bleak edge of the pattern.

They circled back to the antechamber just beyond the
postern gate. The patterned arches reminded her of bones
enameled in garnet. They extended across the ceiling in zig-
zags that became an infinity of golds and reds. Even this
room, seldom seen by outsiders, was designed to be beautiful.
Patterns of force held up the ceiling in a dazzling array of
horseshoe arches, a storm of sacred geometry. She imagined
spadones gliding through the darkest of the corners, testing
the threads of their vital gossip. And the nemones, the ones
without the protection of a gens or the support of a company,
who labored beneath the press of power, hoping to rise. The
arches themselves were a power. The measurements that held
up this fortress, this city. To rise was impossible, she saw,

because the power was an ocean, not a ladder. All you could do was keep afloat.

With Fel in the lead, they climbed down to the undercroft. The limed walls had a smell that wasn't entirely unpleasant. The air was cold and reminded her of fish scales. She shivered beneath her armor. Rows of amphorae and sturdy chests were lined against the walls. This was the stomach of the arx. There were pots of sharp-tasting garum sauce, precious spices under lock and key, eels floating insensate in dark jars. Vessels of oil winked at her in shades of gold and mellow green. Fel lit the nearest lamp with her own and nearly stepped back in surprise. Someone had patterned a black-and-white mosaic in the shape of a rearing dog on the floor. She'd seen its likeness once, in another atrium that now seemed far away. Julia saw it as well and chuckled softly.

"It should be a picture of Latona on her hind legs," she said. *"Beware of Basilissa."*

At the sound of their voices, two figures emerged from the wall of amphorae. Morgan had one hand on Eumachia's shoulder. The basilissa's daughter was dressed in a purple stola, chased through with borders of scarlet. Thousands of bugs and bottom-dwellers had died to produce those dancing colors. Even her sandals were studded with amber and onyx, and she wore a pearl diadem that was a miniature version of her mother's crown. The trains of seed pearls swept through her plaited hair, gleaming with their own uncanny light.

The princess had grown slightly. She was taller, and Fel caught the hint of wiry muscles in her bare arms. Currently, those arms were folded in a parody of her mother's displeasure, which made Fel want to laugh. Then she remembered that Eumachia was more dangerous than all of them put together. She could summon miles in the palace to descend upon them—it was a minor miracle that she hadn't done so already.

"You people," Eumachia said. "Why can't I escape you?"

It was a fair question. They'd first met the basilissa's daughter a year ago, when Latona had attacked Pulcheria. She remembered Eumachia's look as silenoi broke through the windows of the arx. When Latona tried to call the first lares with a horn sacred to the silenoi, Eumachia was there once again, caught in their web. They constantly pulled her toward danger.

Though the girl's expression was cold, Fel could hear the trill of anxiety in her voice. Even now, she was gauging the situation, trying to balance all the ivory weights in order to discover what her next move should be. She didn't trust anyone. That was something that she'd learned from a tender age. So far, it had kept her alive in a world of silk and poison. She'd followed Morgan because some part of her trusted the archer.

Fel cleared her throat. "We've reason to believe that Your Highness is in danger."

"Oh, you've reason to believe, do you?" Eumachia made a face as she adjusted the string of pearls, which must have been uncomfortable. "That's what this one kept saying, while she was pushing me down the stairs. I'll need more than that. I'm the daughter of the basilissa. That means I'm always in danger."

Give me a reason to trust you. The plea flashed across her eyes. Trusting them, giving them even the smallest inch, meant pulling away from her mother. It wouldn't be the first time that she'd done such a thing. Latona had nearly gotten her killed at the necropolis, when she met with Septimus among the die-shaped plots. That rift, Fel assumed, had healed over time. But Eumachia wouldn't be here unless she suspected something.

"Your Highness is wise enough to know that something isn't right," Fel said, choosing her words carefully. "We all may be in danger tonight, but you most of all. Your mother is raising an army, and that has made her powerful enemies."

Eumachia shrugged. "Everyone in the Arx of Violets—*my*

arx—is charged with my protection. Why should I be frightened?"

My arx. Perhaps she was ready to succeed her mother. Fel imagined her on the mechanical throne, small and vulnerable as she rose toward the ceiling. It wasn't something that she wanted. That was clear from her expression and the sting of irony in her voice as she said *my arx.* It wasn't a legacy that filled her with consuming passion. That was something that they could work with. The greatest queens were the ones who'd never asked for power.

"They are the dangerous ones, Your Highness," Fel persisted. "The ones in whom you've placed your trust." *Your family.*

She turned to Morgan. "Is this simply the graveyard all over again? I know that my mother has two faces. I've seen them all my life: the sweet one, and the other." Her expression went dark for a moment. Then the girl was back. "She says that the army is for protection. That she's going to restore the glorious empire and quell the strife that divides the great cities. *Quelling* is a good thing, isn't it?"

Morgan couldn't quite say the words. *She means to give you to the old powers. A sacrifice to spirits of storm and embers.* "We think you'd be safer outside the palace," she said finally. "There's a place that we can take you."

What place? Fel couldn't imagine a place where any of them would be safe for long. No gens, no house, no sheltering tower. All of Anfractus had become a plain of battle. They were stones beneath a royal hand. There was only darkness beyond the pattern, a mist that burned and whispered in the reaches outside the game.

"You can use the house by the wall." Babieca's voice was faint in the dim undercroft. They all turned, as if they'd only just noticed him. "You can take her beyond. I don't know if she'll be any safer, but at least it's far away."

Eumachia looked confused. "Beyond what?"

Morgan turned to Babieca. "Aren't you coming?"

He squared his shoulders. "No. I'm needed here."

"What are you talking about?"

"The sacrifice. It could be any of us. It could be something entirely different. But it's happening tonight, and I have to stop it."

She shook her head. "No. We just rescued you." Morgan said it as if the rules of being rescued were self-evident, and Babieca had just broken them. "We stay together."

"Get her to the house," Fel said. "The singer and I are going to the oecus. If we can prevent this bloody thing from happening, then we have to try."

Eumachia kept looking rapidly around the room, trying to read their shifting expressions. "I don't understand." There was a bleakness in her voice as she said it. Not knowing was the same as losing, and she couldn't afford that. "Who is the—" Suddenly she paled. She hadn't lost after all. The knowledge came to her all at once, and her eyes widened in shock. "Not me. Is it? Am I to be the sacrifice?"

"We can't be certain," Morgan replied gently. "All the more reason to get you away from the palace. And that goes for *all* of us. We're not safe here."

"Fel and I are staying," Babieca said.

Morgan turned on him. "Don't be a horse's ass. What use does she have for a wounded singer? If anyone's staying, it's going to be me."

"Someone has to take Eumachia—"

"I'm staying too."

They all stared at her.

"Your Highness—" Morgan began.

"Don't Highness me, archer." It was her mother's voice. "I am *nobody's* sacrifice. I can help. The guards will listen to me, and I know all the trickiest ways to get to the oecus."

She was right. The girl's logic might save them after all.

"We can't put you in danger," Morgan protested. "We came here in the first place to keep you out of harm's way."

"There is no such thing," Eumachia said. She wished that

it weren't so, but her expression was one of marble understanding.

"Show us the way, then," Fel said.

Eumachia nodded. She'd already put on her fire. "A
detour first, though."

"Weapons?" Julia asked hopefully.

The princess favored her with a sly smile. "Foxes."

THEY MADE THEIR WAY TO THE OECUS WITH
a larger company. Propertius and Sulpicia followed them, a
strange entourage of mechanicals that supported the vanguard.
Propertius kept throwing erratic glances at the walls. Fel
thought that he could probably sense the silenoi that were also
keeping pace with them. Unless they'd gone on ahead.

"Are they following us?"

It took the fox a moment to realize that she was speaking
to him. Propertius and his sister were used to being ignored.
They were treated more like furniture than the original
inhabitants of the Arx of Violets. "You will have to be more
specific," he said at last. "A lot of things are following us at
the moment." His voice reminded her of a brass kettle.

"The silenoi," she clarified.

"Definitely them. And others."

"What others?"

"Best not to dwell on it." The gears in his tail whirred as
it loped along the ground. "Luckily, some of the things
appear to be on your side."

"Don't bother trying to get a straight answer out of him,"
Eumachia said. "He's trained to keep secrets."

Propertius raised his head. "I was not trained at all.
Training suggests taming, and we are not tame things."

"He's very sensitive about that," Eumachia whispered.
The fox's ears swiveled—it was clear that he'd heard her. But
he made no reply.

Sulpicia appeared beside her. She seemed to have a

fondness for humans that her brother didn't share. Or at least a tolerance. "The lares are everywhere," she said. "It puts us both on edge. They have a disruptive presence."

"Are they—I mean—" Fel struggled to frame the question. She wasn't feeling particularly tactful at the moment, with her arm on fire and her shoulder half-numb. "Do you all come from the same source?"

"We are not the same as them," Propertius said emphatically. "We were crafted. They simply crawled out of chaos."

"She wasn't talking to you," Sulpicia snapped. Then she turned back to Fel. "We share some qualities. That cannot be denied. You might even think of us as belonging to the same family. But we do not share their hunger."

"Do you think they'll fight for her?"

Both foxes exchanged a look.

"Too early to tell," Propertius said. If a mechanical fox could be said to have a tone, then Fel heard it. Or something. He wasn't being entirely honest. Like the silenoi, the foxes acted for their own reasons. Perhaps they were simply leading them to Latona. They'd barely been surprised when Eumachia came to them.

"This reminds me of the last time you all were here," the princess said. "And the time before that, as a matter of fact. You're really quite meddlesome, you know. I can see why my mother dislikes you." She looked thoughtful for a moment. Then she turned to Babieca, her expression carefully measured. "I've seen him, you know. The oculus. He's always by her side. He asked about you—when they first brought you to the carcer. He tried to negotiate a lighter sentence for you."

Babieca said nothing.

It was true that they'd barely roughed him up. "Did they ask you about the horn?" Fel softened her words. "I mean, do you remember anything? About what they wanted?"

"Sometimes they beat me," he replied. "Sometimes not. They never asked me anything. I tried to overhear what they were saying, but most of the time they talked of gambling and f—" He blinked. "—of recreation."

They were merely holding him in place, Fel thought. *Perhaps as bait.*

She'd rather not to think about the implications of that.

They were heading for the clerestory above the oecus when two guards rounded the corner. Both stopped in astonishment. Before they could react, the foxes moved to the vanguard. Propertius raised a paw, as if in greeting.

"The singer is to be tortured publicly," he said. His voice was entirely without feeling. "Our basilissa demands it. Her daughter will blood him. A great honor."

The nearest miles frowned. "You've got it turned around. This prisoner stays in the carcer. It's the other who's going to be tortured."

The other. Fel tried not to react. *Who was it?* Her mind raced through possibilities. Had she turned on the oculus? Was it someone else? What if Pulcheria had been captured? She couldn't imagine whipping a rival queen in public, but Latona had proven that she was capable of nearly anything. Babieca had been right, at any rate. The show would go on, with or without Eumachia. She couldn't be the sacrifice.

"Both prisoners are to receive the same treatment," Propertius said. "Questioning the hand of the queen tends to prove fatal. I would take our word, if I were you."

"You don't even have hands," the other miles said. He spat on the ground.

The foxes exchanged another look. Fel readied herself to fight, reaching painfully for the hilt of her sword.

The foxes transformed into comets. They landed on the shoulders of the astonished guards, bronze claws digging into the spaces between their loricae. Both foxes screamed. It sounded like ice cracking, like the roots of mountains crumbling. High-pitched and unearthly, it rippled through the air in painful waves. Sparks burst from their open mouths, and then the guards were also screaming, blind and terrified. Fel clubbed the nearest one with the butt of her sword, while Morgan struck the other once, twice, until he was still. The smell of burnt hair was thick.

Propertius stared straight ahead, as if he were following a scent that kept eluding him. Fel stamped on one of the miles, to put out a small tongue of flame. Then they mounted the steps that led to the clerestory. The broken lion's-head fountain was still there, along with the spiders and rodent droppings that Fel remembered. She almost saw something in the corner, but it vanished before she could register what it was.

"You'd think she'd learn to post guards here," Julia observed. It was the first time that she'd spoken in a while. She was eyeing the two foxes warily, but with a certain level of interest, as well. She desperately wanted to know what power moved through them.

"The palace is sealed up tight," Eumachia said. "It doesn't matter where you go. You might get one clean shot, but you'll never escape."

"I liked her better when she was dusty and optimistic," Fel said, low enough for only Morgan to hear. The archer smiled.

The room below was packed. Latona was their heart. Courtiers mingled around her like clicking tiles, sharing their cold stories as they brushed past each other. They were beautiful in embroidered tunicae, silken head scarves, and networks of finery. The women had their hair teased into miraculous forms, while the men wore golden armbands and scarlet overcloaks. A few meretrices stood out in masks of ivory and jet.

Eumachia leaned over the edge. "Look! It's Drauca!"

She was right. One of the meretrices was leaning on an ivory cane.

Why would she be here?

"Come away from the edge," Morgan said, pulling on Eumachia's gown. They should all keep away from the edges, but they were simply too many. It was all staircases and fountain rims and cliffs that tumbled into the sea. They were always leaning. What choice did they have?

Latona stepped toward the dais. The murmuring stopped. She was surrounded by a spiral of miles, their armor burnished to a brilliant sheen. They curled around her like a snail's shell, and beyond them stood the archers. A cluster of green-robed spadones moved on the periphery of the room. Fel no longer understood what side they were on. Perhaps Narses was down there somewhere, moving things beyond their sight.

"Tonight," the basilissa called, "we have a special performance. A drama to remind us of things to come. Soon we will be at war, and I have arranged this night as a show of faith to our allies. Though you cannot see them, my oculus assures me that they are here."

Fel saw him for the first time, standing behind the throne. He wore a black tunica embroidered with a red swan. He was staring straight ahead, as Propertius had. Distracted and curious at once. Babieca saw him too but said nothing. His dark-rimmed eyes were still.

"Is it true?" she whispered to Sulpicia. "Are the lares here?"

"Yes," she breathed. "Everywhere."

Fel heard a scraping sound. She realized that Propertius was growling. Nobody else seemed to hear it, but she wanted him to stop. It cut her to the quick. It was as if the arx itself were making the terrible noise.

"Bring him out," Latona said.

The prisoner was led across the room. His yellow tunica had been torn in several places, and rust-red patches stood out against the embroidery. Felix swayed slightly as he walked, though his gait remained polished. They'd allowed him to keep his mask. There were bruises and burns decorating his exposed arms, but his face they'd left mostly untouched. She heard Babieca's intake of breath behind her. Drauca continued to lean on her cane. She was a statue in the crowd. He didn't look at her, but he must have known that she was there. His eyes remained fixed on the basilissa. They were the only two people in the room.

One of the spadones lowered his hood. Fel caught the movement. She couldn't help but make a small noise as she saw the ropelike burns on his face and neck, the red skin that seemed to weep as the light caught it. They had done that. On the other side, in a strange library. Her shadow remembered. Flame blooming in the auditor's hand. Mardian's cries. Fel shivered.

Now the threads were being pulled tight. But who had turned traitor? Was it truly Mardian? Or had the oculus betrayed them? The one called Aleo had no expression. She realized that he was watching the lares, in all their glittering danger. He could see the furthest.

Felix approached the basilissa. He was as cold as any courtier, but Fel could see that he was trying not to tremble. One hand clutched the hem of his tunica. He bowed, and winced finally. Perhaps they'd broken a few of his ribs.

"Felix Aurea," she said, lingering over his surname. "You stand accused of high treason. You have colluded with our enemy and straddled the boundary between worlds like the canny wolf that you are." Her green eyes swept over him. "Once you were my favorite. But you have abused our sacred trust. How do you answer to these crimes?"

"I alone am guilty of them," he said.

Now the oculus was looking at him. A lie to preserve what was left.

Latona placed a hand on his head. It was an unexpected gesture. Then, gently, she unlaced his mask. An audible sigh went through the room as she unmasked him. Fel hadn't seen his face in so long. It was as she remembered. The face that she'd seen in the dark, as he stirred above her, flushed like tinted ivory.

The basilissa reached for something. It was a dagger resting on the arm of the throne. She hadn't noticed it until now.

The dagger that had once been Roldan's. Now she was gesturing to the oculus. He approached her, and she placed the weapon in his hand.

"You know what comes next," she said.

He stood before Felix. Neither said anything. The room was waiting. Morgan had readied an arrow, but Fel shook her head. There could be no trick shot this time. No miracle roll. This moment no longer belonged to them.

Aleo knelt before Felix. He leaned over and whispered something into the man's ear. The meretrix nodded slowly. Then Aleo rose. He placed one hand on Felix's head and positioned the knife against his throat.

The foxes stirred at her feet. Babieca was walking toward the edge. She tried to grab his arm, but he kept walking. Morgan was saying something, her voice heavy, but Fel couldn't make out the words. Eumachia had taken off her pearls. Like Babieca, she looked ready to jump. Fel reached for her die. It was a reflex. She didn't even know what she was trying to do. She looked away from Felix for just a second and saw that Drauca had vanished.

"Do it now," Latona said.

Aleo tightened his grip on Felix. "I offer this man to the dark below, to the living skies, to the dancing fire. I offer him to the smoke that swallows all."

Fel saw his hand tremble.

A cry split the silence of the great hall.

Not a cry. A low, attenuated note, rising from the ground and shaking the walls. Her blood thrilled alongside it. The horn. Aleo looked up, eyes widening. The courtiers were nervous now, moving in a wave of finery toward the edges of the room. The armed guards began to herd them like sheep, but they were also uncertain. They looked to the basilissa for clarification. Latona was staring at the entrance.

"You know better than this," she called. "You swore an oath to me. Your princeps will tear you apart for breaking your word."

Septimus stood in the doorway, the horn still raised to his lips. Skadi was beside him. The crowd parted before them in flickers of terror.

He lowered the horn. "I have reevaluated our agreement," he said. "I think you will find that it was flawed from the start."

Now the caela were visible. The lares of air, exiled centuries ago, but freed through the power of the horn. *We stole their place—what did the auditor call it? Their chaos. We're breathing air that belongs to them*. Everything had its chaos. The elements had once belonged to the lares. Perhaps they would again—very soon.

Fel could see the caela as coils of smoke, gathering among the arched ceiling of the oecus. They grew and darkened into slick black folds. They tightened as they lowered themselves, a gyre of burning eyes and blinding grit. As the storm expanded to fill the room, Fel could see mouths in the gray. Last time, it had been the oculus that controlled them. Septimus would not be such a benevolent master.

He pointed at the shield wall surrounding the basilissa. "Show them what you are," he cried, "oh hungry sky travelers, oh spirits of the welkin! Show them!"

The smoke rushed over them, eyes and mouths and insensate screams. It was one scream, one howling note that shook the foundations of the Arx of Violets. Blood fanned against the walls in a grim tracery. It sizzled on the lamps, even as the sound was covered by crunching bone, unraveling marbled by streaks of black. Aleo was yelling something, gesturing wildly. The courtiers ran in all directions. Some of them vanished in clouds of red.

Where was Felix? She couldn't see him. Morgan was sending arrows into the smoke, but they vanished as quickly as she could loose them.

Fel ran down the stairs. Someone was yelling, but she ignored the sound. Her blade was drawn. She cleaved to the edge of the wall, keeping her distance from the caela. In the dim, she could see two black shapes moving. The silenoi. Amber eyes held her and blazed up suddenly. Fel raised her sword. But the shadow moved past her. Now was not the moment.

Then Latona was there. She had Felix's knife.

"Hold him!" Her voice cut across the room. There was blood on her face, and her eyes belonged to something much older, something like the lares themselves.

Two of the miles grabbed Felix by the arms. They pinned him in place, and she advanced, holding the knife.

Where was Septimus? The monsters had vanished into the smoke. Or were they all monsters in this moment? She was too far away. She'd always seen something like this coming, but not *precisely* this. The ashes in her mouth. The blood on her lorica. Felix saw her. Something bright and frail passed between them, and she remembered what held them together. The boy on the other side, waiting for her.

"The oath will not fail," Latona said. She had to raise her voice to be heard above the storm around her. "I offer this man to the dark below, to the living skies, to the dancing fire. I offer him to the smoke that swallows all."

Something rose above her voice, then, above the sounds of the dying. Not the horn, this time. Fel recognized the sound with a start.

A lute.

She looked up. Babieca stood halfway down the staircase. He was playing as quickly as he could. The notes were rough at first. But then they rose. His face was a mask of concentration. Fel could see the sweat on his forehead. He had chosen the perfect spot. The angular walls of the room served to amplify his music, until it crashed over them, a sweet, scalding melody that cut through every other sound.

It was a wordless song. But Fel knew it. Because she had sung this to herself, during the longest nights, when everything seemed to have fled. Morgan knew it too. She had lowered her bow and was listening. Her face was very still. Even Latona was watching him now, and her expression was a secret that she kept. But she heard it.

The guards were frozen. Felix had stepped free of them, but he didn't try to run. Everyone was listening. Somewhere in the staff of notes, they could hear what they'd lost. It hovered just on the edge of their perception. Though stilled, they were reaching. And the singer too was reaching, climbing the fire of the song. Blood shone on the lute, but he kept playing, until his fingers were nothing, a gleaming knot, an unseen promise.

Light moved over the surface of the smoke. It recoiled at first. Then the dragon settled its wings and eyes, and listened. Mangled horrors lay strewn across the palace floor. Some were still dying, loudly, their features obscured by the swirling dust. The song was for them as well, a guiding threnody. It offered its naked body to them, asking for their forgiveness.

A silence settled over them, as if the world were about to begin again. The smoke was still, though not tame. It waited now. Aleo stood in the middle, unsure of what to do. His eyes no longer darted around the room. They were fixed on Babieca.

The last notes were for him. They were a memory, and a promise, and a love on which all of them balanced. It held them up. And even the smoke knew it, and remembered that instant of decreation, that dawn so long ago, when it too had been held fast.

Babieca fell silent, and smiled. There was blood on his hands, tears in his eyes. He seemed to be glowing.

"I told you—"

The air froze. A shadow moved next to Babieca. A trick of the eye, it seemed. But then he stopped. Everything stopped. Fel saw a gleam of silver, like a stitch, move down the singer's chest. *That's strange.* It was her only thought. The stitch made a kind of *Z*, and then she saw that it was a delicate knife. Blood danced in the silver.

Babieca looked down.

He laughed. Then shivered.

Then fell.

Mardian stood behind him. The knife stained wine-dark. He looked down at the singer, now a cut thread.

"The oath will not fail," he said.

PART FOUR

OCULUS

1

CLOSE TO DAWN. THE LIVING SKIES HAD begun to wake in brushstrokes of wild color. Goose song and the *whirr* of insects in the long grass. In the distance, the golden mean of the legislature, now scaffolded, was fading to gray. The whole park was shaking itself from rich dreams. Even the sleepless fish that survived in the toxic waters now circled, listening. There was an air of patience and recognition, a settling of forces. Webbed feet moved over the hill, as clusters of eyes regarded them, sincerely. Everything wanted to know about the body.

Andrew sat cross-legged in the grass, still slightly dazed. His arm ached—the old wound. His thoughts were much slower than usual. The world turned in a cauldron of honey and blood, like the mead of poetry that Odin had once rescued. He flexed his fingers. He was still alive.

The body was not.

It was familiar. Diminished, perhaps, but no more than one who slept deeply. The difference was that its eyes were open. The pupils were receding, the fragile irises beginning to come undone. Already, the humors were escaping their bonds. The body was nude, and he could see the ragged mark where the blade had kissed its heart. A majuscule *Z* with frayed edges.

So quickly and so silently. To look back for just a moment, only to find this. And maybe never looking back would have prevented it. To be as vigilant as those eyes that were shrinking even now, becoming caves where you could hear the low murmur of glaciers. If he hadn't moved. If he'd only moved faster. If the smoke had cleared. If he'd reached for the blade, then it would have been in his hand, not Mardian's.

Like miracles, some deaths were reversible. Some were not. An auditor might swallow seawater and still be saved, though changed forever. A blade to the heart was a different thing, a more precise line break.

What was the right thing to do?

The body was a smooth punctuation to his questions. It gave nothing away. Its edges seemed to swallow the gathering light, the park noise, his thoughts. And it was not beautiful, like bodies in paintings. It was ordinary. It belonged to an order of things ruthless and predictable, banal as dandelions, a cat purring, a kitchen window.

It's different with us.

Everyone was slowly regaining the power of motion. Sam had a dreamlike expression. She stared at the grass, then at her knees, checkered in green. Shelby was looking at the body's pale feet, soles exposed to the damp earth. A pebble between the toes. She frowned at the pebble, as one might at a spider crawling across a picture frame. Ingrid was the only one standing. Like the body, she was nude, though much remained in shadow. Her expression was neutral as it took in everything. She was performing a silent assessment. This was probably not her first time. He noticed the dark bruises gathering along her shoulder, and the way that she favored one arm. The puckered mark along her leg, healed but not forgotten. His own scar ached in sympathy, and he rubbed it, without thinking.

Sam crawled forward. She reached out, uncertainly, to touch the raveled wound.

"Don't move it," Ingrid said.

Sam looked up. "What?"

"It has to stay exactly as it is." Her voice seemed to be coming from far away.

"I don't—" She blinked. Her confusion was bright. "You mean . . . him?"

She gently took Sam by the wrist and pulled her up. "Yes." Then: "We all need to get dressed."

Sam looked down at herself, as if realizing her nakedness for the first time. "They're behind the tree," she said. "The clothes. At least, I think that's where I put them. Sometimes I can't tell the trees apart."

They dressed in silence. The dark lay on the grass next to them, also silent. They covered it gently. When they were finished, a neat pile of clothing remained. Worn jeans, thrice-folded by Shelby, a collared shirt, socks balled up so that they resembled a blind tulip bulb, and boxer shorts. They stared at the pile for some time. The hiking boots were arranged next to it, scuffed toes spaced slightly apart. Everything you needed to make a person.

"What do we do with them?" Sam asked. "Should we dress—" She shook her head. "No. That would be tampering, right? Like in the forensic shows?"

"We'll need to dispose of them." Ingrid's voice was underwater. "There's no blood on the clothes. We can't say that it's a mugging. We'll have to tell the police that we found him like this, in the park."

Sam's eyes widened. "But they'll think—oh God, we can't let them think that, can we? That's not something we can tell his family. His mother."

"I'll talk to her," Shelby said. Her voice was a cut thing. "I'll try to make her understand."

Sam was pondering the boots now. "How do we get rid of them? We can't burn them, can we? Do boots burn?"

Andrew felt himself move. Up until now, he'd been rooted to the spot. He picked up the duffel bag and gently placed Carl's clothes inside. He laid the boots on top.

"We need rocks."

Shelby stared at him. "What?"

"To weigh it down."

Nobody moved at first. But then it became a thing to do, an incredible distraction. They busied themselves, prying up rocks. They loaded down the duffel bag until it felt like a bier. Andrew grabbed one side, and Ingrid grabbed the other. They walked along the edge of the lake. Andrew could feel the others watching. Ingrid said nothing. They made their way down the empty pier.

"On three," Andrew said.

They counted to three and hurled the bag into the dark water. It floated for a moment, then slowly began to sink. They waited until it was gone. Then they made their way back to the clearing. Shelby's eyes were strange. She kept looking at him, as if he were a picture that she couldn't quite comprehend.

"The killer wouldn't have left the clothes," he said finally.

"What killer?" Shelby's voice was low in her throat.

"You know what I mean."

"I don't. I don't know what you mean."

"Shelby."

She stepped forward. "Do you have something to say? Something to clear this up? Please. Go ahead."

He tried to speak, but there was ash in his mouth.

"Was this your plan?"

Every time she said *this*, what she meant was *the body*. But she wouldn't look down. She was careful not to see it. Andrew couldn't do anything but see it. His ears were ringing. Beneath that was a song that he didn't want to hear.

"This isn't the time for fighting," Ingrid said. But she was somewhere else. It was the way you told a child to stop playing with something, even though you couldn't quite see what he was doing. An exhausted plea.

"I'd like to know," Shelby said softly. "Was this the plan?"

Andrew looked at her. "No."

"I seem to remember you holding a knife."

"That wasn't me. I was playing a part."

"It feels like you've been playing a part this whole time."

Andrew closed his eyes. "I thought I could keep it all spinning. I thought it would work. But Mardian—I didn't know. It all went up in smoke. And I could see it happening, but I wasn't fast enough. I couldn't."

Sam's expression brightened. "There must be a trick!"

Shelby looked at her. "What do you mean?"

"There must be. Like—I don't know—some kind of power. We just take him back, and we ask the spirits for help. We give them whatever they want. Blood, our souls, whatever. We just take him back. We just have to take him back."

"It doesn't work that way," Ingrid said.

"It worked for Andrew."

"That was different. He drowned. There was still—something left. We didn't have to fight our way out of the palace just to get back here. We had so much time." Ingrid shook her head. "It was different."

"But that's—" Sam's face contorted. "The park is magic. We're magic. It can't be over, just like that. The basilissa—she's got power, right? She's connected. She could do something. Or the silenoi. They've got powers that we've never seen. There must be, I don't know, a ritual, or a—" Her voice broke. "*Fuck.* Something. There's something. There has to be."

"He's gone," Andrew said.

And as he said it, he knew that it was certain. There was no trick. He was gone because a knife—a gift—had slipped into him like sleep. A gift that he should have kept safe. Felix had said that he would use it, someday. But Felix hadn't known everything.

Shelby struck him across the face.

The blow surprised him more than anything. He touched his cheek. The pain seemed to hesitate. Then he felt it, and swallowed. She stood before him, absolutely rigid, fists clenched at her sides. Everything was slow and white around the edges.

"Do you think you can just say that?" She was flushed. He could feel the burn of her grief, in the mark slowly forming. "You don't get to decide. It's not up to you."

"Shelby—"

"—you don't decide *this*. You're not the center of the goddamn universe, and this is the one thing you don't get to decide, okay? The one thing." Her eyes filled with tears. "He told me that everything would be okay, and I believed him. I fucking believed him."

Her shoulders were shaking. She was taller than him, and he had to stand on tiptoes to embrace her. They swayed in the clearing. Shelby screamed into his shoulder, and he held on, but not too tightly. He rocked her back and forth. He rubbed small circles on her back and whispered in her ear. He didn't know what he was saying. He wasn't sure how long they danced that way. But eventually, a space appeared. The night seemed to separate them of its own accord. There was spittle in the corner of Shelby's mouth, and snot, which she scrubbed at with her sleeve. His face hurt, and his shirt was wet. Something was trying to get out of his throat, but he pushed it down.

"I'm going to call the paramedics," Ingrid said. "I'll say that we went looking for him. That this is where we found him. The police will need to take our statements. We can show them the text message on his phone. But don't add anything. It has to be simple."

Sam looked at her. "Have you done this before?"

"No," she said, looking at her phone. "I'm just a liar."

Then she walked over the hill to place the call.

Sam sat down. She nudged something in the grass with her shoe. It was a piano key. She rubbed off some of the dirt and held it up.

"Is this important?"

Andrew stared at it for a long time, as if unable to comprehend what it was, exactly. Then he took it from her, letting the moonlight touch the ivory.

"That's what they say."

He remembered Septimus screaming. *Find the horn!* It was cold in his hand, slippery with blood. Smoke everywhere, and a smell like the end of the world. He'd seen Felix for a moment, only to lose him. The memories were burned around the edges, like abused parchment. Septimus had carried the body. No. It was Skadi. She'd lifted it with no expression, no hint of strain. The brass foxes at his feet. Eumachia crying, but Latona had her by the arm. Smoke. Hundreds of eyes watching. Hunger and questing curiosity. Gore-slick armor, a forest of cries. The bundle in Skadi's arms. And where was the knife? How had he lost it? Why did they trust him with bright things?

"What did he say to you?"

It took Andrew a moment to realize that the question was meant for him. "What?"

Shelby turned. "He said something. I couldn't hear it, because I was too far away. But he was looking at you. What did he say?"

I told you.

"It was too loud to hear anything," he said. "But I think he was happy."

"What was that song?" Sam asked. "Was it—a blessing?"

"I think it was different for everyone."

"What did you hear?"

Andrew looked at his hands. "There were no words. Just a feeling. I knew—who I was. Who we were. For that second, I knew. And I wasn't afraid."

"When you were mostly dead," Shelby said, "we tied you to him with a belt. And he rode that way. He couldn't believe how light you were."

Babieca had been light in Skadi's arms, or seemed that way. Latona's expression had been a mystery as they'd carried him through the smoke. Out of the chaos and toward the edge of the world. Even now, the memories were fading. Eumachia's broken cry. The knife in Mardian's hand, as if it had never left. Babieca's astonished laugh.

Andrew leaned over the body. It was hard not to touch, and he was surprised by the desire. He knew there was no warmth left. But he wanted to reassure himself that something was there. He brushed the hair with his fingertips. It was soft, limp. Doll hair. The body seemed to forgive him this trespass. He followed the curve of the breastbone, to the ruin of the heart. He remembered the feeling of being in those arms. The darkest moment of the night, and his head in that warm crook, drifting, half-asleep.

I'm essential, am I?

The tomcat smile. Knowing the answer.

You're the song that begins it all.

But he'd been wrong about that. Not a song of beginnings. No one should ever trust him again. But the song was still in his ears. The mouth on his. The wild roll and the woven quiet between them. And the salamanders, so demure. The feeling that everything could be saved, if the night, and the wheel, if only the wheel, if.

And now Ingrid was walking back down the hill. How long had she been gone? He couldn't say. Had she actually left? It seemed as if she'd always been there, ghosting around the edges of their family. Now they were four. Or maybe less. Any of them could walk away. There was no shame in that kind of logic, not now.

"What did you tell them?" Shelby asked.

Ingrid blinked, as if she hadn't heard the question. She stared at the object in her hand. *How did this get here?* The slim brick that could solve anything. But it was just her phone, and she realized that. Her expression changed.

"Something," she said. "I don't know."

Shelby frowned. "You were gone for a while. You must have told them a lot."

"It was only a few minutes."

"No. It was a long time."

"Really?" Ingrid shook her head. "I don't think I said much."

"We found him in the park," Sam said. She hadn't spoken in a while, and her voice was strangely loud in the clearing. "That's the story? Just that?"

Shelby shrugged. "There's nothing else."

"What was he doing in the park? Without his clothes?"

"The police will draw their own conclusions," Ingrid said.

"But they'll know that he died tonight. They know those kinds of things."

"He died in another world," Ingrid replied. "Who knows what they'll find? Dust from Anfractus, maybe. Living smoke. This is where we found him. This is the only story that we have. If we say it enough times, it will be true."

"Isn't that—what do they call it—perjury?"

Shelby turned to her. "If you want to go, just go. We won't say anything."

Sam looked down. "That's not what I meant."

"It's fine to be worried about these things. You should be worried. None of us will think less of you if—" She made a vague gesture. "It's fine. It'll be fine."

"You don't need me."

Shelby blinked. "What?"

"That's what you're really saying. *We don't need you.* That's how you've always felt."

She winced slightly. "That's not true."

"It is. But it's okay. I'm with you now, and I'm not going anywhere." Her expression was grim. "We carried him this far. I'll say what I have to say. You don't have to wonder about me anymore. I'm part of this company."

His replacement.

Andrew couldn't help thinking it. Sam balanced the equation. She made them a true company again. He wasn't sure what he felt about this. All he could see was the pebble between the toes. But he couldn't touch it. Not anymore. It was like a piece of writing now. The type was set. Nothing could be redacted.

Strangely, he thought about Carl's apartment. The dust bunnies, waiting for him to come home. The blast radius of his bedroom. The books that he'd stolen from the library, tucked into inoffensive corners. The tin can on the balcony, where he ashed quietly, when no one was looking. The whole place humming unexpectedly with love, washed in red light from the sex shop below. He imagined how long it would take to collect the remains, all the dust and papers and broken things that even he'd forgotten about.

Sam crouched next to the body. She was only partially looking, the way you might watch a coyote who was following you home. Her expression was difficult to read. Not fear, exactly. Something closer to disbelief. But there was also a dark gleam of curiosity that made its way to the surface.

"I thought it would be different," she said. "The first time I saw this. I thought it would change everything. My cousin. She had pancreatic cancer." Sam swallowed. "It wasn't good. And afterward, when I saw what was left of her, I thought it would be something. Like an answer, or maybe an argument that I couldn't win."

Strange to think that, among them, it was Sam who'd seen a body before. The cry in her voice earlier had suggested that this was all new. But maybe it just brought back memories that she didn't want to deal with.

"Was it?" Shelby asked.

Sam looked at the canyon in the body's chest. "No. I don't know. They say that something leaves. That it's smaller. Not them. But it was still her. I was twelve years old. When they put her in the ground, I thought she'd wake up. I listened at the window."

Andrew struck the tree. First with his hand, then with his head. The pain dazed him. It was hot and sweet. He would have done it again, but Ingrid grabbed his arms. She was surprisingly strong, even on this side of the park. Still dizzy, Andrew stared at the tree bark. It was spotted with blood. He touched his throbbing forehead, and his fingers came away wet. He thought he might be sick.

"What was that?" Shelby demanded.

His tongue was thick, which made it hard to speak. "I . . . don't know. I wanted to do it. I wanted to hurt. Everything in me is screaming to do it again."

"But you won't," Ingrid said gently. She had one cool hand against his forehead and was stroking it absently.

He shook his head.

Ingrid let him go. He sat down on the grass.

"I used to think," he said, "that the world was full of falcons and fur-lined cloaks. That it was like a medieval poem. All you needed was a good dictionary." His eyes, which normally demurred, moved across the faces staring at him with surprise and concern. "Is this what it is? How it works? Because I don't understand. He knew I didn't like tomatoes, so he picked them out of my sandwich. Ate them right in front of me, like he was taking a bullet. He liked dogs, and buttons, and when he was drunk, he taught me how to say bad things in Spanish. I can still *hear* him. And I don't understand how this works. It's not in the dictionary."

They were silent for a while.

"Why do you think he did it?" Shelby asked.

Andrew didn't quite comprehend the question. "Who?"

"Mardian." She nearly choked on the name. "Felix was supposed to be the sacrifice. But it could have been anyone. Why did he do it?"

"To hurt us," Ingrid said.

"No." Andrew looked again at the tree. "Not us. Me."

Shelby gave him an odd look. "I know what I said before. But this isn't your fault."

"Isn't it? I scarred him. I shamed him. It wasn't Roldan. It was me." Andrew shook his head. "He was the basilissa's ensign. He followed us all the way to the university library. And I'd forgotten it all. I was so stupid. The power was there, and I just—" He shook his head. "He screamed. I remember the smell. And the salamander, breathing fire. When I saw him again—as Aleo—I knew. His face was unmistakable. All those lies about fomenting revolution. He never stopped being her engine. It wasn't enough to kill Felix. This was his revenge. We burned him and left him for dead."

"He was trying to kill us," Ingrid said. "What else could you have done?"

Andrew shrugged. "Anything? But Carl kept yelling about the salamander. And I thought"—a smile quirked the edge of his mouth—"*he sees it too*. It was such a relief. And for a moment, I thought the fire would just dance around us, and we'd all be okay. But lares are hungry. I should have known that."

He believed in meter, and mosaics, and the sound of dead languages coming back to life. He believed in libraries, and bars where you could be anyone. He believed in the compassion of stories, even the bad ones. Beyond that, he wasn't sure. He'd also believed that his mother was gone, and now—it wasn't simple. He couldn't dive into the water and wash himself free of these doubts. Simple had never been possible.

"They'll be here soon," Ingrid said. "The paramedics."

"Is our story straight?" Sam asked.

"None of them are," Andrew said. "But they're what we have to work with."

Now he could hear the sirens in the distance. And there wasn't enough time. There was never enough. He couldn't say it all. He couldn't disturb that smoothly punctuated sentence. No time to hold the hand, to kiss the mouth, to breathe, breathe, hoping for the heart to sing. Wasn't that what it was for? Couldn't he still hear the song everywhere, in his bones, in the leaves, moving the world?

The sirens drew closer. He could see the flickering lights at the edge of the clearing. In a moment, there would be strangers here, taking apart the silence. There would be questions and the straightening of stories. The lies that they lived with.

Blue light dazzled the trees. This had been him. Insensate on the ground, his lungs full of water. Still swimming. But he'd come back. Did he remember? Was there something he'd seen in that ocean, something to change him forever? It had seemed like a second, like a wave of time, crashing over him until he was dark sand, abalone, all inside.

"They're here," Ingrid said.

He surfaced, water in his mouth, the song in his ears.

It was time.

2

THERE WAS A DIFFERENCE IN THE STREETS. IT
wasn't a perceptible shift so much as a subtle change in
vibration. People gathered near the white paving stones,
murmuring in what shade they could find. They wore
hooded expressions and spoke in low voices. More than a
few were masked. Night was on its way. Soon the sky would
turn on them, red-rimmed clouds swallowing the sun in
anticipation. The shadows would grow longer. Dove song
among the insulae would be replaced by the trill of breaking
glass. The people of Anfractus—some of whom weren't,
strictly speaking, people—recognized that something was
coming. Nervous machines skittered across the cobblestones, trying to keep up with their makers. The street-side
popinae were shuttered, while the tavernae remained open
under guard. No one wanted to spend too much time outside
if they could possibly help it. A storm seemed to be brew-
ing in the heart of the world, and they could feel it in the
gray spaces, the cracks between the stones. A celebrant was

selling half-priced garlands. Soon her stock would have to be replenished.

The lares were also out. Gnomoi lingered in the alleyways, tasting the bricks. Their dark eyes might have been blind, but Aleo couldn't tell. Perhaps they saw everything. Undinae hissed among the fountains, their webbed fingers gripping the marble rims. He could no longer hear what they whispered. That gift had been lost. But he could see them now, and he wasn't sure which sense he preferred. They watched him with their lamplight eyes, their graven faces, closer to stone or seaweed than flesh. They too were waiting. The smoke above them had become a constant presence. He adjusted the ivory horn on its leather strap. Septimus would demand its return, but for now, it was his to wear. The caela watched him from jewel-encrusted clouds, drifting near. The oath had not failed. But to whom did they pledge fealty? All he could remember was blood and smoke.

It wasn't long ago that he'd been running downhill, away from the Arx of Violets. Now he was walking toward it, climbing the shallow steps that led to the wealthiest quarter of the city. He could see the firewalls that crisscrossed the Subura, dividing it from the stately homes of the elite, with their servants and painted blue doors. He nearly turned around. It would be a simple matter to visit the black basia. To seek answers. Felix would be in the undercroft, licking his wounds. The briefest of detours. His hand strayed to the dagger. He'd pressed it to the pale neck of the meretrix. He'd steadied himself. The blade feather-light. Anything was possible in that moment, beat thin, like brittle foil.

But it would not be that simple.

He kept walking. It was not smart to be here, exposed like this. Not their most sterling plan. Success meant stealing time, and possibly even answers. Failure was a cell in the carcer, whips and starvation, a final, guttural *yes* in answer to whatever questions they posed. He would not be able to endure torture. He'd died once, and now, a stubborn part of him clung to this second life. It was a persistent desire that would eventually betray him.

The lemon trees were fragrant. He heard the lapping waters of the fountains, the rustle of silk as a domina passed him on the street. Her hair was covered by a jeweled scarf, and gold flashed on her bare arms. She belonged here. Aleo wasn't so sure if this was his home, or if he'd lost it in a bet. The wheel crackled with light as it turned above him, singing on its world-axle. He was a small thing moving in the middle-yard below, while Fortuna looked on. Had she spoken to him once? He had a very dim memory of her voice. But it was so faint that it might have been a dream. Maybe she'd spoken to the other one. They shared space in this life, but there was almost no trace of him left. Just a pale outline, beginning to crack beneath the force of the sun.

The path narrowed. Soldiers in burnished loricae emerged from the line of trees. They watched him closely but didn't reach for their weapons. Latona was curious. She wanted to know why he'd come back. He'd spent some time in her palace, and the one thing he'd managed to glean was that she enjoyed puzzles. That curiosity was keeping him alive. He didn't nod or make eye contact with the guards. He pretended that they were lemon trees with sharp branches. The gate was in his sight.

Violets carpeted the walls of the arx. They flamed in purple profusion, spreading across wood, stone, and glass until they were a part of everything. He trailed his hands across the bloom. The petals were soft. Most of the beauty in this city was dissimulation, but these, perhaps, were a rare exception.

The guards admitted him. The sun was sinking, and it painted their armor, flickering across the gold and enamel of their stylized buckles. The barest word from Latona would send his head rolling among the red horseshoe arches. He couldn't afford to look at anyone, to register any expression. He remembered the shock of the crowd when Felix had been unmasked. The gleam of his eyes, the curls against his brow. He could never again be what he was. They'd seen him, judged him. What remained?

He passed through the courtyard, with its brightly painted walls and soaring ceiling. Lanterns burned in subtle niches, throwing light across the colored expanse until it danced before his eyes. Two salamanders were basking in a corner. He nodded to them, and they flicked their tails. Being an oculus was somewhat like being a shepherd of spirits. He couldn't speak with them, not in the strictest sense, but he could influence them. The lares would follow him down the corridor—he had only to wish for it. But what they did next would be their decision. That was the tricky bit. Latona didn't understand this. You could raise an army of lizards and water sprites, and even a dragon made of smoke, but *following* and *serving* were different concepts entirely. The lares would follow her, because she smelled like power, because her actions might benefit them. But they wouldn't serve her. Whatever they did, once gathered, was their decision. If the salamanders had a purpose, they remained silent about it.

One of the lizards blinked, and he knew that the miles was behind him. There wasn't time enough to act. He turned, and the guard stopped short. A flicker of surprise played across her face. She'd thought that he wasn't paying attention. Two others joined her. They could move quietly in their sandals. He'd forgotten that.

"You are to come with us," the commander said. Her eyes were slate. He wondered what she'd been told about him.

"I have an audience," he said, and it sounded like a lie.

"We'll take you there."

Aleo hesitated. If this was a trick, then it was a relatively subtle one. Latona had a hundred ways to kill him at her disposal. She might have riddled him with arrows long before he entered the courtyard. Leaving him to water the lemon trees with his blood.

The miles closest to her twitched. His hand strayed to the pommel of his gladius, a bronze apple carved with an invocation to Fortuna. Not everyone agreed that he should arrive at his assignation in one piece. Aleo glanced at the salamanders. One had fallen asleep, but the other kept a golden eye on him. Fire was within reach.

He opted for cool reason. "I suppose an escort is appropriate."

The commander said nothing but remained within an inch of him. They made their way down a series of hallways with painted frescoes. He realized, after a few moments, that they were heading away from the oecus. He knew that it would be pointless to say as much. They had their orders. They could drop him in the carcer or throw him off the battlements. Now he was entirely within their power. He should have made that deal with the salamander.

They brought him to the baths. It was unexpected. He couldn't imagine what their purpose was. Unless she thought it fitting that he should drown.

"Our lady wishes that you be prepared for your audience," the commander said. "Appropriate garments will be delivered. In the meantime, we'll wait by the entrance. Don't be too long. She doesn't like waiting."

She's the one prolonging our conversation, he thought. But he remained silent. The guards assumed their place. He felt very odd. The general emptiness reminded him of a dream. Something with snow and fire, but he couldn't remember it now. He stepped into the apodyterium, whose floor was heated by the hypocaust below. Outré pictures decorated the walls. Flying phalloi, disembodied breasts, men and women joined like a snake, circling. A graffito near the bench accused someone of *devouring middles*. He undressed swiftly, feeling awkward. The room was vacant, but that didn't mean he wasn't still being observed. He placed his clothes in a niche painted with a leaping fish. No need to remember. Most likely, he wouldn't get them back.

He grabbed a thin robe from the peg and went straight to the caldarium. Rising steam made the coffered ceiling shimmer. The last rays of sunlight came through the circular window, moving across the water. The pool was empty, the floor so hot that it nearly burned his feet, but he liked the shiver of pain. It reminded him that he was still alive. He'd come this far without giving up everything. Just something.

Aleo dropped the robe on the ledge and eased himself into the water. It wasn't quite scalding, but only just. He breathed deeply, flushing as his body grew used to the temperature. He could feel his muscles uncoiling like frayed rope. The wound on his arm was a tree-branch pattern, blurred beneath the water. He looked up, watching the dance of the suspended lamps, hazy from the steam. *Are the caela here too?* he wondered. Smoke was their domain, but he wasn't sure about steam. He relaxed his vision, trying to see anything that might be moving, any dark passengers upon the air. But there was only the wink of glass and the warm glow of the bronze coffers. He relaxed.

A memory came, unbidden. Babieca moving alongside him, stained with ash. His own cry echoing through the devastated house. Aleo tried to stare past it. He spied the golden lizards clustering near the edge of the pool. He appreciated their fiery contentment. Happiness shouldn't have to be so complicated.

"Oh."

At first, he thought he'd been the one to speak. But then he looked toward the entrance and saw that he wasn't alone. His face became a blank.

"A lot of people have audiences today, it seems."

Felix managed to look uncomfortable for a moment. He was thin beneath the robe. He'd lost some weight, but it was more than that. He was diminished, somehow. Aleo saw the dark hollows beneath his eyes, the muscle jumping in his throat as he spoke. Bruises formed an almost delicate pattern on his cheek, and one eye was still red-rimmed. He favored one leg as he stood there, stiffly, about to speak. But *oh* was all he'd managed to deliver.

"Come in," Aleo said. "It's a big pool. You'll see me coming if I try anything."

It was meant to be funny, but Felix winced slightly at the suggestion. He rubbed his throat unconsciously. The blade had left no mark. Aleo remembered its weight in his hand. The meretrix crouched before him, staring straight ahead. Gracious in his acceptance.

Only he wasn't a meretrix anymore. He was unmasked. Aleo had grown so used to seeing the mask that he'd imagined it being there.

Felix disrobed and slipped into the water. He no longer moved with grace. Several parts of him had been broken, and he couldn't hide that fact. But there was still something playful about his bearing, as if this too were a part that he'd decided upon. Wounded wolf.

"Where is it?"

Felix looked at him for a moment. Then he knew. "Gone."

"Did you leave it in the undercroft?"

"No." A beat. "She made me destroy it." He stared at the water.

Aleo said: "It was beautiful."

"It outlived its purpose."

He drew closer. "What do you think her game is? Did she think we'd try to drown each other? Poetic, but impractical."

Felix looked at him. "Did you mean what you said? When you were holding the knife?"

He met the man's gaze. "Yes."

Felix watched droplets of water fall from his fingers. "I'm very sorry. I know what he was to you."

"What was he to you?" He didn't mean the question to sound like a challenge, but there was a kind of growl behind it.

Felix didn't look sad. His expression was impossible to translate. "Music. A stone in my sandal. We didn't fit, but we appreciated each other."

"Maybe you don't fit with anyone." He wasn't trying to be cruel, but his mouth formed the words, regardless. He was still very angry, though not at this man.

Felix simply looked thoughtful. "It's always been a possibility."

"The plan wasn't flawed," Aleo said. "The flaw was in us. We thought we could stay one step ahead, but here we are, wet and stupid. Surprised to both be alive."

"It should have worked. All the right bribes were made. Nobody should have remained loyal to Mardian. That was the one card that we had to play. His exile."

"And what made him so dangerous. His desire for homecoming. That's a weakness that we all have." Aleo touched his bruised cheek. "Does it hurt much?"

Felix didn't move. "Only when I smile."

"Then you'd better not."

He winced. "I never could help it. I was always pleased with myself."

Aleo looked at him. "This is what she wants," he said.

"What do you want?"

They were very close. Steam rose from their bodies. Now he was convinced that this must be a dream. The salamanders observed him from far away. The question wasn't rhetorical, he realized. Felix didn't know the answer. His face was curious, but not expectant. For the first time, he wasn't at the center of a secret network. The whispers had gone silent. He was naked and uncertain, with scars visible on his body. No longer the house father of the black basia, the favored courtier. Something entirely different now.

Aleo told him.

They kissed on the shoulder, as was the courtly custom. Then they dressed in silence. Beautiful tunicae had been left for both of them. Felix's was white—a jest, perhaps—while Aleo's was black with a bloodred die at the throat. No more swan, then. He would be known for his gens only. The real die against his chest was cold as winter, but he'd grown used to it.

For a moment, he thought about rolling. Something brilliantly wild and unexpected. A roll to turn back the flood, to reverse every doom and guarantee their safety. Even if it meant dying twice. He realized that Felix was thinking the same thing. The comedy of changing the world in a room meant for changing clothes. Maybe it was possible. But there was something necessary about living in the flaw. The smoke afterward. A part of him wondered if they were spinning the wheel, and Fortuna merely watched.

The group of miles escorted them. Cool air rushed in through the impluvia. Lemon scent, the murmur of fountains. Felix was beside him, silent, matching him step for step. The fallen courtier, the hand that held the knife. They moved through the dazzle of the palace, two flaws that formed a crystal. Yes, Aleo thought, he'd meant what he said. Not just then, but now.

He'd thought they were walking toward the oecus. It would be fitting for Latona to meet them on her hydraulic throne. Instead, they found themselves emerging into sunlight. They were on the Patio of Lions. He wasn't sure why it was called that, since there was only one lion, rearing in white marble. Aleo remembered being here once before, but it was veiled by distance, like something that had happened to him when he was still a child. There were patterns in the lilies that he seemed to remember. The fountains sang. They were powered by water from the massive aqueduct whose granite bows pumped in water from the twin rivers. All of the city's energy seemed to coalesce in this oddly serene place, with its delicate topiary and scent of summer fruit.

He looked at Felix for a sense of what to do next. The

courtier had been here many times, after all. He'd once been a fixture in the palace. But Felix was staring past him, frozen in the act of saying something. Aleo followed his look. Six paths radiated from the white marble lion, meant to represent the six spokes of Fortuna's wheel. At the center of the patio, amid the cool spray of the fountains, two women sat on pillows. There was a board between them, and Aleo realized that they were playing acedrex, the game of queens. They could play nothing else. Latona wore a sleeveless stola, embroidered with purple dragons. A heart-shaped brooch gleamed at her throat, studded with carnelians. She'd removed her slippers, and her bare feet were tucked beneath her.

This was not so surprising. The basilissa had always been a contradiction, and it was only natural that she would shed her armor to disorient them. The real surprise was her adversary in the game. Basilissa Pulcheria calmly considered her pieces. Her expression gave nothing away. Her hair was teased high, in the late-imperial style, and held in place by a series of winking jade combs. She looked quite formal in comparison to her opponent. Aleo had seen images of her in the palace—icons of gold and painted wood—and Felix had told him about her reputation as the ruler of Egressus. She was young, studied, fair-minded. After a botched assassination attempt, she'd also become Latona's enemy. He couldn't imagine what had brought her to this place, or why she'd consented to move gold and silver acedrex pieces in an alien court.

Latona didn't look up from the game. "Have a seat. You're late, and I'm in the middle of doing something with my elephant. Though I haven't decided precisely what." She squinted beneath the cloudless sky. "One hopes for inspiration. Or distraction."

"She likes to talk," Pulcheria said, tapping a golden vizier with her nail. "From what I can tell, it's part of her strategy."

"Have I bored you, sister?" Latona nearly moved her

elephant, then drew back her hand at the last moment. "It's a flaw of mine, this need to tell stories. Perhaps diplomacy is better served by silence."

"This game has nothing to do with diplomacy."

Pulcheria took a sip of wine. Her goblet was engraved with a forest scene—Aleo thought he could see a silenus emerging from a forest grove.

He looked at Felix again. *Do you understand?* He felt as if he'd arrived late to a performance, and now he had to try to follow along. Latona's army was poised to march on Regina. No doubt, Egressus would follow. She would conquer what lay on either side of the park. Basilissa Pulcheria should be raising her own army, sending messages to the distant basilissae, who might follow her into battle. What was she doing here, playing a game on the Patio of Lions, with a woman who wanted her dead?

"Confusion is natural," Latona said, as if reading his thoughts. "More than anyone, the two of you have resisted a certain understanding. You've moved down unexpected pathways. That's why you're here. As witnesses, of a sort."

Pulcheria said: "Are you going to extemporize all day? If so, I'll need more wine."

Latona flashed her a grin. "I thought you were the patient one."

They might have been speaking another language, for all that Aleo understood. Latona had been screaming the last time he'd seen her, covered in blood and ash. Now she was sweet as honey, as if she hadn't spent the last month trying to set fire to both worlds. *A happy ending.* When she'd said that earlier, at the house by the wall, he'd thought it was a jest. Now he wasn't so sure. He had to remind himself that this woman had planned to kill Felix. Babieca was dead, if not because of her, then as a result of her actions. There was no grief in her expression. Just a strange sense of play that he found infinitely more unnerving than the rage that he'd seen before. She looked up then. She might have been a painting in that light. Every inch Fortuna, with one hand dipped in blood, while the other rested lightly on ivory.

"You're looking well," she said to Felix. "The water did you good."

"You tried to kill me." Felix's reply was the first sane thing that Aleo had heard. He said it without inflection. A bare statement of fact.

"Of course. A ruler decides these things. And someone always dies." Latona finally moved her elephant, taking one of Pulcheria's heralds. A grandiose move for a minor victory. Surely there was something behind it.

Felix stared at her. "That's all you have to say?"

"Do you need me to explain how death works?"

Pulcheria made a sound. "There's no use torturing them. You can't expect them to see things from your position."

"Now who's extemporizing?"

Pulcheria captured her vizier. "At least I arrive at a point."

"What . . . *is* this?" Aleo's voice was hoarse, as if he hadn't spoken for years. "You bring us here, throw us together, play games. Are we meant to be some kind of audience?"

Latona considered the board. "I could say something about it all being a game, but surely you're tired of that by now. I will remind you, however, that I didn't bring *you* here. You came of your own free will, bearing my property."

He seemed to remember the horn for the first time. He'd brought it as a kind of insurance, but he was no longer sure against what. Up until this moment, he realized that he'd considered returning the horn. It would depend on what he received in the bargain. But as he watched the pieces glide across the board, he knew that it was folly. She could pick him up just as easily, smash him against the ground. There was no deal to be made. There was the chance that he might not leave here alive.

"You both swore an oath to me," Latona said. "You broke that oath. Felix betrayed me, but that was a long time in the making." She looked at Aleo then. "Your betrayal came as something of a surprise, though. I gave you everything that you asked for. I kept your friends alive. I offered you the power that you needed. Not enough, it seems."

"You asked me to commit murder."

"I asked you to pass sentence on an oathbreaker. The lares needed blood—you knew that. It's always blood."

He looked at Felix, whose expression was empty. "There had to be another way."

"Yes." She moved a horseman. "The spado found it. The oath held."

Aleo felt a chill pass through him. "What you did," he said softly, "was monstrous."

"What *I* did?" Latona shook her head. "You did it, Aleo. Don't you see? A sacrifice requires love. It couldn't have been anyone. It needed to echo. You set the terms, and you don't even remember. It had to be one of them."

"How could he?" Pulcheria chided. "He's been several different people. Who can keep it all straight?"

"What are you *doing*?" Aleo realized that he was screaming. "Why are we here? What can this possibly serve?"

"We're passing time," Pulcheria said. "She's always late."

Aleo wanted to smash the board. He nearly stepped forward. But then he heard the soft crunch of gravel behind him. The basilissae rose in unison, leaving the game half-played. He couldn't tell who was winning. Every piece seemed to be in danger.

A woman was walking across the courtyard. She stopped at the nearest fountain, letting her hand trail through the water. Aleo felt something part him on the inside, like a knife paring an apple. He knew her, but he couldn't say her name. The way that she walked, the silver in her hair, was like something from a dream. Light played upon the twin brooches that fastened her cloak. She was dressed for an entirely different climate, as if she'd come from far away.

Each woman stood on her own spoke, her own path. For

a moment, they were still, silently assessing each other. Then the newcomer raised her hand, and the others echoed her motion. She came to join them by the white lion. Her eyes swept over the abandoned board, and she smiled slightly.

"I prefer stones to acedrex. There are fewer rules."

"You always did play on the margins." Latona inclined her head. "Well met, Pharsia. The sun has given you some color, I see."

She shrugged. "The dark has its possibilities. I like the cool silences. Nobody bothers me, unless I want them to."

"I suppose misanthropy suits you," Pulcheria said.

Pharsia gave her a look. "I thought you died of a bee sting."

Pulcheria gestured to Aleo. "This one helped me. Though he doesn't remember."

Aleo frowned. "That wasn't me."

Pharsia was close enough to touch him. Her hand trembled, as if she might. For a second, they were the only people in the courtyard. "Sweet boy," she said. "You're nothing but possibilities. Don't forget that."

He felt a stab of memory. A hand rubbing circles on his back. *Sweet boy, some things are riddles. You can't solve them all. Just remember that you're nothing but possibilities.*

Before he could say anything, Latona and Pulcheria stepped forward. Their movements were oddly choreographed. They mirrored each other in the water of the fountain. They each sat on the marble rim.

"We're close to the end of a story," Latona said. "Few remember its beginning. Worlds emerged out of darkness and mist, joined by a great axis. A root system linked them together. Green grass, stone buildings, and the spirits that haunt the gaps. Many were lost in the voyage between. Some wanted to be lost. They dreamed of empires. They chained the elements. They too passed away, when night fell."

A breath later, Pulcheria took up the thread. The story seemed to live in their collective memory. Perhaps they'd never spoken it aloud until now. Perhaps they'd always been telling it, a slow shiver beneath the skin of things. "Three queens rose to preserve the pattern. One in the north, one in the south, and one who ruled among the roots. Grand-dame to mother to fierce young domina, they kept the weave going. They kept watch over Fortuna's seal, which divided the possibilities. They laid aside their loves for the loom, knowing that one day, every thread would meet its opposite. The seal would break."

Pharsia laced her hands together. She spoke to the court-yard as if it were a packed theater, but her eyes remained on Aleo. "War is one of the endings," she said. "One possibility in the ocean where fates glide like dark minnows. Every story has an end. But an end isn't a blank page. A story is a wheel, after all. We must all endure the turn. What it brings, not even we can say. We three queens who dance on its rim."

"I don't understand," Felix said. "What's our part in this? Are we just pieces on your board? Insects crushed beneath your wheel?"

"This one likes metaphors," Pulcheria said.

Latona favored him with a smile that was almost kind. "You'll have to fight," she said. "You'll have to roll. You may even win."

"What if we refuse to play?" Aleo demanded. "I have a company. A family. People who keep forgiving me. They're what I care about—not your war."

"You will care," Pulcheria said, with a trace of sadness. "Or they will be lost."

Then he realized. He stared at Felix's white garment, stark against his own. The ritual waters, meant to prepare them. The cutting sorrow, and the debt unpaid. Felix was no longer a member of the night gens, or any gens. He'd been stripped of his die. He belonged to nobody, and for that reason, he was dangerous.

Though perhaps Aleo was the dangerous one, after all.

A look passed between then. It wasn't what he expected.

"It shall be war, then," Latona said. "And right on schedule."

Pharsia inclined her head. Then she walked down the gravel path. As she passed Aleo, she brushed his cheek with her fingertips.

His mother's touch chilled him.

3

PAUL'S EYES NARROWED. "WHAT DO YOU MEAN
dragons?"

They were still dressed in black. Sam picked at the cheese
tray, while Andrew rubbed his hands against the dress pants.
The wool was driving him slowly mad. He thought about
taking his pants off, in the middle of Ingrid's living room,
and realized that Carl would have approved of this mightily.
Pantsless grief. Neil arranged gemstones on the carpet. His
hair was getting shaggy. Andrew, not usually one to notice
such things, realized that he'd grown quite a bit in the last
year. It had happened while he was distracted. Time was
always getting away from him. Ingrid used to be able to
throw the boy over her shoulder like an outraged potato
sack. Now, even Paul struggled to lift him. Andrew had once
watched them carry Neil to bed in tandem, like an unconscious reveler. Three bodies shuffling delicately down the
hallway.

"Dragon *singular*," Ingrid corrected. "And it's made of

smoke. Though I suppose there are a lot of eyes and mouths. You could think of it as a hungry collective."

Carl's mother had read Borges aloud. "Street with the Pink Corner Store." The sky swallowed her voice, low, incantatory:

Su inquietud me deja
en esta calle que es cualquiera

The joy of being surprised by light from a pink cross-roads. She'd moved through so many cities. Carl had once told him that she took pictures of her hotel rooms, sending them first as Polaroids, then as attachments. He had a collection at home. Now it belonged to Andrew. The apartment was silent and smelled of lemon cleaner. He could remember the sweat, the aching muscles, the task of moving everything in plastic totes that would barely fit in the truck. Where had it all come from? Where was it going? He touched his left pocket, where Carl's phone was wedged like a small brick. The only account that he hadn't closed. An archive of sorts that he carried around, since he didn't know what else to do.

"And the dragon's controlled by . . . the ballerina?"

"*Basilissa.* Actually, they're plural."

Neil had arranged the gemstones into a fortress. He was humming something to himself as he built up the walls. Andrew didn't know if he was listening or not. His eyes narrowed in concentration as he surveyed the mosaic. Light fired the stones, and he smiled.

Andrew stood up and grabbed his bag. As he walked down the hallway, he heard part of a question: ". . . the nice one?"

As soon as the bathroom door was closed, he tore off the pants, nearly ripping them apart. His fingers trembled as he unbuttoned the dress shirt. The starched collar left a ring around his neck. He stood before the mirror in his underwear. As a child, he used to practice facial expressions in the mirror. He would laugh, as if he'd just heard the funniest joke, and then study the shape of his mouth, the crinkling around his eyes. He stared at the face in the mirror. It made less sense than the array of reversed objects in the bathroom: the rubber duckies, the shampoo bottles shaped like cars, the Waterpik that seemed to be collecting dust. The urge to wreck things had passed, but there was still a dark energy that made him twitch. He touched his forehead to the mirror. If he pushed hard enough, he might slip through. He'd probably need clothes for that.

He emerged from the bathroom in jeans and one of Carl's shirts. Shelby noticed this but said nothing. The shirt didn't smell good. That was why he chose to wear it.

"When were you going to tell me?"

Ingrid smoothed her skirt. "Every time I imagined this moment, it was different. There was yelling, and explosions, and possibly running. But now we have no choice. What happened—" She swallowed. "I couldn't lie about that. I couldn't spin it. There's no going back now, Paul. If we're going to get through this, we need your help."

Paul breathed in. Then out. He didn't say anything for a while. His eyes were a little wild, and there wasn't much color left in his cheeks. Andrew wondered if he might throw up and thought about going to fetch something. Ginger ale? A receptacle? There didn't seem to be enough time. Surely, Ingrid had planned for this. She had sharp reflexes.

"How do I know you aren't all crazy?" Paul asked finally.

"Mummy has a sword," Neil observed from his circle of gemstones.

Paul looked at him. All he could manage was: "A sword?"

Neil didn't bother to look up. "I have seen it in mine dreams. Mummy's sword. It has a very beautiful crack in it, like . . . a *mineral*." He seemed pleased by his own simile. "We are all inside of her force field, which has quite a lot of range."

Ingrid knelt beside Neil. "Did you really see me in your dreams?"

He looked up finally. He touched her cheek. "It was so lovely to see mine mummy there, in her armor. Protecting us all."

Andrew could remember when he used to say *betect* rather than *protect*.

Shelby emerged from the kitchen with a tray of coffee. "There you have it. Dream evidence is admissible in court, right?"

Paul took one of the cups. He turned it around in his hands, like a polished stone. His eyes were unfocused for a bit. Then he said: "Let me get this straight. You're telling me that Wascana Park leads to another world, a place where you're all heroes."

"I wouldn't go that far," Shelby replied. "More like advanced meddlers."

Paul blinked. "You go to this world every night. While Neil and I are asleep, you traipse around this fantasy world, solving quests."

"We don't *traipse*," Ingrid said. "You can't really traipse in armor—" He gave her a long look. "Sorry. Continue."

"Now the evil ballerina"—Paul grimaced—"sorry, *basilissa*—has raised some army of lizard demons and smoke monsters, and she's going to attack the capital of Saskatchewan. Because of its global importance. So you need my help to protect Regina from the insane Muppet Queen who's going to unleash an army of reptiles and Fraggles and other things that I can't see—because what you need in a situation like that is someone who can make chocolate ganache. Or maybe you just need me to babysit Neil while you ride into battle."

"We don't have horses," Ingrid murmured.

Paul's color had returned. "And you chose not to tell me about any of this, so that you could secure free day care. You put yourself in danger every other night, you got hurt and scarred and nearly killed, and you didn't tell me about any of it. Because your little brother can be a parent, but he's too stupid to be part of this. And you're only telling me now because Carl—" He hesitated. "Because something went wrong. You're telling me as a last resort. Have I got this all straight? Because I'm not a graduate student who knows how to take perfect notes. I may have missed something."

"That's about it," Ingrid said. Her voice sounded slightly hollow. They were all exhausted. Andrew couldn't even tell what was keeping him conscious, except for a burning along the edges of everything.

"Ingrid—" Paul couldn't quite look at her anymore. "This all sounds like some kind of nervous breakdown."

Andrew stood. "Show me where the furnace is."

Paul frowned. "Seriously?"

"Please."

"I—" He shrugged. "Sure. Why not? It's downstairs."

They went down to the basement. Neil followed them with mild interest, still counting gemstones in his palm. The furnace was in the corner of the laundry room, surrounded by plastic bins full of toys that Neil had outgrown. He began digging through them.

"Don't turn the light on," Andrew said. "Just give me a second."

He knew that lares could cross over. He'd seen the salamander at the university library, and once—out of the corner of his eye—he'd also seen a dripping undina in the bathtub. It must have had something to do with the paper-thin barrier between worlds. Or maybe the lares had always existed on both sides. He scanned the room. After a moment, he was able to make out a flickering ember, beneath the pilot light. He crouched on the cement floor. The salamander was very faint. Only part of it seemed to be here, or perhaps they were simply harder to see on this side of the park. But the amused golden eyes looked up at him.

"What's he doing?" Paul whispered.

Ingrid didn't reply. They'd moved past explanations.

"Oh!" Neil joined Andrew on the floor. "How sweet!"

Andrew looked at him in surprise. Then he remembered the children in Anfractus, who'd watched the salamanders feeding at the shrine. "You see him."

"Her," Neil corrected.

Paul sucked in his breath. It must have felt like he was in the middle of a horror movie. Something with prophetic children and nightmares living in the basement.

Andrew opened his clenched fist, revealing a piece of apple that he'd liberated from the kitchen. The salamander approached. He held out the treat. He could feel the lizard's heat. It opened its mouth, revealing a row of needle-sharp teeth, and snatched the apple. The sound of its chewing reminded him of a cat eating dry kibble.

"What the—" Paul stepped forward. "How did you do that?"

"Put your hand right here," Andrew said. "Slowly."

Paul knelt beside him, looking confused.

"Don't be afraid," Neil soothed. "She's not that hungry."

Slowly, Paul reached out his hand, until it hovered near the salamander's unseen head. She sniffed it cautiously. Paul's eyes widened.

"It's *warm*."

The lizard sneezed. A tongue of flame burst out of the darkness, and Paul cried out. He sat down heavily on the concrete, staring at the tips of his fingers.

"Sorry," Andrew said. "They do that sometimes."

Paul looked at the empty space in front of him. "What is it?"

"One of the Fraggles."

"And"—he'd gone white again—"it lives in our furnace?"

"Salamanders like warm places. She's harmless. Mostly."

Ingrid touched Neil's shoulder. "Bubs, have you always been able to see her?"

He shrugged. "Sometimes I can hear her scratching. Sweet little Chordata." His eyes suddenly widened as he stared at the furnace. He gripped Ingrid's hand. "But I don't like this room. It is a bit too much like Hatshepsut's funeral bier."

JUST PAST SUNSET, THEY GATHERED OUTSIDE Darke Hall. The downtown campus of Plains University was a crumbling beauty, full of old brick buildings that had been commissioned after the cyclone that nearly destroyed Regina. Oddly enough, the venerable hall with its stained-glass windows had become the administrative center for online programs. It made no sense that something called "digital delivery" would house its offices in a haunted auditorium. Or perhaps it made perfect sense. The campus was quiet, almost derelict. Surrounded by Wascana Park, it seemed to be sinking into the woodland without complaint. Fat insects buzzed around the landscaped green. The parking lot was empty, save for Shelby's truck.

It was an unlikely spot for a battle.

"You're sure about this?" Ingrid asked. "The main campus seems a more likely target. Why would they come here?"

Andrew squinted at a spiderweb. "Because it's old. And ghosts live here. That's like catnip for lares. The basilissa wants to overrun our world with the spirits of Anfractus. But Regina has its own lares—they've been crossing the border for centuries. Maybe they've always been here. They won't take kindly to a breach of their territory. Darke Hall is as good a fortress as any. We can defend it."

"With all of the weapons that we don't have," Shelby clarified.

Paul unzipped his hockey bag. "I've got sticks and bats. And a lacrosse stick." He frowned. "Not sure what good that'll be."

"This wouldn't be a problem if we lived in Utah," Shelby said.

Andrew frowned. "This is the hunting epicenter of Canada. If we wanted guns, we could find them. But they won't do much good. We need something else."

"Is he coming?" Ingrid asked.

She meant Oliver. He'd left a cache of weapons at the library. They'd thought of stopping there first, but nobody knew the code to the safe. Andrew shifted nervously from one foot to the other. "I'm not sure."

"I thought you'd come to some kind of arrangement."

"That's not precisely how I remember it."

You know him better than I do. Care to guess what his next move will be? Andrew didn't voice the thought aloud. Ingrid's speech to Paul hadn't included any mention of Oliver. It didn't seem like the right time to open up that particular box. He hadn't objected to leaving Neil with a last-minute babysitter. Like the rest of them, he was pale, but present.

A car pulled up. Oliver stepped out, carrying what looked like a cooler.

"Sandwiches?" Ingrid asked.

He laid it on the ground. "Swords."

"Even better."

Something passed between them. A question asked and answered. Oliver looked at Andrew. He didn't quite smile, but the corner of his mouth twitched. Like he was remembering something funny. Andrew thought about everything he didn't know about Oliver and the few things that he did. They were both unpredictable pieces. His hand curled around the piano key in his pocket. It wasn't a horn, but it might still work. All of their plans seemed like beautiful hypotheticals. Mere outlines that would burn beneath the shock of color. He reached into his other pocket. Carl's phone was heavy and certain. A suitable grave gift. Death hovered nearby, fog on a windowpane. He couldn't stop it. Best to invite it in.

Sam emerged from Darke Hall. "All clear," she said. "Everyone's gone home for the day. It's a Scooby Doo ghost town in there."

"It really is," Andrew replied.

Sam gave him an odd look. "Can you see them?"

"No. But the lares can. It's creeping me out, to be honest."

"My grandma says that we don't have to be afraid of ghosts," Shelby said. "They're citizens, just like us."

"Let's hope she's right." Ingrid held open the door. "We could use the reinforcements."

Latin scrolled across the stained-glass windows. It was warm inside, and the air smelled like an old closet. The auditorium made him dizzy. Plush velvet chairs rose like a wave. The pipe organ loomed above the stage, a sleeping automaton with serrated teeth. He could almost hear spectral music clinging to the rafters.

Andrew gave the piano key to Ingrid. "You're good here?"

She nodded. "Go do your thing."

"And if it doesn't work?"

She flashed a smile. "We'll all laugh about it, just before we die."

"That's soothing."

Oliver followed him outside, while the rest of them finished setting up. Their shadows crossed on the cement floor, trading stories. Carl had never trusted him. For a moment, he thought about dialing Carl's number. *Can you clear this up?* As if his distracted voice mail message would have answers.

They descended the stairs that led to the faculty offices. The hallway had recently been painted a buttery shade of yellow. It was so still that he could hear his own breathing. All the doors were closed. Oliver stood very close to him. Their hands were nearly touching, and he wasn't sure what to do about that. *Carl, who am I without you? Am I a good person? Am I sane? Tell me what I should do. Play me something. Air Supply. Elevator music. I don't care. Just tell me how this works.*

"You're sure about these tunnels?" Oliver asked.

"I'm not sure of anything."

"It wasn't meant to be a metaphysical question."

Andrew turned to face him. "What are you sure of?"

The fluorescent lights made him look overexposed. "What?"

"Are you sure that you want to help us?"

He frowned. "There's no other option."

"That's the answer you're going with."

"What do you want from me, Andrew? I've always been on your side. Whatever I used to have—it's gone. All I can do now is fight."

"She could restore your position. If you switched sides."

"Do you really believe that?"

Andrew searched his expression. It wasn't difficult to look him in the eyes, which was strange in itself. Oliver had chosen. Andrew skated along the edge of disaster, like always. He thought about power, how vital it was, how bright. Maybe he'd been the variable all along. The one who couldn't be trusted.

He walked down a short flight of stairs without answering. There was a brief corridor, which ended in a bricked-up wall. He smelled water and decay. This was a limb that the campus had forgotten about. The tunnels were supposed to be haunted, but that no longer frightened him. Being haunted wasn't the worst thing in the world.

Andrew pulled out a geode from his knapsack. He'd bought it years ago at the mineral fair, intrigued by the way that its crystals caught stray light. He set it next to the brick wall. Nothing happened at first. Then, after a few moments, he saw small shadows gathering. Two gnomoi emerged from a gap in the brick. They had lamplike eyes and brittle white hair. One of them picked up the geode, tapping it with his talons, the way you might test a watermelon at the supermarket. He tasted it. Andrew saw his shy tongue, the color of quartz, as it flicked across the surface of the stone.

The gnomoi looked at him expectantly. The offering was suitable. He pointed to the brick wall and imagined it melting, like ice cream on a summer sidewalk.

The lares nodded and began to eat.

After the brick was gone, they stepped into the narrow tunnel. They used the light of their phones to guide them. Andrew pulled out Carl's phone as a backup light, but Oliver didn't say anything about it. They walked slowly and in silence. The gnomoi followed, curious, picking stones from their teeth. Andrew stopped.

"We've crossed College Street," he said. "We're below the park now."

There was a large access panel in the ceiling. He could just make it out in the triple light of their phone-torches. It was locked. The gnomo who'd taken the geode looked at him thoughtfully. His eyes were green in the semidarkness. Andrew swallowed his fear, trying to find the desire beneath it. He flattened everything into a striated need. The gnomo cocked his head in understanding. Then he ate the lock in one bite, as if it were a low-hanging plum. He spat out liquid metal on the ground.

Oliver took a step back but said nothing.

Andrew opened the metal doors. He could feel a breeze and hear the ducks, hissing in the grass. They were near the gazebo. The park cared little for what was going on beneath it. Everything kept moving forward.

Oliver gave him a boost, and he crawled to the surface. He extended his hand, pulling Oliver up after him. They both emerged feeling strangely disoriented, like criminals who'd engineered a daring escape.

"If we can herd the lares underground," Andrew said, "we might be able to minimize the damage to the city. The caela will sense that the horn is nearby. I'm hoping that the others will follow them. Out of curiosity, if nothing else."

"And what are we supposed to do, once we've got them down there?"

"Run faster than the hungriest ones."

Oliver exhaled. "Now I remember why I hate your plans."

"The gnomoi will keep them busy. I hope. We're pitting the lares of Anfractus against the ones who live here. I guess you could think of them as a spiritual diaspora. There aren't as many, but they're territorial. That should at least buy us some time."

"And you can control them?"

He laughed. "Control? No. I can bribe them, and reason with them, but they'll do what they want in the end. I'm counting on the fact that Latona isn't willing to admit this flaw. There's still a chance that we can turn her army against her."

Oliver's eyes widened. "I think we're going to find out."

Three shadows were moving across the surface of the park. A woman rode ahead of each army. Latona was dressed in a lorica of ebony and jade, with hundreds of shining segments that flickered, like stars. She was riding a bronze horse. It took Andrew a moment to realize that she'd liberated Queen Victoria's mount, which normally stood in the garden across from the legislature. Mardian rode with her. A dagger gleamed against his silken belt. Andrew shivered when he saw it. The spado's face was a web of scars, a leaf of scoured parchment. There was nothing in his expression. A peculiar emptiness, far worse than the keening rage that he'd expected to see.

They were surrounded by lares. Salamanders left flaming footprints in the grass, while undinae slithered through stagnant puddles. The turf buckled and writhed as gnomoi burrowed beneath it. Pulcheria followed on her right. She moved a bit more slowly, since she was riding a stone frog. Its back was a mosaic of winking tesserae. Andrew remembered seeing it near Darke Hall. Engineering students had damaged it years ago, but now it had a new set of legs and was making good time as it terrified the ducks. A smaller group of lares followed Pulcheria—spirits still loyal to the city of Egressus. On the far left, Pharsia rode in a chariot of scrap metal, pulled by rusted, faceless sculptures that surged across the ground like blind worms. A pack of furs kept pace with her, dressed in patches and carrying an assortment of unlikely weapons.

"We may need to call the fire department," Andrew said. "And everyone else."

"I can see them," Oliver said. His voice held a note of astonishment.

Andrew turned. "You mean the lares?"

He nodded. His expression was almost childlike. "There are so many different kinds. No one ever told me that they were beautiful."

"They also want to eat you."

Oliver shook his head as if to clear it. "Why can I see them? And—is that a frog?"

"The walls between worlds are like damp newspaper. They're stretched to capacity, and everything's getting in." He looked up. "Absolutely everything."

The caela swirled above them, a cloud of eyes and searching mouths that was spreading across the sky. In no time, they would blot out the moon. An engine of furious appetite revolved within the heart of the smoke. He knew what it wanted.

He sent a message to Shelby: Start playing.

At first, nothing happened. Then, a cluster of gnomoi put their shriveled ears to the ground. The salamanders heard it too. Their tails whipped back and forth as they strained to locate the source of the vibration. The undinae stared at the surface of Wascana Lake, as if they could divine a message in the glass of the water. Even Latona's stolen mount paused in midstep, flicking its ears.

It was beginning to work.

Sam had come up with the idea. She'd been fascinated by the piano key, which had once been an ivory horn. She knew that it summoned the caela, but its form here was entirely different. The park was like a door frame, a boundary that kept things in order. But as that boundary declined, anything that crossed the threshold would begin to vibrate with hesitation as it shifted between forms. There had to be a way to put that to use. It was Sam's idea to replace one of the organ keys with the artifact. The vibration from the pipes, she reasoned, would amplify the call of the horn.

She'd been right. All of the lares heard it. Then something unexpected happened. The gnomoi began to sing. They called out in unison, and their voices matched the dark cadence of the magnificent organ. It *thrummed* across the ground and into the air, a single note that sent shivers across Andrew's body. The park itself was awake now. He could feel it in the patient movement of the trees. Wascana Lake churned beneath the moonlight, a stained-glass window alive with rills of blue. Latona hesitated. He could see it in her expression. The caela were moving away from her, following the sound. Her army was splintering.

It was Paul who played.

His fingers danced across the keys, playing the only song he knew: "Baby Beluga."

Pulcheria chose that moment to charge.

Andrew realized that a stone frog could move a lot faster than he'd thought.

A few evening bystanders gathered on the edge of the lake to watch. They assumed it was a movie or some drug-fueled reenactment of a scene from *Game of Thrones*.

That was when the silenoi burst from the line of trees.

The princeps carried a spear. Andrew felt his arm ache, remembering when the silenus had clawed him. That scar was forever. Black hooves churned the earth as the princeps's followers massed around him. On the other side of the clearing, Septimus and Skadi ran at the head of a smaller pack. Everything slowed down for a moment, then sped up with a crash that jarred him to the bone.

The bystanders couldn't remember which episode this was supposed to be.

Lares from Anfractus were attacking the elemental spirits of the park. It was a vicious battle for territory. Salamanders burned like will-o'-the-wisps, biting and clawing in golden flashes. Their blood seared the grass. Undinae skated across the surface of the lake, slashing with needle-thin blades of congealed ice. Andrew watched in horror as one of them was cut to pieces and burst into a spray of black water. The gnomoi used their talons, and sometimes their teeth. They screamed and whirled through a mist of slate-gray blood. Latona's horse reared back, and she nearly fell. Pulcheria had already dismounted. A salamander leapt at her, hissing, but she struck it with her distaff. The lizard unraveled into fine gold seams that burned against the air, then vanished.

The silenoi were a dark, terrifying wave that moved across the battlefield. Skadi and Septimus led a loyal—or foolish—pack against the forces of the princeps. The lares burned around them, but these monsters only had eyes for each other. The princeps was vertiginous murder, a dance of glorious edges. Green blood sizzled on the tip of the royal spear. The silenoi howled and bucked and tore at each other. Septimus gored an oncoming warrior with his spiral horns. Brilliant green sap burst from the ruined throat, and the silenus convulsed as he fell. Skadi was contending with an opponent twice her size, which didn't faze her in the least. The silenus clawed her shoulder. With a low snarl, she drove her fist beneath the attacker's ribs. The warrior stumbled backward, and she leapt on him, twisting his body until he was face down in the mud. She used her weight to drive his head into the sodden turf, screaming liquid syllables that must have been wild invective.

Now the princeps had begun to hesitate. His eyes took in the chaos. He hadn't expected his own people to move against him. Septimus had been his right hand, Skadi his left, and now they were both cutting an emerald swath through his ranks.

Latona and Pulcheria faced each other on the green. Their distaffs were raised. Spirits writhed at their feet. In the distance, he could hear sirens. Oliver, he realized, had taken seriously his suggestion to call the fire department.

It was then that Andrew had a profoundly stupid idea.

It would depend on several variables, and also how fast he could run. It was a roll worthy of his name. Possibly, it would kill him for real. But some part of him had always been ready for that.

He ran toward the chaos.

"Andrew!"

There was no time to stop. He remembered running like this ages ago. Sandals dancing across uneven stones. And Babieca's voice. *Follow that bee!* It wasn't his memory. It belonged to his shadow. But he claimed it as his own. This time, he would be fast enough. This time, the song would not fail.

He knew that Oliver was chasing him. But there was nothing he could do. No chance to turn back. Fate moved. The salamanders looked up as he approached. Their spines glowed like coral beneath stretched golden skin. They hissed and reared.

Ages ago, it seemed, the lizard in his dream had asked: *What do you desire?* The question was always the same. He'd answered over and over, but not to anyone's satisfaction. *What do you desire?* The eyes that had seen empires fall. The dark pupils that threatened to swallow him. The claw against his heart, always waiting. Now he knew.

We want the same thing. And we'll have it. Just follow me.

Some of them paused. Some ran toward him. One hissed a cloud of flame that singed the hairs on his arms. He felt a storm of claws. Oliver screaming his name. Babieca laughing as the final note settled.

He ran.

Light bloomed on either side of him. Latona swung her distaff. He fell to his knees and rolled, like he was tumbling down a hill. The earth bit into his knees. There was blood in his eyes, but he ignored it. All he saw was the dagger.

Mardian turned on him, fumbling with the belt. It was more of a sash. Decorative, but not very efficient. The dagger was caught by a thread.

There was a salamander at his feet. Andrew almost thought that he recognized it. There was something familiar about those hourglass pupils, the tail curled in a question mark. He struck out with his pain and need and fear. He flung it like a javelin, screaming something, a word, perhaps a name. It was hot ash, a note burning on its way out. He was crying, he realized. Tears stung the cuts on his face.

The salamander joined his cry. It puffed out a cloud of flame that danced in the air between them. He felt its purifying heat. Mardian dropped the dagger. He was terrified of the flame. Andrew grabbed the weapon and stood up. For a moment, he loomed over the spado. Mardian's expression twisted in astonishment. Then something changed in his eyes. Something gave way. He made no sound. He stayed exactly where he was, half-kneeling on the ground.

I'd do it again, he seemed to say. *Fate moves.*

And Andrew saw him as he was. Not a proud spado, cold in his passions, but a person who'd given up everything for power. He remembered that night long ago, when Mardian had pledged fealty to Latona, before the shivering fountains. He would have done anything. Even the basilissa was startled by his desire. Andrew saw it now, beneath the frozen look, which was the real mask. They were the same. Like him, Mardian had searched for something beyond the pale network of his life, beyond the long days of working in a hospital or wandering monklike through a library. Surrounded by pain and confusion, he had reached for something that only the park could give him. They had both made wild rolls. There was no sense in regret any longer, no reason to be so scared. Magic was dangerous and alive. There was nothing else.

Andrew stood with the dagger in his hand. There was a spot of dried blood on the serrated hilt, like a careless drop of paint.

He might have brought the blade down in one smooth motion. That was one ending.

Instead, he drew it against his palm. The pain was sharp but momentary. As his blood kissed the dagger, everything stopped. The lares craned their heads. Even the silenoi felt what was happening. Septimus and Skadi were watching him. The caela had already fled, but the remaining lares were frozen before him. A breath between chaos and the unlikely body that stood in front of it. Blood trickled down the hilt. This was the knife that sealed the oath, the knife that stole Babieca's life. It was wild with possibilities. In Mardian's hand, it was an instrument of destruction.

But it didn't have to be.

He raised it above his head. The lares followed his every movement. This was where Latona had faltered. They couldn't be commanded. But, like all things old and reasonable, they could be convinced.

"Follow me!" His voice was the organ note. It surged in all directions, once a little song, now leonine as it climbed. "Follow me, and this world is yours!"

The gnomoi moved first. Then the salamanders. The frog and the horse followed. They were all heading toward him.

The princeps yelled something. His warriors charged the hill, descending like a murderous herd. Septimus and Skadi followed. They were also screaming something. It took him a moment to realize what it was.

Run!

Latona's expression was difficult to read.

Oliver grabbed his hand.

Then he was stumbling through the tunnel, with an army at his back.

He hadn't even tried the profoundly stupid thing yet.

4

THEY RAN THROUGH THE DARK, LOSING EACH other, stumbling over stones and roots, barking shins on imprecise corners. Everything was chasing them. Andrew couldn't turn around. He kept telling himself that the tunnel was short, that they had a head start. But that wasn't quite true. Clusters of lares had already come ahead of them. Salamanders had scorched the walls, and gnomoi had burrowed through the floor of hard-packed earth. Stray wires sparked around the access panel. Had someone tried to eat them? Lares were unpredictable creatures. He knew that salamanders preferred oranges, but what did the undinae snack on? Hopefully seaweed, not people. Smoke hung heavy in the air. The caela had left a mark on this place as well. Everything was hurtling toward his friends, every nightmare beneath the bed, every not-so-blithe spirit with an appetite for this world.

He heard scraping in the distance. It might have been the stone frog.

What did they eat?

If he kept running, it would be fine. It would all be a dream.

The dagger was hot in his hands. He could feel the blood drying on his palm, the faint but persistent sting of the cut. No matter. He was all scars now, running through the dark with a lightning rod for spirits. Oliver kept pace with him. A former meretrix who, most nights, preferred numbers to sex. He'd been a librarian once. There was a joke there, something about *Archive Fever*, but he couldn't quite crack the punch line.

He wondered if he'd die in the dark. Had that been the plan all along? Maybe it should have been him. What difference could he possibly make? He'd looked into the heart of smoke and realized how small he was. He'd made empty promises. Now he was leading an army to a forgotten auditorium, with no idea what to do next.

Except for the stupid idea.

It might work in a fairy tale, or on an episode of *DS9*. Commander Sisko singing in the dark. *Come on, Andrew. The whole Gamma Quadrant believes in you.*

He felt heat on his back.

Latona's vanguard was upon them.

He could make out light coming through the hole in the wall. He no longer knew if Oliver was still behind him. Everything had flattened to a plane of need. This was how it felt to run from a woolly mammoth. The surprise of the survival instinct, rattling through you in a cascade of neurotransmitters. The clarity of knowing, in your blood, that you would live, that you would damn well thrive, even if you had to run across molten lava. Which, at this point, was already a distinct possibility. Knowing that you could kill something, no matter how ancient, or how beautiful it was. Fingers tightening around the blade.

The chokecherry trees making shadows against white brick, warmed by sun. The possibility that every park might be connected. That they were living things, breathing across the surface of a world covered by cellular towers. Regina had built a park over a graveyard of bones, and now it was haunted by history. The stories greening to perfection beneath the earth. The memory of buffalo. *There are no truths,* Coyote said, *only stories.* That much he'd learned from Thomas King. The park was a story that needed to be told. It belonged to everyone.

He'd never have met Carl, if not for the park.

He'd never have seen Neil petting an invisible salamander.

He'd never have felt the stories turning beneath him, those persistent whispers, warp and weft that knew him, truly. The stories that were fireworks. The stories that were cats' paws kneading. Those ones that were a long, slow kiss, and those others that were fat drops of rain falling on your book, even as you read on, skipping every class, pulled forward by bright need and fear and delight. Stories that had no beginning or end, because they were a touch under twilight, swampy laughter, a gloaming of naked possibilities.

They burst into the light. Oliver was still with him. Out of breath, he turned in circles for a moment. The faculty offices remained silent. The basement had no idea what was about to happen. Andrew looked down and saw two gnomoi sharpening their claws on the brick. He snapped his fingers to get their attention. The gesture was not appreciated.

"The wall! We need it again!"

The gnomoi stared at him. Then they murmured something to each other in a language like clicking tiles.

Andrew pointed desperately to the open space. He tried to imagine every wall that he'd ever seen. Reinforced steel, crumbling stone, blushing drywall, even a house that he'd once seen on TV whose walls were covered in tomato tins. Anything to slow them down. They'd tear through it in a moment, but a moment was all that he needed.

The gnomoi looked at him expectantly.

He dumped out his knapsack on the ground, frantically searching for an offering. There were books, and wrappers, and paper clips, and dead highlighters. Finally, he found what he was looking for. The flat rock that he'd taken from the micropark on the day when he'd told Carl that he was dreaming of salamanders. There'd been a sculpture there, overgrown with grass, that had reminded him of a tumulus. He'd spied the rock near purple flowers.

Andrew placed the rock on the ground.

It's all I have.

The gnomoi considered it for a second. Then one of them snatched up the offering, while the other began patching up the wall. His claws moved with the speed of an electric loom. *Snick-snick-snick.* The wall reappeared.

"Will that hold—" Oliver began.

But Andrew was already pulling him up the stairs. No time. No miracles left. They were like the dwarves leaving Bag End, forgetting to bring weapons. Everyone had left the dragon out of their calculations.

The auditorium resembled the set of a postmodern music video. Salamanders had set fire to a few of the velvet chairs, while undinae hung from the curtains, screaming watery imprecations at each other. The caela had broken the stained-glass windows. Their enormity swirled around the vaulted ceiling, dimming the room. A dragon without a hoard. Paul was still playing "Baby Beluga," since he couldn't think of anything else to do. His face was pale as he watched the smoke congealing above him.

Andrew heard humming.

His eyes widened. "Shit. I was right."

A burning white filament hung above the stage. It looked like something from the heart of a plasma globe, nearly dancing as it stuttered in the air. He rubbed his eyes to make sure he hadn't imagined it. Oliver made a sound next to him.

Being right didn't feel as comforting as he'd thought.

As he looked into the thing, he could see flashes. Indistinct ripples of color that might have been places, or people. He thought he saw a familiar alley, then a grove beneath a steel-blue sky. He saw flashes of other worlds. Towers of glass that rippled beneath unfamiliar constellations. Lush forests with sinister flowers. Cities that flamed and trembled and demanded forgiveness, naked before dazzling windows. They turned and toiled. They sang, erred, screamed in their foundations. It was all there. Even his own story, a fiber-optic point, winking in the smog. The city was betrayal, but it was also solace.

He couldn't have moved faster.

The song hadn't failed.

Shelby was beside him. "What's happening?"

"What she's always wanted," Andrew said. "Chaos. But I think we can use it. I think there's still a way out. If you trust me."

The caela shrieked. It was the sound of a dying star. He remembered the death of a cherubim who'd unmade himself to save a teenage girl. The death of a white hole, bursting his claudication, so that there could be light to read by. The caela were older than imagination, and their scream was the sound of every hinge being unlatched, every atomic bond shivering, breaking away from its mate. They moved as an inky cloud, flowing through the pipe organ. Andrew felt his insides turn to ice.

"Paul!"

Ingrid knocked him off the bench just as the organ exploded.

The pipes burst with an inhuman bellow.

In the rubble, something gleamed. An ivory key. But it was changing now, in the strange light of the auditorium. It trembled like a root, about to burst forth.

Shelby moved faster than he'd thought possible. She grabbed the key. Nearly fell. Turned and ran, her expression entirely blank. Claws of smoke raked the space where she'd been a second ago. Ingrid followed her, pulling her brother along. Paul had the dazed look of someone who kept expecting to wake up from a particularly confusing nightmare.

Sam stood before the cloud of smoke, holding one of

Oliver's prop swords. She seemed to have forgotten that its edge was useless. Her expression was set.

"This thing is really starting to piss me off," she said.

"Sam!" Ingrid made a desperate motion. "Now's not the time!"

The engineering student cast a final look at the dark thing that seethed before her. Then she stumbled over to join them in the middle of the room.

"Safety in numbers?" she asked. "Or will they just eat us more efficiently this way?"

"We need to get to the stage," Andrew said.

Sam glared at him. "Did you not notice the *crazy thing* that's happening there? You want to get close to that inter-dimensional twister?"

He exhaled. "I want to go through it."

"The shearing forces alone would tear you apart. Trust me—I study this shit for a living. And even if we did survive—where is that thing going to take us?"

"I think—*everywhere*," he said. "Unless I'm wrong. Then we'll be spaghetti."

It was Paul's turn to swear. "*That's* your plan? You want us to go through some kind of cosmic pasta maker, and out the other side?"

He heard a rumbling. Something was moving beneath the floorboards. Two gnomoi burst from the ground, clawing blindly. The other lares regarded them with interest.

"Is that a frog?" Shelby asked.

Pulcheria rode her mount into the auditorium. Pharsia was directly behind her, spurring on the scrap-metal creatures that drew her chariot. Andrew heard the sound of bronze hooves, cracking against the antique floor. Latona was coming.

All of his dreams were here, and they wanted to tear each other apart.

Silenoi were crawling through the broken windows. He heard a noise above and saw that a group of furs had climbed in through the roof. Then he noticed an arc of water through the doorway. The undinae had gotten to the plumbing.

The caela saw the three queens.

All of their eyes narrowed.

"Now now *now*!" Andrew screamed. "While it's distracted!"

They stumbled across the debris. Mouths snapped at them; water and sparks leapt at them. Gnomoi spit jagged stones in outrage. Pain flared along Andrew's arm, but he kept running until he was up the stairs. They reached the stage. Tendrils of smoke followed, curling at their feet. At any moment, they could turn hard as steel.

The filament seemed to turn before them. A ballerina in a music box, strangely beautiful, even as it vibrated with horror. Images skittered and blinked within it. The rim of a marble fountain. A coffered ceiling, resplendent with lamplight. A narrow cell whose empty bed reminded him of a tomb. He looked closer, and thought, for a moment, that he could see himself, leaf-tossed in the storm.

He did not see Carl.

Was he waiting in the wings, somewhere? Behind the lightning?

Then, Andrew saw a body, pale as boxwood, floating.

Roldan.

Or maybe it had always been him. Two threads in the same pattern.

He'd given something to the hungry spirits. Something, but not everything.

"We need to join hands," he said.

Shelby gave him an odd look. "What exactly is your long game, here? Are we all supposed to perform *You're a Good Man, Charlie Brown*? I don't think the ravenous smoke monster is going to be charmed by musical theater."

Andrew held out his hand. "I know I'm dumb. But just trust me. Please."

She took his right hand, while Oliver took his left. The others followed suit. Paul had a death grip on Ingrid's hand. He was holding on for dear life. Sam took Ingrid's remaining hand, completing the circuit.

These were his friends. The people who saved him. The people who knew him and didn't turn away. Because their flaws fit together.

"We choose to roll," he said.

Nothing happened.

"Are you crazy?" Shelby whispered. "We don't have dice. Paul isn't even a member of the company. Roll with what, exactly?"

"I don't think we need them anymore."

"Not to rain on your charming RPG fantasy," Paul hissed, "but I don't think a twenty-sided die is going to make us any less dead!"

Andrew repeated, more loudly: "We choose to roll!"

Latona's bronze horse leapt through the air. He saw fire and ice and shadow on the edges of everything. The world crumbling like parchment. Oliver's hand in his own. Shelby's reckless faith. Sam, the spark that continually surprised, making its way through layers of doubt. Ingrid's patient love for them all.

Then it was Paul, strangely, who said: "Everyone!"

They all spoke: *"We choose to roll."*

They all chose. A company as unlikely as it was unbreakable.

He saw an unexpected face in the tear. Just for a moment.

Then they dove forward. It was just like discovering the park for the first time. All the hope that lay on the other side. Before, they'd wished to be different.

Now they knew who they were.

The light swallowed them, while every other thing screamed.

He saw the brick first.

It was hard to look at. He tried to concentrate, but the blocks kept shifting. Yellow moss trembled in the cracks. It was too quiet. The familiar city noises were gone. Something was cutting into his knee, and he realized that he was sprawled on the ground. The uneven paving stones reminded him of cooled lava. Shelby was struggling to rise next to him, and he helped her up. Paul maintained his grip on Ingrid's hand, while Sam looked around, searching for a clue that might make sense.

She frowned. "This isn't my alley. But it's familiar."

Andrew looked for the hole in the wall, but the bricks refused to yield. There was no packet of goods waiting for him in the dark. Just warm stones that kept blurring beneath his vision. He also remembered this place, or some version of it. The shadows filled him with a sense of unearthly nostalgia that he couldn't quite explain.

Someone had scratched a *B* into one of the walls.

He didn't know what it meant.

"It almost feels," Ingrid said, "like this is everyone's alley."

"Is there a way out?" Sam peered down the corridor. "I don't see anything. It's just brick going on forever. I'm going to check."

She disappeared. Her footsteps faded for some time, then came back. She peeked around the corner. "I don't think it ends," she said. "At least, there's no exit that I can find. No city. Just alley."

"The city of infinite alleys," Ingrid said. "I guess we found the infinite one."

Paul threw up noisily in the corner.

Everyone turned away politely. Ingrid offered him a handkerchief from her pocket and said: "Don't worry. That's normal."

"None of this is normal." Paul wiped his mouth. "Where are we?"

"It's called Anfractus."

"I'm not entirely sure that's where we are," Andrew said. "This is more like an in-between space. A waiting room."

"I don't understand," Paul said. "Why are we here? What's

going on back in the park? Are those monsters going to set fire to the city?"

"Regina has survived cyclones and floods," Sam said. "And once, a rain of frogs. I'm sure it can deal with some angry salamanders."

"All of you seem extraordinarily chill about this," Paul snapped. "Forgive me for losing my shit here, but I was nearly killed by an exploding organ. Then a bronze horse tried to trample me, and now I'm in some infinite fucking alley." He was breathing hard. He leaned against the wall. "And I think I'm having . . . a panic attack . . . in your nightmare world."

"Hey there, mister." Sam took both of his hands gently in her own. "Look at me. Repeat after me. I am the barbecue master."

"Shut up."

"Just say it."

"I . . . am the barbecue master."

"My frosting is sick."

"Sam—"

"Don't argue with an engineer." She rubbed his thumbs. "Say it."

"My frosting is—" He frowned. "*Sick* really isn't the right word. I'm not even sure what that means. Is it some kind of gaming term?"

Sam smiled. "And you're back."

He laughed softly. "You're right. I feel better."

She kissed him on the cheek. "Good. Because we're trapped in an alley while the world is going to hell. We need you to keep a tight lid on that anxiety, until we think of a way out of here. I'll run out of mantras, otherwise."

Paul nodded slowly. "Sure. Tight lid."

Andrew ran his hands along the brick walls. "It's so quiet. Like we're in some kind of beta-testing space. Maybe this is the first alley."

Shelby punched him in the shoulder.

"Hey! What was that for?"

"Because you convinced us all to jump, and you don't even have a plan. Jerk. I really need to stop trusting you."

"I do have a plan. It's just . . . kind of theoretical at this stage."

"Great," Paul said. "Why don't you write a paper about it?"

Ingrid snorted. "How long have you been waiting to say that?"

"How long have you been in grad school, again?"

"That's a hostile question."

"I just—" Andrew frowned. "Did anyone else see all those different things flickering in the tear? I didn't think we'd end up in this place."

"I thought we'd be naked," Sam said. "Kind of stoked that we're not."

Oliver suddenly stepped into the alley. "Hey."

Everyone screamed.

He winced. "Sorry. I was way down there."

Sam glared at him. "Were you hiding? I walked for a while, and didn't see you."

"I'm not really sure where I was. Or where I am now. It all looks the same." He glanced at his clothes. "I guess the rules no longer apply."

Shelby held up the horn. "You're telling me. I almost impaled myself on this thing. I liked it better when it was a piano key."

Andrew noticed the dagger in his pocket for the first time. His blood formed a rust-colored patchwork on the blade. He could no longer see the original spot. His hand pained him, but only slightly. If the rules were coming undone, then anything was possible.

He hadn't seen Carl in the tear. He'd seen everything else.

But some part of him might still be here.

"I remember everything," he said. "Not just my own memories, but Aleo's. Even"—his eyes widened—"Roldan's. I remember the water, and Babieca's bloody nose, and the undinae whispering. It's like two hemispheres coming together."

"That's all well and good," Shelby said, "and I'm also starting to remember some pretty funky things." She glanced at Ingrid. "And some swell things too. But we can't just stand here, enjoying the slide show. We have to do something."

"There's only one way out," Oliver replied. "Maybe we should just keep walking."

It seemed like a reasonable idea. They walked down the unchanging corridor. After a while, they started to pick up the pace. Then they were running. It felt good. It felt like something was possible. They ran until their feet hurt, until they had shin splints, and all they could do was lean against the brick. They were no closer to escape.

"Should we go back?" Oliver asked.

"Thanks a lot, Google Maps," Sam said. "You're full of bright ideas."

"It was better than suntanning in an alley."

"Wait." Ingrid was examining the nearest wall. "If Andrew's right, and the rules no longer apply, then maybe we need to make our own exit."

"That's very meta," Sam replied, "but how do you propose we do that?"

"I think we need to change our perspective. That's what I do when Neil won't see reason. I shift his attention. We keep looking at this from one angle, but what if the exit isn't in front of us? What if the whole place is one big exit?" Ingrid laid her hands on the brick wall. "Help me push."

Paul rapped his knuckles on the wall. "It's solid."

"You'll accept a smoke dragon, but now you choose to believe in physics?"

"Fine," he replied. "Everyone push on three."

They all braced themselves against the wall.

"One—two—*three*—"

Something yielded.

Andrew felt dizzy, as if he were just waking up from a

deep sleep. The world around him shifted violently on its axis. The brick dissolved. Then he was falling forward.

They were in an entirely different place. But Andrew knew it well. Lemon scent still clung to the floors. The bookshelves were bare. A girl sat on a stool in the middle of the empty living room. It was her face that he'd seen in the tear.

"Eumachia," he breathed.

She winked. "I knew you'd all figure it out, eventually."

"This is Carl's apartment." Shelby's voice was soft. "Why are we here?"

"I thought you'd appreciate something with less brick," Eumachia said. "From a design perspective, it's a bit too industrial."

Latona's daughter was dressed in flared jeans and a *Library Voices* T-shirt. Gone was the pearl diadem, the embroidered stola. She also wore bright red Crocs, which was somehow the most unsettling thing of all.

"Are we back in Regina?" Andrew asked.

Eumachia stood. "You're kind of everywhere. I know. *Matrix* jokes are so millennial. But there isn't really a dimension that corresponds to this one. If all the parks and all the cities under twilight were a ladder, this place would be the stuff that the ladder's made of."

"What does that make you?" Shelby asked.

Eumachia smiled. "You really haven't guessed?"

"Your psycho mom is trying to destroy our world," Sam said. "The least that you could do is give us a clue about what to do next."

"Do we know this little girl?" Paul asked. "Is she . . . part of this?"

"Technically, I'm a lot older than you," Eumachia replied. "Though I realize that this outfit isn't doing me any favors." She glanced down at her red foam shoes. "I wanted to appear nonthreatening, but I may have gone overboard."

Andrew heard a noise from Carl's bedroom. Two mechanical foxes emerged from the hallway. Sulpicia and

Propertius walked over to where Eumachia stood. They moved in a slow circle, as if testing the ground, then curled into balls and fell asleep. The sound of their snoring reminded him of a bubbling percolator.

"They're exhausted from all these transitions," Eumachia said. "I don't know whether I should take them to a vet or an auto mechanic." She laughed, and shrugged. "Listen to me and my secondary-world problems."

"I know that laugh," Shelby murmured. "When I rolled to save Pulcheria from the silenus—to make the shot—a voice spoke to me through the fountain. Your voice."

"How talented of me," Eumachia replied, "to have been in two places at once."

"That's the thing, though." Shelby stepped closer. "You've always been there. When I rolled that night above the oecus. And later, when Andrew rolled on the stolen die. You were there when Oliver nearly died, and when—" She stopped herself from saying it. "You've always been in the background. The foxes were supposed to be Latona's pets, but they follow you around like—"

"—like she was their maker," Sam finished. "I always knew that she had an artifex vibe. I couldn't quite explain it. But I felt something."

"She told me how the fountains worked," Shelby continued. "She knew the Arx of Violets better than anyone else. She knew too much."

Eumachia rolled her eyes. "So says the grad student."

"Who are you really?" Shelby demanded.

A tremor passed through the floor of the apartment.

The walls broke down the middle, as if it were a gingerbread house. The ceiling flew away, and stars boiled in the night sky above them. No pollution to obscure their dance. They were surrounded by constellations that burned like fantastic Lite-Brite sculptures. A mosaic brought to life and electrified in the hallowed darkness. The floor was a giant wheel, and each of them stood on a spoke. The wheel was alive. It was made of branches, and thread, and bone polished by immeasurable time. Animals whispered among its cells. Parts of it were water, and parts were flame, and some parts remained in beautiful shadow. It breathed but was oddly still as it hung in the void.

"I've paused it," the girl said, "so that we can gain some perspective."

"I don't understand," Andrew said. "You made all of this. If you're the artifex, then why would you let it fall apart?"

She shook her head. "No. I'm a word in a book, just like you. All of these possibilities were here before me, and they'll be here when I'm gone. I'm only their steward, for a little while. My mother—" She frowned. "Well, let's just say that she played her part with too much expertise. The basilissae were supposed to counter each other. To preserve the balance. Like quarks. Up and down spinning in tension, with one queen under the world, who waited."

"My mother," Andrew said. He thought of her waiting beneath the earth. Hadn't he been the one who was waiting for her, above?

"It's hard to be loved by a queen," the girl offered. "It's not always what you'd expect. Now we've come to the end of this rotation. The wheel will turn back on itself, and everything will start over. Latona doesn't want that. Like any good story, she refuses to be forgotten. I tried to point her in another direction. She loved me the best that she could. But there's no going back now. She's broken out of the margins, and into your world. She'll destroy them both if she has her way."

Two stars collided above them. A ring of purple flame exploded across the black sky, and they had to shield their eyes. Andrew felt the wheel tremble.

"There's not much time left," the girl said. "You came here for a reason. You rolled without a die—and without a net. That sort of collective risk deserves an answer. But the wheel can't remain still for long. Choose your question wisely."

"What kind of *Last Crusade* bullshit is this?" Sam

demanded. "We're just supposed to choose a question? What if we can't?"

Ripples of plasma spread across the dark. The stars seemed to be getting brighter, drawing closer together. Maybe stopping the wheel meant stopping the universe. If everything ground to a halt, then—what?

Anything was possible. But that was far from comforting.

Oliver stepped forward. "You're saying that if we ask the right question, then you'll stop all of this? You'll save both worlds?"

The girl smiled. "Is that your question?"

"No." He frowned. "This seems like a trick."

"It won't in a few moments," she replied. "Trust me."

"Okay," Sam said, "it's like writing an essay. What's our thesis statement?"

"Are you kidding?" Shelby glared at her. "I've been stuck on my thesis for a year. If I knew how to write an argument, I wouldn't spend all my time on cat blogs."

Oliver turned to Andrew. "This was your idea."

He managed to look uncomfortable. "It was just a theory."

"Well—make it concrete. What's your thesis?"

People had been asking him that for years. *What's your thesis on?* And he'd been asking himself the same question. What was the point in studying Anglo-Saxon poetry that had dissolved into fragments over time? What did it matter that Wulf bore a bundle to a storm-tossed grove, that a small, bright voice waited in an earth-cave? What could all of those iron links possibly add up to? *What have you done with your life?* That was the real question. Why had he chosen this inconvenient path, which would probably end in a shared basement suite rather than a white picket fence? His own private earth-cave, full of books and notations and bills from debt collectors. It was a strange and unlikely thing. It was maybe the wrong thing, and always had been. If he had moved faster, glanced behind, if, only if. Would he have chosen differently? Was any choice possible?

He knew the question that he wanted to ask. His chest ached with the need to ask it, to know, even if the answer wasn't what he expected.

The stars were so close now. The universe awash in startling light. He could see into the hearts of those giants. They reminded him of the salamander's eyes.

Andrew didn't ask the question.

Instead, he turned to Paul. "You should do it."

Paul stared at him. "What? Why?"

Because you know better than all of us. Because you aren't weighed down by every bullshit desire that we've attached to this world of possibilities. Because I'm not the center of the universe, and my question won't save us. Even if I ask it for the rest of my life.

"Because you'll choose right," he said. "You love Ingrid. You love all of us. Your frosting is sick. We know you'll choose right."

Ingrid gave Paul a long look. She squeezed his hand.

The girl waited.

The light was becoming unbearable. This was what the heart of the story felt like, the place where they all came from. The joy and grief and star-matter that connected them all, holding them together, even across unknowable distance.

Paul asked: "How can we do better?"

The wheel shuddered and began to turn. Andrew nearly lost his balance. The constellations danced.

The girl reached up, grabbing one of the smaller stars. A red dwarf that burned like a carbuncle in her hand.

"Start with this," she said.

Then she tossed the star at him. Paul, who had never been afraid of a flying puck, caught the fiery ball in his hand. It shimmered, and cooled, and became a glass die.

"Wars have been ended by less," she said.

The wheel spun faster and faster, until they were all forced to hold on to each other. The light crept over them. Andrew smelled smoke.

Then they were on the stage.

Narses had arrived with spado reinforcements. They were holding back Latona's silenoi, dancing in green with their slender knives. The furs joined them, stabbing like murderous acrobats. Septimus and Skadi were fighting with the princeps. Skadi bled emerald. *That's my supervisor,* Shelby thought with pride. Septimus clawed at his own master, who was also wounded. Sometimes they were raging monsters, but beneath a certain light, they were also delicate. Their shadows embraced on the ashen floor, which was coming away in places.

Pharsia and Latona were engaged in single combat. Pulcheria was wounded and struggling to collect herself. She grasped for a weapon on the ground. Mardian was there, moving like an asp. He nearly brought his blade down, but Narses leapt between them. Their weapons sang in a voice that rose to the rafters. All of this happened in the moment of transition, when they were still rubbing their eyes. Death moved on swift feet. Lares were tearing each other to bits, while Darke Hall shuddered. The ghosts were surely awake now, and placing bets. Andrew heard the sound of the fire trucks outside. They'd have a devil of a time breaking through all the stone that the gnomoi had erected.

His mother fought with steady grace. She and Latona were evenly matched. They could dance like this forever, while all the worlds burned.

Paul held up the glass die. "What do I do with this?"

The caela saw them. Andrew watched the smoke as it moved toward the stage. Every incarnadine eye was fixed on the thing that Paul held. All its mouths opened, and a scream filled their ears, filled everything.

"It's not a weapon," Andrew said. "I think it's—"

"—a key," Ingrid broke in. "A key to the world."

Andrew sat down. "Give me the die. And the horn."

"Why are we sitting?" Shelby demanded.

"Because we have to change the story."

They sat in a circle while the smoke coalesced around them. Andrew refused to see that network of hunger. He realized that they'd bound it centuries ago precisely for that reason. It was starving. It wanted to consume everything. They'd tried to lock it up, but, as Eumachia had said, every system needed its flaw. You couldn't bury entropy. But you could spread it out, over all of the worlds, until it was an ocean rather than a cloud. The flaw that held up the masterpiece, indistinguishable from the beauty that it supported. Another deep, unsoundable place from which they'd all emerged, when the possibilities were still so very young.

He placed the die next to the horn. He laid the dagger atop them both.

The question rattled around inside him. It clawed at him, trying to get out. A million times he would ask it. Every dream, every hesitation, would hone that question, until it was pearl, until it was all he had.

It was the hunger of the caela. Latona's need. The survival instinct of every story graven in rock or tattooed on flesh.

But the story had to belong to everyone.

He let go.

He thought of the park, instead. Of how it was common space. A *hortus conclusus*. Anything could happen there. It was borderless and green with possibilities. He had stumbled upon its magic by accident, but it couldn't be his secret anymore.

"I give up the park," he said.

And it was the magic that he gave up. And it was Carl's sweet care, the puff of smoke between them, the purple flowers on the ground.

The die began to glow.

"I give up the park," Shelby repeated. And he saw that she was giving up her pain as well, the burn of insecurity, the imposter syndrome, the drive to be more, always more. Letting the moss cover it. Letting others hold on to it for a while.

"I give up the park," Ingrid said. And in that moment,

she knew the question she would have asked, and knew its answer. She gave up on the voice that said she was a bad parent, that she was doing it all wrong, that her words couldn't possibly make a difference.

"I give up the park," Sam said. And in that moment, she heard the wind in the trees, the forces that could tear you apart, billow laundry on the line, stir your lover's hair. And she gave up feeling lost, because the map had always been drawn on air.

"I give up the park," Oliver said. His voice was thick as he spoke. He was giving up distance, and cold calculation. Giving up the fear that what he'd left behind would no longer want him. What the mask had always concealed. Andrew took his hand. There was a whole tapestry of questions to consider, and he didn't have to do it alone.

The caela dove, grasping and crying. But its scream was more desperate now. The eyes were also asking, imploring. Andrew could see its thread for the first time, and it was necessary. The gleam before the loom. The first throw.

"I—" Paul paused. He'd never had the park to begin with. How could he give it up? But maybe that was wrong. Maybe, through Ingrid and Neil, he'd always held a piece of it. Or it had always held him. "What they said. Take it. None of us is big enough to hold this. Let it belong to everyone!"

The die was a star again. It hummed, louder and louder, until it was the crashing of the wheel, a storm that was all around them.

It went nova.

The caela's scream became a wild song. They exploded through the broken windows. They swirled ever higher, until they were the living skies.

The remaining lares sang as well. Gnomo, salamander, and undina, raising their indescribable voices to the air. They harmonized amid the wreckage.

Latona dropped her sword. Mardian turned from Narses to watch. The silenoi stopped and drew a collective breath. The princeps helped Skadi to stand.

Dazed, they began to file outside.

Pharsia and Pulcheria joined their sister. The lares followed them, putting out flames and floods as they went.

Sirens moaned around them. Firefighters stared in confusion. Reporters were looking around in wonder, as if they'd just seen something out of their dreams. Hours might have passed inside Darke Hall, or centuries. Now the city was responding.

They crossed the street and stepped into the park. It was alive. It had been built, but that didn't make it any less a part of the planet. It was an improbable, moonlit jungle. Salamanders perched in the trees, flicking their tongues in search of low-hanging fruit. Monsters played games in the water. Clouds moved above them, no longer ominous, but drenched in subtle fire.

They gathered in the night, before the water, now streaked with light from police cars. Andrew stood next to his mother, while Latona placed a hand on Pulcheria's back. The silenoi were watching the skies. The princeps leaned on his spear. A reporter had begun to approach them. Shelby could only imagine what form that interview might take.

Ingrid joined her. "Should we explain to the reporters about the silenoi—and the fire lizards? Oh, wait." She winced. "One of them just found the scrap-metal chariot. It's cranky."

"Not just yet," Pharsia said.

They listened to the ducks and the startled cries of onlookers.

Andrew smiled.

He couldn't wait for the new semester to begin.

GLOSSARY OF TERMS

aditus: An intersecting avenue.

Anfractus: A city controlled by Basilissa Latona.

artifex: A member of the Gens of Artifices. They build machines, which they can occasionally infuse with life.

arx: The palace of the basilissa and the seat of the court.

auditor: A member of the Gens of Auditores. They are able to speak with lares (though they cannot see them).

baculum: A ceremonial staff carried by some auditores and oculi.

basia: A brothel that serves a diverse clientele.

basilissa: A hereditary position and a vestige of the former empire. City-states such as Anfractus and Egressus are governed by a basilissa. The position is matrilineal.

caelum: A lar whose natural habitat is smoke.

carcer: The dungeon beneath the Arx of Violets.

caupona: An inn that offers food and entertainment.

chlamys: A ceremonial robe fashioned of leather and worn by the basilissa.

cloaca: The extensive sewer system beneath Anfractus, which contains a system of tunnels.

domina/dominus: A wealthy landowner who administers a large house (domus).

Egressus: A city controlled by Basilissa Pulcheria.

Fortuna: The goddess of chance, whose wheel determines fate.

fur: A member of the Gens of Furs. They are thieves or peddlers who serve the Fur Queen.

gens: A guild or "family" of members devoted to a particular mastery. There are six gens devoted to the day (miles, sagittarii, auditores, trovadores, medica, and artifices) and six gens devoted to the night (spadones, meretrices, sicarii, furs, oculi, and silenoi, the last constituting a wild gens).

gladius: A short sword generally carried by a miles.

gnomo: A lar whose natural habitat is earth. They are rarely seen.

Hippodrome: A complex that features chariot racing, duels between miles, and performances.

hypocaust: A furnace designed to heat a domus (larger versions heat public baths).

impluvium: A basin in a house designed to catch rainwater.

insula: A block of apartments, often with shops on the ground floor.

lar: An elemental spirit.

lararium: A roadside or indoor shrine to lares.

lupo: A slang term for meretrices, meaning "wolf."

machina: An automaton built by an artifex.

medicus: A member of the Gens of Medica. They are surgeons and chemists.

meretrix: A member of the Gens of Meretrices. They are courtesans and sex workers who offer their services at the basiorum.

miles: A member of the Gens of Miles. They are soldiers and law keepers who also guard the grounds of the palace.

nemo: An individual who does not belong to a gens.

oculus: A member of the Gens of Oculi. They can see lares (though they cannot hear them).

oecus: A great hall with windows.

Oscana: The territory covered by Wascana Park.

pedes: A servant under the protection of a wealthy dominus or domina.

popina: A street-side bar that offers food.

sagittarius: A member of the Gens of Sagittarii. They are archers who patrol the battlements of the arx and are considered the first defense against intruders.

salamander: A lar whose natural habitat is fire. They are generally amenable.

sicarius: A member of the Gens of Sicarii. They are assassins who sell their services.

silenus: A satyr (half humanoid, half hircine) who hunts at night. They comprise the Gens of Silenoi, though they do not respect the tradition.

spado: A member of the Gens of Spadones. They are eunuchs who serve as palace officials in addition to supervising archives and libraries.

Subura: The entertainment district of Anfractus.

tabularium: A room for storing books and parchments.

triclinium: A formal dining room, which is named after a style of slanted couch upon which guests can recline while eating.

trovador: A member of the Gens of Trovadores. They are musicians, entertainers, and poets.

undina: A lar whose natural habitat is water. They are natural tricksters.

via: A main road.

vici: A neighborhood.

Learn more about the work of Bailey Cunningham
by visiting his website: cunningbailey.com.

THE ULTIMATE IN FANTASY FICTION!

From magical tales of distant worlds to stories of those with abilities beyond the ordinary, Ace and Roc have everything you need to stretch your imagination to its limits.

Marion Zimmer Bradley/Diana L. Paxson

Guy Gavriel Kay

Dennis L. McKiernan

Patricia A. McKillip

Robin McKinley

Sharon Shinn

Steven R. Boyett

Barb and J. C. Hendee